SILENT BETRAYAL

CJ WOOD

What readers say about CJ Wood's books…

'Really enjoyed this read, wasn't able to put it down! The author clearly understands the justice system and uses it to great effect. Brilliant, highly recommended!'

'Good pacy thrillers.'

'Yet again, another great book from this author; I would say that it is even better than the first one. Once you start, it is hard to put down and moves along quickly and dramatically. I recommend it if you like fast-moving detective novels.'

'The author is clearly in the know and is a great writer. The characters are relatable, and I got immersed in the story. It is well written and highly recommended.'

'The plot twists and turns and keeps you riveted throughout. The author obviously knows his way around the law and higher echelons of the crime industry. It's big and bold and almost impossible to put down. A master class in crime writing.'

I love all 3 of these talented writers' books. It's hard to put down with gripping storylines and characters. Can't wait for book 4!'

Copyright © C J Wood 2025

All rights reserved.

No part of this book may be reproduced, or stored in a retrieval system, or transmitted in any form or by any means, electronic, mechanical, photocopying, recording, or otherwise, without express written permission of the publisher.

This is a work of fiction. Unless otherwise indicated, all the names, characters, businesses, places, events and incidents in this book are either the product of the author's imagination or used in a fictitious manner. Any resemblance to actual persons, living or dead, or actual events is purely coincidental.

ISBN: 9798310096684

Editor: Kathryn Hall – cjhall.co.uk
Cover art: Joseba Altuna – seklevdesign.com
Formatting: Catherine Arthur – catherinearthur.com

IN MEMORY OF
JAMES WOOD

1

Richard Flannagan-Smythe woke with a start, his legs tangled in the duvet, indicating another restless night's sleep. The eerie silence of the house lingered as he fumbled for his mobile phone and squinted at the screen, his eyes playing catch up: twenty past nine. He lay still for a moment, staring at the ceiling, assessing the extent of his hangover from the night before. Relief washed over him. It wasn't debilitating, just a manageable dull throb in his temples. He untangled the duvet and rolled out of bed.

He ambled towards the window, his eyes scanning the vast gardens below. The sprawling lawns and flower beds looked impressive. The gardener's noticeable absence irked him. He was probably running late again and Richard decided that words were needed to lay down the law and remind him who was the boss. The lawn was beginning to look a little shoddy and unkempt; it wasn't good enough. Was the cretin deliberately testing his patience? Seeing how far he could push him?

His wife's car was absent from its usual spot beside his SUV. He remembered they'd left it at the hotel last night. As usual, Jane had left the function by herself after the meal. It was no secret that she detested the after-dinner drinks with his political cronies, potential party donors, and hangers-on. And in all fairness, he hadn't missed her; it's how it was these days.

Once dressed in his slim-fit blue Oxford shirt and chinos, he headed to the kitchen where he found Mandy, the cleaner, sitting on a tall stool at the kitchen island, nursing a coffee whilst scrolling on her phone. His eyes focused on her pink T-shirt, struggling to contain her breasts. He'd always thought she was a good-looking young woman but that she had too much to say for herself. She looked up at him and placed her phone on the worktop.

'Morning, Richard. Would you like a coffee,' she asked dutifully, unable to hide her insincere tone. She slid from the stool as if anticipating his usual answer of yes.

'No, I'm going to have one of those fruit smoothies. Besides, you've got work to get on with. You can't be sitting around all day scrolling on your phone, can you?' he said, turning away from her to fix his drink. 'Give my bedroom a tidy, will you? You seem to have forgotten about it.'

Mandy didn't reply to the barbed comment and climbed back onto the stool, giving him a disparaging look as he opened the freezer door. 'Has Jane left already?' she asked.

'I don't think so. She's probably not up yet. It's her day off,' Richard replied before switching on the blender. Both remained silent, unable to compete with the high-pitched, irritating whining noise that filled the kitchen.

Mandy sent a text: *Sleazebag has just shown his face, text u later.*

Then she dropped her phone into her handbag and admired her new black cherry-coloured fingernails.

Richard poured the contents of the blender into a tall glass and then hovered by the kitchen island, casting an eye over Mandy's long black hair. A while ago, he'd considered making a move on her in the local pub but had thought better of it, fearing a one-night stand didn't justify the risk of her telling her mates in the village or, even worse, disclosing all to the journalists, at the red top national newspapers.

Mandy laughed. 'What are you staring at, perv?' she asked.

'Don't flatter yourself,' Richard replied. 'My mind was elsewhere, and I have bigger fish to fry than a cleaner. I'm sorry to disappoint you,' he added smugly, eyebrows raised.

'Yeah, right,' Mandy said, pulling her cardigan over her bosom.

Richard's head was elsewhere already. Something didn't feel right. Jane was usually up and about; maybe she was waiting until he'd gone to the leisure club. He had a recollection of pissing her off at the function, which wasn't hard. He left the kitchen and headed for her bedroom. He needed to find out if she had gleaned any helpful information or gossip while working the room last night. *She probably failed, as usual,* he thought, as he wondered why he paid her to be his secretary, suspecting he could do better. Maybe a secretary with benefits, he pondered.

He placed his ear to the bedroom door and listened but heard nothing, so he pushed the door open gently and peeped into the room. She wasn't there, and the bed looked like it hadn't been slept in. Where the hell could she be? He walked into the room, aware of no tell-tale smell of recently applied perfume. She obviously hadn't arrived home last night, he concluded, as he glanced around the room as if looking for clues. But nothing looked out of the ordinary.

He began to feel lightheaded, and the nervous twitch in his eyelid suddenly returned. It flicked, and he cursed, rubbing his eye, willing it to stop. This had been happening frequently lately, and it distressed him. He knew colleagues would detect it as a sign he was struggling with stress, a weakness to be exploited.

He turned about and headed back to the kitchen, his anxiety swelling, his mind now totally preoccupied by Jane's absence. Where was she? She'd never done this before. His mind raced through the events of the previous night, remembering they'd had cross words as usual, nothing new there. She just didn't listen to him, so it was no wonder she messed up so often. Images of Sebastian flirting with her, one of the party's new independent special advisors, flashed across his mind. From what he could remember, she seemed to be relishing the attention. His mind simmered for a moment; there was no way anything could be going on between them. Either way, Richard decided to make it his business to ensure that Sebastian's stay was short. Some misinformation in the right ears would ensure his demise.

'She's not upstairs,' he announced, pacing the room, ever more conscious of his twitching eyelid.

'Probably left early,' Mandy suggested nonchalantly, not bothering to look up from the magazine she now seemed to be engrossed in. *I don't blame her. She probably just needed time away from her prick of a husband,* she reflected, not giving a toss about Richard's predicament.

'She can't have,' Richard spat back, irritated by the useless suggestion. He studied his phone, checking for any missed calls or texts. None. He selected her number from the contacts and began pacing the room again. 'Bloody answer machine!' he shouted. 'Bollocks.'

Mandy retrieved her phone from her bag and began texting: *OMG, Jane didn't come home last night.*

Out shagging??? Who could blame her? He treats her like shit, Lol.

The reply: *WTF good on her!!!*

'It keeps going to bloody voicemail,' Richard fumed, slamming his mobile onto the work surface.

'I'll call her. She might answer me,' Mandy said. 'Have you two been arguing again?'

Richard stood still, his eyes on Mandy. Slowly shaking his head, he said, 'No, we've not been bloody arguing.'

'No, straight to voicemail again,' Mandy reported back, with a tone of disappointment. 'What are you going to do? Call the police?' she asked, her tone going up a notch as she appeared to revel in Richard's discomfort.

Richard was pacing again. 'Not just yet; there'll be a simple explanation. I'll make some calls first.' Jane's absence was gnawing at him, his anxiety growing. 'I'll be in my office,' he muttered, leaving the kitchen. The wave of paranoia overwhelmed him. Something wasn't right, which made his anxious mind race towards the worst-case scenarios that could have happened.

He sought sanctuary in the lounge, rather than his office, picking up the broadsheet newspaper that Mandy had placed on the coffee table.

The previous night had started badly before they'd even reached the party function at the hotel. Richard couldn't even recall what started the row, but it raged into a full-scale domestic, with Jane refusing to attend the function with him, flicking on the television and telling him to fuck off. He pleaded with her to attend for the sake of appearances and buttered her up, saying she had an important role to play. Eventually, she reluctantly agreed, probably just to shut him up. An uncomfortable silence had lingered in the car on their journey to the hotel, and he couldn't help wondering if he should have gone alone after all, because things didn't get any better during the event.

The incident that Richard had been successfully suppressing until now suddenly replayed, increasing his anxiety and tense disposition. Had he overstepped the mark…again? The images in his mind were all too vivid for comfort. He willed them to stop, but the scene painfully played out in his mind.

His thoughts placed him back at the function. The room buzzed with activity, donors mingling, drinks flowing, and a string quartet playing in the background. Jane looked impeccable in a long, black, figure-hugging dress, the softest satin caressing every curve and accentuating her firm breasts, a hint of cleavage commanding the attention of the guests as she made her way around the room, as popular with the guests as ever.

She caught Richard's eye while chatting warmly with a donor, Caleb Lavelle, a long-time supporter of Richard's political career. He approached them, his smile polite but strained, noticing the fear in Jane's eyes. She knew what was coming, which justified Richard's irritation. She knew she was receiving too much attention and letting him down.

'Jane, honestly, how many times must I remind you not to monopolise the conversation? Mr Lavelle doesn't need a lecture on… what was it?' Richard asked, frowning at Caleb. 'Charitable tax reform?'

Jane smiled calmly. 'I wasn't lecturing, Richard. Mr Lavelle was sharing his insights on how—'

Richard cut her off loudly enough for others nearby to hear. 'Spare me the excuses: your job is to support, not sidetrack. Stick to the agenda.'

A few guests standing nearby glanced over, having heard the raised voice. There was an awkward pause between the three of them, tension thick in the air. Jane's face was flushed, but she kept her composure. Caleb Lavelle's face tensed before he looked towards the floor.

'Of course, Richard, my apologies. I will leave you to discuss other matters,' Jane said, smiling politely at Caleb before walking away.

Richard watched as she made a beeline towards Sebastian. Then his recollection faded and he was back in the moment, considering whether she had finally left him this time. Had she had enough? An alternative, darker explanation for her absence hovered on the periphery of his mind: Had Hargreaves taken him seriously after all, following their drunken night in his den?

2

DS Lee McCann huddled close to DI Andrea Statham to avoid the downpour. Their umbrella was barely holding back the relentless rain, weather that mirrored the sombre mood of the gathering. Lee's gaze remained fixed on the funeral cortege, its slow, deliberate process halting at the crematorium doors. For a moment, time seemed suspended before the lead car door opened, the hushed murmurs of those in attendance lost in the noise of the rain.

Rachel Higgs was the first to step out from the back seat, dressed head to toe in black. Her children closely followed and took each of her hands. She paused a moment, smiling at those in attendance closest to her before leading the children towards the entrance. Lee felt tears welling up and a flowing wave of sadness.

He squeezed Andrea's waist. 'Are you okay?'

'Poor woman,' she replied, dabbing her eyes with a tissue. 'This can't be easy for her.'

Lee nodded and remained silent, fearing his words were inadequate to capture the depth of the situation. The assembled mourners began to shuffle towards the entrance and Lee and Andrea strolled in line. No one appeared to be in a rush. They reached the reception area, where a solemn-looking, apologetic staff member asked mourners to file down the sides of the chapel. It was standing room only already.

Lee and Andrea were among the last to squeeze inside the crematorium before the doors clicked shut behind them. As if on cue, the celebrant began proceedings.

'Welcome, everyone. We are gathered here to remember Peter Higgs and the good times we shared with him…'

As she continued addressing the mourners, Lee's mind took him back to the rooftop where he last saw Pete alive. Lee still grappled with regret and guilt that he hadn't managed to save the man's life. Waking up from a nightmare in the middle of the night as Pete's body hit the floor with a shuddering thud was a common occurrence for him these days. He'd since read accounts of people finding extraordinary strength in critical situations, such as lifting vehicles to release a person trapped underneath.

He couldn't reconcile why he hadn't mustered the strength needed to pull Pete back to safety before he committed suicide by falling to his death. Maybe just a little more effort would have saved him. In his mind, Lee was back on the warehouse roof, struggling as his grip on Pete loosened. Then, watching him fall to his death, Lee's tormented mind was in overdrive, assessing what he could have done differently to prevent what had happened. But maybe Pete didn't want to be saved. There was no doubt his corruption in running with the organised crime gang would have led to a lengthy jail sentence.

Lee felt Andrea squeeze his hand, bringing his attention back to the service in time for the first hymn. He was relieved at not having been handed a hymn book, satisfied that he didn't need to put others through the torrid experience of listening to his dulcet tones. Instead, he found himself looking at Pete's photograph on the cover of the order of service; Pete, once a respected, seasoned detective, and now leaving this world with his professional reputation in tatters: a corrupt cop.

'Didn't expect to see him here,' Andrea whispered, discreetly nodding towards the back row of the congregation.

'Me neither,' Lee replied, his eyes fixed on Frank Burton, Pete Higgs's former shady acquaintance and lawyer to the Manchester underworld. Burton gazed straight ahead, unaware of the attention he was receiving.

'He's got a bloody nerve,' Andrea said between clenched teeth.

Lee nodded. 'Don't let him get to you; his time will come.' He wasn't in the least bit surprised by her animosity towards Burton.

Following the celebrant's closing speech, a palpable tension lingered as mourners dispersed, having paid their last respects and said their goodbyes.

Andrea sighed. 'That was tough,' she said, as they walked to the car park through the gardens. 'We were colleagues for years and shared some great times. He wouldn't listen to me or let me help him towards the end. I just hope Rachel and the kids can get on with their lives now, best they can.'

'Me too, they'll still have lots of great memories of their dad, hopefully. His demise from the police will fade with time. They won't be affected by the gossip. The kids will give Rachel a purpose and some focus while she grieves. She's a good mother. She'll pull through.'

'She will. He was a great dad; he doted on his kids.'

'You did all you could for him, Andrea. You went above and beyond to help him. Never forget that. Once his addictions took hold, he was on a downward spiral.

He didn't do things by half, either. Gambling, drugs and booze, the full set. The debts he rocked up must have been massive. Money from corruption must have appeared to be his only option.'

Lee heard hurried footsteps approaching from behind them and he instinctively spun around, unsure of what to expect. A breathless Frank Burton slowed down his pace as he reached them.

'I just wanted to express my sincere condolences to you both. Pete was a top man and a bloody good detective,' Frank said. 'I wish I'd known just how troubled he was in the end. Taking his own life took us all by surprise. I wish I could've done more to help him.'

'You've got a bloody nerve—' Andrea fired back.

Lee stepped forward and interrupted her. 'Pete was backed into a corner by you and your cronies, Frank. He deserved better than being dragged into your world. Were you blackmailing him? Threatening to expose him?'

Frank shook his head. 'It wasn't like that. Pete and I had a good professional relationship, I gave him good intelligence, but things spiralled out of control with his vices. He didn't do things by half: drink, drugs, and gambling. Believe me, I did try to help him,' Frank said, getting his breath back.

'Of course you did, Frank. You alerted the organised crime group to his vulnerability and steered him towards corruption. Some help that was,' Lee said with a sneer. He turned back to Andrea and nodded towards the exit. They left Frank Burton standing, lost for words, but only momentarily.

'Pete made his own decisions,' Frank said to Lee's retreating back. 'Don't you dare pass judgement on me.

Perhaps you should look in the mirror. Where were you when he needed help?'

'Keep walking,' Andrea said, guiding Lee with her hand on his back. 'He isn't worth it.'

3

Richard closed the door and slipped into the chair at his desk. He ran his hand through his unruly lock of blond hair and sighed. His mind swirling with anxiety over Jane's inexplicable absence. Should he go to the club for lunch as planned and try to distract himself or confront the gnawing fear that something terrible had befallen his wife? Maybe she'd be back home by the time he returned.

His mind continued to ruminate, grappling with the unsettling void of unanswered questions. No innocent explanations were forthcoming, just a blank. Drunken discussions with his one-time friend Tony Hargreaves resurfaced from the dark recesses of his mind, but that's all they were—discussions, nothing more. Still, they made him feel uneasy.

This had never happened before; she'd never stayed out overnight without first letting him know. And now she wasn't answering her phone. Something was wrong. Names of adversaries he'd crossed swords with flashed across his mind. He'd always known it was impossible to get this far in politics without treading on a few toes, and Richard had stomped on quite a few on his way up the political ladder. One associate in particular, whom he'd allowed himself to get too close to, now left him with a justified feeling of vulnerability. A sickening feeling in his gut indicated his involvement was a realistic possibility, but surely Hargreaves wouldn't sink that low, his name reaching Richard's conscience for a second time.

With a mounting sense of dread and his gut knotted, he selected Ethan Nash from his contacts. It was not a call he relished making—the party director of communications needed to be made aware of potential personal problems at the earliest opportunity so he could work on damage limitation strategy. Nash wasn't called the Rottweiler for no reason. He had the party leader's ear and ensured that things ran smoothly. Richard couldn't allow the situation to fester and then face Nash's wrath when things came on top for him. That was not a viable option.

'Nash speaking, who've you been upsetting now, Dicky-boy? I always seem to be putting the wheel back on for you these days,' came the curt voice on the other end.

Richard stood and began pacing around his office, mobile to his ear; his breath caught in his throat as he struggled to form the words. 'I thought I'd better give you the heads-up, just in case there's a problem. My wife is missing. She didn't come home last night.'

'She must be having an affair,' Nash replied, clearly lacking any empathy. 'I couldn't blame her myself. You're highly skilled in pissing people off. She's probably overslept and is working on her excuse for you as we speak.'

'This is serious, Ethan,' Richard snapped, his voice trembling with urgency. 'It's totally out of character; something's wrong. That's why I called you.'

Ethan's tone hardened in response. 'Have you made the obvious calls to family, friends and work colleagues?'

'Yes, with no joy. The last time I called Jane's mobile, it was switched off. That never happens; this isn't good,' Richard said, dropping back into his seat, feeling deflated.

'Are you telling me everything, Dick? I need to know every detail, no omissions. If it transpires you've given me half a story, I'll come down on you like a tonne of bricks, and your missing wife will be the least of your problems. The party doesn't need any more negative media or scandals right now.'

Richard's pulse was racing. He was sweating; the combination of being grilled by the party enforcer and the fear of any skeletons emerging from the cupboard made him feel sick. The word *scandal* resonated in his head, as if he didn't already have enough on his plate with his wife having gone missing. Richard hastily decided to hedge his bets; it wasn't time for unnecessary disclosures to Nash, regarding his worst fears yet. He had his political future to consider, his eyes fixed firmly on the top job. 'There's nothing else to tell,' he said with conviction.

'I hope so, for your sake. Have you or Jane experienced any conflicts or received any threats from anyone?'

Richard's heart began to beat faster and he felt lightheaded. 'No, only the usual hassle with constituents… and Jane hasn't mentioned anything.' Then he buckled under the pressure, deciding he'd better mention Hargreaves. 'I had a run-in with the property developer, Tony Hargreaves, but you know about that already. It got pretty nasty, but surely, he wouldn't take revenge by targeting Jane, would he?' Richard's mind was in overdrive, recalling the acrimonious dispute and threats after he had reneged on promises to steer Hargreaves' building development application through protests, red tape and bureaucracy. Hargreaves was furious when the application was declined and blamed Richard for the massive financial losses.

'I doubt it, it's very unlikely. More likely to be some crackpot or terrorist organisation, but we've got to consider all angles. Give Hargreaves a call and find out if he's involved.'

'Christ, Ethan, I only told you she's missing, and now you're escalating it to terrorist activity.' Richard struggled to compose himself, which was showing in his quivering voice.

'Calm down, Dick, old boy, I'm just covering the bases; we've got to consider all eventualities. What did you expect when you called me? Tea, custard creams and sympathy? I've got to go. If there's no news by this evening, I'll ask the police to make discreet enquiries.' There was a slight pause, then Ethan added 'You've told me everything, haven't you, Dick? If she's buried in the rose beds, now's the time to tell me.'

'I'll call if there's any news,' Richard said, letting the last comment slide in fear of responding with something he'd later regret. He looked at his watch, remembering he had another call to make. He selected Beth, his team leader in Westminster and mistress, from the contacts.

The phone was answered on the third ring; she must have been waiting. 'I can't make it tonight. Jane's gone missing,' he said.

'Gone missing, what do you mean?' Beth asked, sounding surprised.

'What the hell do you think I mean?' Richard replied with irritation. 'She didn't come home last night, and I haven't a clue where she is right now.'

'You don't think she's found out about us, do you?'

Richard didn't like the speck of satisfaction he detected in Beth's voice, and feared she would see this as an opportunity for him to leave Jane.

'Give me a break, Beth. What are you suggesting?'

'Nothing. I'm just helping you to think things through. She could be having an affair, too, I guess. Maybe she's left you?'

Both of them were consciously skirting around the thought that she may have come to harm or even harmed herself.

'I need to make more calls and find out where she is. I'll call you tomorrow.'

'So, we're not meeting at the hotel tonight?' Beth sounded disappointed.

'I'm too busy. I need to get this sorted.'

'I'm here if you need me. As always, just call.'

'Thanks, Beth.' Richard slid his mobile onto the desk and sat forward, leaning on the desk. What the hell was Jane up to? Was she trying to create problems for him? He started to scroll through his contacts assuming someone must know where she was. He decided to start with her friends and then progress with work colleagues.

4

Andrea decided to ditch the car in favour of the Metrolink for the morning commute. It made her life easier when she was heading into the city. The tram station was a stone's throw from her house; luckily, it wasn't raining. She fastened the buttons on her coat and placed her hands in her pockets as she approached the station. *The judge will probably wrap up proceedings early today*, she thought, assuming he'd have his Friday round of golf booked with his Manchester associates before returning to London for a weekend off. The idea of staying in town after work, having drinks and maybe eating out appealed to her. She no longer enjoyed late nights out, preferring instead to get home at a reasonable time and make an early start the next morning. Maybe it was the drunken crimes committed in the early hours that she was accustomed to dealing with over the years, usually influenced by too much alcohol. It wasn't uncommon for one punch to result in a manslaughter charge. What a needless waste of life and trauma for the families of both victim and offender. She decided she'd run it by Lee, knowing the suggestion would be music to his ears. Andrea stepped onto the platform and made her way to the usual spot, learning from experience exactly where the tram would stop.

The yellow Metrolink tram, now a familiar part of Manchester's infrastructure and still expanding to towns further afield, appeared from around the bend and slowly glided towards the platform. The brakes squealed and hissed as if announcing its arrival. It came to a smooth and steady stop at the platform's edge. Andrea followed other passengers into the virtually empty carriage and sat at the rear, her back against the bulkhead.

She took out her phone and tapped Lee's number, placing the phone to her ear whilst glancing around the carriage, checking for privacy.

'A bit early this, boss. I'm not even on the clock yet,' Lee teased.

'Cheeky. I was checking in to see if you remembered that we're starting work at Crown Court this morning,' Andrea said. 'Just having your back as usual.'

'And it's always appreciated, thank you. I'm on the tram. I should be there in fifteen minutes.'

'Me too. How do you fancy a few drinks after work?' Andrea asked.

'Sounds like a plan. It's been a while. We could grab something to eat as well, if you fancy.'

Andrea smiled, knowing eating out would be the next thing on Lee's mind. He hadn't stayed over at her place for a few days, so hopefully that would be his next thought, she guessed.

'Have you given any more consideration to selling your flat? I think it would be a good move. It can't be easy living there with the memory of Jason Hamilton taking you hostage in the lounge. It must be like living at a bloody crime scene,' Andrea said, then laughed.

'That's true. It would probably help with the nightmares, too. I can't decide. I'm still toying with the idea of getting tenants in. It would be a nice little earner.'

'Do you really want the hassle of tenants? I've heard some horror stories of them being a pain in the arse and even trashing places before they move out.'

Lee had a flash of mental images: Pete Higgs and himself fearing for their lives and being held at gunpoint in his home by Jason Hamilton. An organised crime boss they were investigating. 'You're right, probably best to sell it and move on, it would help to deal with the post-traumatic stress and all that.'

'I couldn't live in a flat after experiencing a nightmare like you did there,' Andrea pointed out. 'Some people feel the need to move if their house has been burgled, a violation of their space. It's no wonder you have nightmares.'

Their conversation was interrupted by Andrea's phone bleeping, indicating a call waiting. 'Samuel's calling me. I'll call you back,' she said, looking at the screen display. She lifted the phone to her ear. 'Morning, boss, how are you?'

'Still finding my feet in the new role, I wouldn't have taken this promotion had I known how many meetings it involves. Still, it won't harm my pension in the long run.'

Andrea laughed; she wondered if Samuel had made the right move, knowing he still enjoyed the hands-on rush of investigations. But she knew he was an excellent appointment for the Serious Crime Squad staff working under his command. An experienced, safe pair of hands was now at the wheel, following the last incumbent who had been "moved on" for career development opportunities. 'I'm taking it this isn't a social call. Please tell me it's not a Friday clusterfuck investigation coming my way, is it?' Andrea wasn't joking: Friday afternoons before a rostered weekend off were notorious for being allocated a complex investigation that necessitated sixteen-hour working days over the weekend.

'No, of course not,' Samuel confirmed. 'It's a request from the Chief Constable. Can you come over to my office? I'll bring you up to speed with what he wants. In all fairness, it shouldn't take you long to sort it out.'

Famous last words, Andrea mused. 'Is it urgent? I'm just about to meet with prosecuting counsel at Crown Court. It looks likely the trial will continue into next week. I just wanted to check in and ensure no unpleasant surprises are looming from the defence.' As she finished speaking, she feared she might have come across as if she was trying to avoid the incoming task. Something she never did. Her commitment was unquestionable.

'No, that's fine. I'll see you when you're done at court.'

Andrea ended the call and called Lee back. 'Well, it sounds like the Chinese or Indian we were looking forward to has been cancelled.'

'What's he got lined up for us?' Lee asked. 'I've checked the Force daily summary: there were no major incidents overnight.' He was relieved to occupy his mind with something other than being held hostage in his flat, which hadn't dissipated since Andrea mentioned it.

'It's the ominous "quick task" from the Chief Constable,' Andrea said. 'No further details were given.'

'The officer in the case, DS Fraser, has things in hand at court. We can meet with him and the prosecution team for a briefing and then get one of the team to drive us over to headquarters.'

'Yes, that should be fine,' she agreed. 'Our case is solid and straightforward. I don't anticipate the defence coming up with any eleventh-hour challenges.'

Andrea's team had undertaken the investigation during their weekend on-call cover duties. The defendant had punched the victim to the floor outside a pub and killed him. Initially, the outcome looked like a one-punch manslaughter charge. But some fine detective work established that the offender had been bragging to other pubgoers that he had a lethal punch he'd acquired from martial arts training. The witness also provided a statement saying the offender had previously punched another person to demonstrate his claim. Luckily for the previous victim of assault, he survived. However, the newfound evidence suggested a sinister intention and a motive, not just a pub fight with a fatal ending. It ensured the offender faced the more severe charge of murder rather than manslaughter.

Andrea was the first to arrive at Crown Court and decided to wait for Lee in the foyer. She stood in the shadows, watching people arrive. The lawyers and staff were easy to identify, probably because of their air of familiarity with the place and system, and she recognised a lot of them, anyway. She could also pick out victims and witnesses with little effort, those who weren't used to the system. Circumstances, perhaps being in the wrong place at the wrong time, had interrupted their day-to-day life and landed them in the justice system as reluctant participants, and they often looked like rabbits caught in headlights, unsure of what to expect and fearing cross-examination at the hands of the defence barrister. The attendees that irked Andrea were the frequent flyer criminals who showed no respect for law and order, and who treated their appearances here with disdain and a sense of mockery. Such behaviour just seemed to be the norm these days.

'Hey, how long have you been here?' Lee asked, slightly out of breath.

'Only a few minutes. I've just been people-watching.'

'Have you seen any of our witnesses arriving?'

'No, not yet. Let's hope they all show up,' Andrea said, looking around. Losing a case was one thing, but losing it because of witness no-shows was a sickner.

'They will. That's probably what the defence is checking right now. Once they know all the witnesses have turned up, they might offer a guilty plea and save the need for a trial.'

She shrugged. 'I don't see that panning out. I reckon they'll offer a guilty on manslaughter or run the trial. They've nothing to lose.'

Andrea and Lee headed up the stairs and onto the long airport-like concourse, windows on the left and entrances to the courtrooms on the right. The remainder of the concourse was lined with uncomfortable-looking metal seating bolted to the floor. They'd both been here many times, sometimes on the winning side and sometimes puzzled by a not-guilty finding or lenient sentence. The judges seem unpredictable these days, and consistency in sentencing appeared to be a thing of the past.

DS Fraser spotted them and made his way over. 'Didn't expect to see you two here,' he said.

Andrea replied, 'Funnily enough, we won't be stopping. Samuel wants to see us. A hush-hush job is coming our way from the chief's office.'

Fraser's smile dissipated. 'We were on call last weekend,' he said with a heavy sigh. 'My missus won't be happy with me. We planned on going to Durham to see her folks this weekend.'

'She must be used to your weekends being cancelled at short notice by now, it's par for the course. Anyway, are we all set for the trial?' Andrea asked.

'Yes, all witnesses have arrived. I've spoken with our lawyer, and we're good to go. The lawyers have just gone to the canteen for a coffee if you want to speak to them,' Fraser responded.

'No.' Andrea shook her head. 'You've got everything in hand here. We'll crack on and meet with Samuel. I'll call you at lunchtime and see how it's going.'

*

Richard scrolled aimlessly through social media. He couldn't concentrate on anything more meaningful. He felt mentally exhausted with having been up until the early hours trying to establish Jane's whereabouts and bury gnawing fears that Hargreaves was somehow involved. He'd then ended up falling into a whiskey-induced restless sleep.

Beth's name flashed on a call notification, blocking the dross content he was looking at.

'Any news?' she asked.

Richard glanced at his watch. 'Christ, it's eight o'clock already. No, nothing. I've spoken to most of her friends; she's vanished into thin air.'

'Is her phone still switched on?'

'Nope.' Richard sighed.

'Have you called her family? You need to tell them.'

'Her mother and father passed a long time ago. She only has a brother, and they've not spoken for years. I don't think I've even got his number.'

'Maybe it's time to call the police?' Beth suggested.

Richard felt a hot flush wash over him. 'This is the last thing I need, Beth. Once they get called in, the press will get hold of it, and God only knows what will blow up. What a mess!' It was, however, a comforting quantum of relief that Nash had approached the police via contacts through the back door. Looking down at the desk, he placed his forehead in his free hand.

'Oh my god!' Beth exclaimed. 'I'll be uncovered as the other woman, the MP's mistress! I can see the headline in the red tops: *"Love affair in the chamber, MP and advisor caught with their pants down."* If Martin finds out, he'll go ballistic. Christ, I dread thinking about what he would do to you. Do you think the press will come after me too?'

'Great to see you have your priorities sorted, Beth. My career is in imminent danger. At the very least, the party will ditch me to avoid bad publicity.' Beth's self-concern irritated him, making him feel like ending the call and hanging up.

The conversation turned sinister as Richard's mind raced through all possibilities. 'Beth, you didn't contact Jane, did you? Have you told her about us?'

'How dare you ask that, Richard,' she snapped, clearly affronted.

'I had to ask. You've always said you wanted me to leave her for you.'

'Don't you think I would have mentioned it, you moron?' Beth shot back, still clearly pissed off with the accusation.

Richard let it slide, but his tired, anxious mind wouldn't let it go and questioned whether he could trust her. His thoughts escalated his fears further. Was Beth working alongside Hargreaves to ruin him? She'd met him at functions, and they appeared to get along. She could even be having an affair with Hargreaves. Richard willed his internal chatter to stop and switched his focus to Ethan Nash. 'Nash will see this as an opportunity to get rid of me. He's made no secret of the fact he detests me and alleges that most of the party hate me too.'

'It's not just about you. Ethan Nash wouldn't be too pleased with me either, and I'm easier to let go. Jane must have found out about us. It's the only explanation. Maybe she'll call you when she's calmed down... Or is it possible she's left you for someone else? We may need to take a break until we know what's happening. At least you won't have to worry about Martin seeking revenge and turning up on your doorstep.'

'Your pathetic husband is the least of my worries. I need to call Tony Hargreaves,' Richard announced.

'What... do you think Jane is having an affair with him?'

The thought hadn't occurred to Richard before, but his mind began churning through memories of drunken parties before their big fallout—surely not, no way. 'No, I don't think so,' he mumbled, not sounding convinced. 'But he always swore that he'd take revenge on me for the construction deal collapsing. Shagging my wife would just be the start for him. He'd want to ruin me good and proper. He's a ruthless bastard who'll stop at nothing.' The fear of Hargreaves' involvement was genuine, and Richard felt physically sick. He'd suspected Hargreaves would come for him sooner rather than later; the dormant fear was now revived. His survival instinct flicked to the subject of Beth's husband, a second threat to cope with as if one wasn't enough.

'Are you okay?' Beth asked, breaking the silent pause.

'What do you think?' Richard said, rubbing his forehead, his head foggy with tension and anxiety. 'Would you call Hargreaves for me, Beth? Maybe try and establish if he's involved in Jane's disappearance. He might let something slip to you.'

'Sod off, Richard. It's got nothing to do with me. I'm not getting drawn into that battle. It's between you and him.'

'I'll call you later; I need to think things through.' He hung up and refilled his glass to calm his racing mind, Beth forgotten in an instant.

Before he could take a drink, his phone began to ring. He felt battle-weary as he picked it up.

Nash's abrasive tone greeted him. 'Still nothing?'

'No, I've tried every one I can think of. This isn't right—'

Ethan stopped him in his tracks. 'We can't have the local plod all over this. Word will get out to the press. I've contacted the Chief Constable. I've asked them to take a low-key approach for now. Before they speak to you...are you sure you've told me everything I need to know? Last chance, Dicky-boy.'

'There's nothing more to it. I'll await their call; thanks, Ethan,' Richard said, struggling to keep his eyes open. He lay his head in his arms on the desk.

*

The lift stopped on the top floor at the Serious Crime Squad Command Suite. Andrea led the way to Detective Chief Superintendent Samuel's new office. The corridors were empty as usual, not bustling with as much activity as the lower floors, which were home to the investigation and operational teams. 'It's quiet up here. I suspect some weekend breaks have commenced already,' she said whilst passing the second glass-fronted empty office.

'I've only ever been up here to parade on when I've been in the shit,' Lee said, taking in the unfamiliar surroundings.

Andrea glanced back over her shoulder. 'You've never told me about getting in the shit,' she said with a hint of mockery.

'You never asked. Anyway, it's confidential, so I can't tell you,' Lee responded in kind.

Andrea knotted her eyebrows and shook her head. 'What have I got myself involved with? I'll never learn. I always go for the bad boys.' She knocked on the door and pushed it open.

Mr Samuel rose from his seat. 'Ah, Andrea, thanks for coming at such short notice. Grab a seat. I'm sorry about the mess. I'm still unpacking and sorting things out.'

Lee stepped forward from behind Andrea. 'Hey, Boss, long time no see. Congratulations on the promotion, by the way. But you'll be lucky to get beyond the building's exit door from now on unless it's for a meeting.' They laughed as Lee took a seat, and Samuel returned to his desk, surrounded by stacks of cardboard storage boxes.

Andrea placed her casebook on the edge of the desk and clicked her pen, ready to go.

'Right, let's get on with it,' Samuel said. 'Force Command has received a call from one of their political contacts. The wife of a local MP has been missing for about twenty-four hours. She's not been seen since they attended a party fundraiser together.'

'Apologies for stating the obvious, but isn't this something that uniform and local CID should be dealing with? It's a missing-from-home enquiry,' Andrea said.

'Fair point. Normally, it would be, but the Chief has asked us to deal with it, probably to keep things low-key for now. You know what the media are like in these situations.'

'But we'll still need local resources for searches and the like,' Andrea said. 'It's going to become public knowledge whether they like it or not, sooner than later. Anyway, I get it. We'll go and meet up with the MP and make an initial assessment. So, who is he?'

'It's Richard Flannagan-Smythe. Not a very popular character, from what I'm told. He always manages to piss his constituents off when he meets with them. I believe he needed a police presence at his last public surgery,' Samuel said, shaking his head.

'That's what I've heard,' Andrea agreed. 'Since then, he's spent very little time in his constituency while enjoying the grace and favour trappings of Westminster. The consensus is that he's failed to deliver on his election promises and tells lies when backed into a corner.'

Lee replied, 'I've got to be honest: I've never heard of him. I gave up on politicians a long time ago. I don't trust any of them.'

'He doesn't impress many people in Westminster, apparently. He was booted out of his job in the environmental department and is now skulking about on the back benches,' Samuel said before continuing with the briefing, while Andrea noted what little detail had been passed on to him.

'I'll go and run some intelligence checks on the main players before we set off,' Lee said, getting up from his seat and leaving the office.

Samuel leaned back into his chair. 'That's about it — no doubt there'll be more to it than we've been told. Keep me up to speed with developments. By the way, you've got a good one there: Lee McCann. Top detective, one of our best.'

'I know, boss, he's good to have on the team.' Andrea left the office wondering whether Samuel had given her a gentle nod to signify his awareness of their friendship away from work or whether she was overthinking it.

In years gone by, the Force didn't approve of couples working together and the like, but those authoritative days were long gone. Some would say that standards had slipped. It didn't matter anyway; they weren't officially an item, and neither wanted to rush into things. It was just fine as it was, taking things one day at a time.

5

Richard's head dropped and he sighed, just about to give up and put the phone down as it was answered.

'What the hell do you want, more money? I can't believe you've got the nerve to call me,' Tony Hargreaves said in a seething tone.

'Have you seen Jane, Tony?' Richard asked in a beat, instantly regretting how desperate he sounded; his question had just come out wrong. He winced but listened attentively for any signs that Hargreaves knew anything about Jane.

'What? What are you suggesting? Do you think I'm shagging your wife? Have you been drinking?' Hargreaves laughed. 'Jane, your husband is on the phone. Can you get dressed and come down, please,' Hargreaves theatrically shouted over his shoulder. 'Bring the Moet down with you,' he mocked.

Richard sensed the disdain in Hargreaves' attitude, and self-doubt swelled around him, questioning himself whether making the call had been a good idea. 'This is serious, Jane has gone missing and if I find out that you're involved—'

Hargreaves raised his voice and interrupted. The tone of mockery had vanished: 'You'll do what, exactly, you maggot?' His strong Yorkshire accent made the challenge sound even more intimidating.

'You threatened me and warned me to watch my back. What was it you said? You wouldn't rest until you'd got payback?' Richard spat out, trying to justify his suspicions.

'You need to calm down, you prick. Making wild accusations will land you in serious shit. The only person who ever mentioned harming your wife was you, don't you remember?'

Richard felt a wave of nausea; he remembered the moment too well. He'd repressed the memory to the darkest vaults of his mind. His regret was palpable as he shifted in his chair. Of all the people he could have asked to arrange a hitman, why did he choose Hargreaves?

'Shall I remind you?' Hargreaves continued. 'You asked me if I knew any contacts who could be trusted to sort things out for you. Maybe that's something the police would be interested in hearing. "Make her disappear" was the phrase, if I remember correctly.'

'I wasn't serious. I was pissed. We'd been drinking all day at the races.' Flashbacks of happier times filled Richard's mind: champagne-fuelled parties in the VIP enclosure. Hargreaves lavishly throwing crazy amounts of money at the horses. 'Jane and I were having marriage problems at the time. I was venting. That's all,' he spluttered.

'But that isn't true, is it? You lying piece of shit.' Hargreaves' quiet tone had a sinister edge. A silence hung in the air.

The magnitude of Hargreaves' words instantly zapped the energy from Richard's body. He loosened his tie, feeling dizzy and vulnerable. Panic overcame him, and he sank forward, leaning on the desk and recalling Hargreaves' threats at the height of their conflict. He'd claimed he had possession of recordings of their conversations and Richard had naively assumed the subject of these recorded discussions was Hargreaves' party donations and the building development. But then his heart sank at the realisation they were more damning... conspiring to kill his wife.

Hargreaves continued, 'It sounds like you're still having relationship problems...what have you done to her, Richard? Did you finally snap?' A silence filled the void of an answer. 'You still there, Richard?' Hargreaves taunted. 'Or have you run away, as usual, you fucking coward.'

The door bell rang, Richard felt a shot of relief and seized the opportunity to take time out. Not unlike a boxer pushed against the ropes at the end of a tough round.

'I've got to go; someone's just arrived at the house,' Richard replied, relieved for the welcome distraction.

'Bullshit, running away again? You ripped me off. I lost a massive income because of your false promises that the building applications would be passed without a problem. Just remember, what goes around comes around. You owe me a lot of money, you worm.'

'We've been over this already; my hands were tied,' he said, trying to disguise the irritation in his voice. 'There was nothing I could do to save the development plans. I did all I could for you. Look, if you hear anything, call me,' he added then hung up, picked up his glass and knocked back the remnants of his whiskey in one gulp, before heading to the front door, cursing the day he had met Hargreaves.

*

'This must be the one,' Lee said, pointing to the open gateway on his left. The six-foot Victorian red brick stone wall was shadowed by the dark mass of Rhododendron bushes hanging over it, concealing any view of the gardens and house beyond. 'They reckon this is the most expensive road in the town. Most of the houses here were built for the wealthy mill owners during the Industrial Revolution,' Lee said as Andrea turned off the road and drove along the driveway towards the imposing dwelling ahead of them.

'While the workers lived in tiny terraced houses, with whole families sharing a bed. Cotton wasn't king for them, was it?' Andrea replied as she brought the car to a halt next to a top-of-the-range SUV.

'Ever the socialist,' Lee mocked

'Not really, just taking the side of the underdog as usual,' Andrea said, giving him a sideways glance. 'The treatment of the workers during the so-called glorious days of the Industrial Revolution seems to have been forgotten. Anyway, when did you have an interest in socio-economic history, Professor McCann?' Andrea laughed.

'Knowledge is power. You'd be surprised at what I know,' Lee said with a wink.

The loose stones crunched underfoot as they headed for the door. 'Shouldn't we be going round the back to the tradesman's entrance?' Lee asked, raising a mocking eyebrow.

'It wouldn't be the first time I've been asked to do that,' Andrea said sardonically, glancing over her shoulder. She rang the doorbell and stepped back from the door, glancing around at the expansive gardens.

'Nice house,' Lee said, looking up towards the first floor. 'I bet it cost a few quid. How many bedrooms do you reckon? Six?' Andrea didn't have time to answer before the door swung open.

Lee caught the occupant's eye, a slim, anxious-looking man fidgeting with the top button of his shirt. Lee presented his warrant card and said, 'Good morning, sir. I'm Detective Sergeant Lee McCann, and this is Detective Inspector Andrea Statham. We have come to see Richard Flannagan-Smythe.'

'That's me; you'd better come in,' Richard replied, turning to head back into the house without any further pleasantries. Andrea gave Lee a knowing smile as they followed him down a long hallway.

'Beautiful tiles,' Lee said, taking in the pristine, elaborate design underfoot.

'Yes, they're original encaustic ceramic tiles, not copies,' Richard replied, gesturing towards the kitchen door. 'We might as well sit in here, take a seat.'

Lee hung back, waiting until Richard had taken a seat first, wanting to sit in the best position to observe his body language. As Lee pulled out a stool next to him, he smelled a strong waft of alcohol and wasn't surprised. The MP looked like he was struggling with the situation. His unruly blond hair looked like it hadn't seen a brush for days.

Andrea sat opposite Richard and leaned forward. 'I understand you wish to report your wife missing. Are you concerned about her safety?' she asked.

Richard stood up from his stool and leaned back against the kitchen worktop. He gazed towards the floor, stroking his chin. A momentary silence hung over the room and he began fidgeting with his shirt buttons. 'It's a bit over the top, isn't it? A Detective Inspector and Detective Sergeant. I expected a visit from your uniform colleagues.'

Lee looked up from his notepad and placed his pen on the worktop. He was surprised at Richard's opening gambit, almost killing time with an irrelevant observation. Just how concerned was he about his wife?

'This is what happens when the normal procedures are circumvented. I believe a representative of your party approached the police command team directly,' Lee said, cutting to the chase.

'Well, you know how things go, media intrusion and speculation frenzies—'

'So, would you like to run us through the circumstances leading up to your wife, Jane, going missing?' Lee asked with a tone of impatience.

'Of course, we'd been to a party fundraising event, nothing unusual. At about midnight, Jane told me she was leaving, and that's the last time I saw her.'

'Why did she leave early? Was there a problem?' Andrea asked.

'No, on the contrary, the evening had gone well. She was in good spirits. It was her usual routine at these events. She didn't care much for the after-dinner drinks, drunken tales of derring-do, and political bravado. She'd done her bit, presenting as the loyal, dedicated wife and working the room for me.'

'Why do you suspect she didn't come home? Is it unusual behaviour?' Lee asked diplomatically.

'Look, we've had a stressful year: local elections, campaigning and everything that comes with that. We've been under a lot of pressure. It takes its toll on the strongest of relationships. We've probably not given each other much attention, but that's how it is. If you are ambitious and want to succeed, sacrifices must be made.'

'You've been having domestic arguments?' Andrea suggested.

'No, I'm not saying that...just the usual trials and tribulations of marriage, like any couple with a lot on their plate.' As Richard backtracked, Lee scanned his face and hands for any signs of scratches or cuts. 'Maybe she's felt the need for time out...gone to see a friend? We all need a break at some stage,' Richard added, not convincing either of the detectives of his conviction.

'When was the last time she failed to arrive home?' Andrea asked.

'She hasn't done this before. It's out of character, so I'm concerned,' Richard replied.

Lee glanced at Andrea and then back at Richard. 'Do you mind if I have a quick look around the house? It's just a routine requirement. It's always the first place to be checked.' Richard made a "carry on" gesture with his hands, holding a puzzled expression and folding his arms.

'Right, let's get some details,' Andrea said, pen ready as Lee left the kitchen.

Lee slowly walked through the entrance hallway, checking for anything unusual or suspicious, such as signs of a disturbance, while also satisfying himself that Jane was not on the premises. It wouldn't be the first time the police had overlooked the most prominent location of a potential missing person.

He entered the lounge, a large rectangular room with a feature bay window at the far end overlooking the garden. A comfy-looking four-piece suite dominated the room, and there was nothing else besides a fifty-inch television and display cabinet. It didn't feel homely; it felt more like a utilitarian space.

Lee returned to the hallway and headed for a closed door, unsure where it led. As he opened the door, a woman shouted from within, 'I've not finished in here yet, Richard. I won't be long. Give me five minutes.'

He stepped inside and found himself facing a startled-looking young woman.

'Sorry, I didn't mean to surprise you. I'm DS McCann. I'm just having a look around the house. It's standard procedure for a missing person enquiry.' It was apparent to Lee that this was Richard's office: a grand oak desk with a red leather inlay, sprawling bookshelves, and an array of photographs on the wall, including the obligatory cringe-worthy pose of the MP with a constituent's baby while out canvassing for votes, framed newspaper articles and other self-promoting wall hangings.

'I'm Mandy, I'm the cleaner.'

'Nice to meet you, Mandy,' Lee said before casting his eyes around the room, taking in the ego theme of the place.

'What do you think has happened to Jane?' Mandy asked eagerly, placing the duster and surface cleaner spray on Richard's desk.

'Too early to say. Do you know her well?'

'Not socially, but obviously, I've got to know her from working here.'

Lee tried not to be too obvious, taking in the office's surroundings. 'Are you surprised to hear she's gone missing?'

Mandy looked towards the door, unsure whether it was safe to talk. 'Maybe it's not my place to say, but she deserves a medal for putting up with Richard. He can be a right self-centred prick at times. If she's got any sense, she'll have found someone else and eloped.'

Lee raised his eyebrows, inviting more disclosure. But he sensed her unease at talking inside the Flannagan-Smythe's home and gave her a business card instead.

'So, you're not concerned about her safety? That's the priority I'm focused on.'

'No, like I say, she'd be better off without him.'

'Do they argue much?'

'I suppose so, but nothing more than that, if that's what you're asking,' Mandy said.

'If Jane contacts you or you think of anything that might help us find her, please call me. I'll be in touch anyway at some stage, if that's okay. Somewhere you can talk more freely.'

Mandy smiled and slid the card into her pocket, and Lee left the room to continue his search of the premises. He was confident that had the cleaner known anything significant, she would have shared it immediately, but he suspected a further chat would lead to relevant background information.

A short time later, content that Jane was not on the premises, Lee returned to the kitchen and said, 'I think it's safe to say she isn't here.'

'I could have told you that and saved you the trouble of looking. You could have spent your time looking elsewhere,' Richard replied, looking back towards Andrea.

Richard's condescending manner irritated Lee, but he let it slide. There was no point in getting his back up. According to the cleaner, the man was under pressure and also had form for being a "right self-centred prick".

'Well, I think I've got enough background information to get on with it,' Andrea said, with the timely intervention. Call me if you recall anything further that may assist us or if there are any updates.'

Lee watched as Richard stood to show them out. He noticed the sweat marks spreading on his shirt from under his arms and that he looked on edge, failing miserably at concealing his twitching eyelid.

'We'll be in touch,' Andrea called as Richard closed the door behind them.

Lee clicked his seat belt fastener as Andrea set off along the driveway towards the road. 'What's your gut feeling?' he asked.

'There's more to this than meets the eye,' Andrea replied. 'He could have shared much more relevant information with us but chose not to. He appeared to be very cagey. That wasn't just the emotional fallout of his wife having gone missing.'

'I bumped into the cleaner, a young woman called Mandy. She didn't appear to be a fan of his. She seemed uncomfortable talking at the house. I'll get one of the team to speak to her as soon as possible, in a more comfortable environment.'

Turning left into the next road, Andrea replied, 'I've set up a team briefing; they should be assembled for us by the time we get back to the nick. In the meantime, I've asked for a fast-track enquiry to be undertaken at the venue where she was last seen. Some CCTV footage would be a great start. Can you arrange for the Tactical Aid Unit to search the gardens and outbuildings here?'

'Yes, I'll call them now,' Lee said, selecting the number from his contacts. 'I'll also put them on standby to search the grounds at the hotel. Let's see what the CCTV footage offers us first; it might capture her leaving, with a bit of luck.'

Andrea's mind drifted back to why the enquiry had been escalated for allocation to the Serious Crime Squad in the first place. Sure, as Samuel suggested, it was a low-key approach, but she suspected the politicians or the command team were probably holding some other cards close to their chest for now. Something wasn't right; to that end, she recognised that she must ensure her investigation was meticulous, not leaving any stone unturned.

Lee finished his call. 'The search team is allocated; they'll be attending within the hour,' he announced.

'Nice one. Let's get the teams briefed and find Mrs Flannagan-Smythe,' Andrea replied as they pulled up into the police station's backyard.

6

The team was assembled and ready for the briefing as Andrea and Lee entered the major incident room. Lee sensed an air of indignation in the room. Maybe it was because they were undertaking a missing persons investigation, which was usually a local CID matter, or maybe because their rostered weekend off was about to be cancelled.

Lee also suspected Andrea had felt a sense of indignation because of her motivating opening line: 'Right, everyone. You've probably heard we've been allocated a missing person investigation. But we need to switch on and focus. I suspect there's more to this than meets the eye, and it's a high-profile family. The CCTV Evidence Unit are on the ground already carrying out a trawl for footage, starting from the hotel, our last known confirmed sighting of her. So, we can expect that to generate further lines of enquiry soon. We'll get those allocated to you as soon as they come in and fast-track anything time-critical.' She then looked over to Lee.

'Thanks, Ma'am,' Lee said, scanning the detectives in the room, relieved to feel the indignation had been replaced with an air of focused interest in the briefing content. 'We are aware of no known threats or risks, either external or domestic. Simon, will you look into that further?' The detective nodded and began tapping on his keyboard right away. 'You'll need to contact the Parliamentary and Diplomatic Protection Command at Scotland Yard. They'll be alive to the case already.' Simon looked up from his computer and nodded.

'Dave,' Lee continued, 'will you please look at the communications and social media of the missing person, Jane, and her husband?'

'Yes, Sarge, will do,' Dave replied.

'Louise, will you look at the victim: Day-to-day routine, habits, friends, family and the usual, please.'

'Including media?' Louise asked.

'Good point, not just yet. Force command has asked us to keep this under the radar for now, but it'll be constantly under review. A thorough media appeal would be of significant benefit to us, so the sooner the better for me,' Lee said, glancing over to Andrea. 'Everyone else, see me after the briefing, and I'll allocate the remaining actions.'

'Thanks, Lee. Right, everyone, let's get stuck into this. We've got more than enough to get on with. Let's find Jane Flannagan-Smythe.'

*

When the briefing concluded, the sound of chairs being pushed back and plans of action being discussed filled the incident room as the detectives prepared to hit the streets. Andrea and Lee retired to the Detective Inspector's office to review the situation and ensure they had covered all bases for the investigation.

Andrea sat at her desk and fired up the computer. Lee pulled out a chair and placed his mug of coffee on the round meeting table.

'He looks like the ambitious type,' Andrea said, looking up from the internet search results. 'He's also punching above his weight; Jane Flannagan-Smythe is a bit of a looker.' She pushed the screen around to show Lee the media publicity images of the couple. 'That's interesting, "Local MP pulls the plug on retail and residential development". I remember seeing that on the local news. The was crying out for the development of a cinema, gym, restaurants, and apartments, and he kyboshed it.'

'Yes, I remember, too. They ended up building those huge industrial storage facilities instead. I suppose it came down to who was paying the biggest back-hander. No wonder Mr Flannagan-Smythe can afford a house like that.'

'Listen to Mister Cynical, there,' Andrea said with a smirk as her mobile phone started to ring. She broke away from the computer, grabbed the phone from the desk, and activated the loudspeaker.

'Hi, Ma'am, it's DS Booth from the CCTV Evidence Unit. We've made a good start. We have footage of Jane Flannagan-Smythe leaving the hotel grounds on foot, alone.'

'Excellent, great work.'

'It gets better. We see her next on Priory Lane, near the hotel entrance. Unfortunately, the footage isn't the best quality; we retrieved it from a garage forecourt. A car can be seen pulling into the kerb alongside her. She can be seen talking to the driver momentarily and then getting into the front passenger seat. The car then heads off towards the motorway junction.'

'Does anything look suspicious or out of place?'

'Not on the face of it. It looks like someone she knows. Hopefully, we should be able to sort this out pretty quickly. I've got a team working on the timeline of her movements from arriving at the hotel until her departure, and another team is investigating the car's route as a priority. It's possibly someone from the same function who stopped to give her a lift somewhere.'

'Or a pre-arranged meeting,' Andrea pondered out loud. 'Their destination will shed more light on things. That's a great start. Keep me updated on anything significant, and I'll fast-track actions out to the team.'

'Will do. I'll email you the footage of her getting into the car.'

Andrea hung up and asked Lee, 'What do you think?'

'It sounds feasible, but why didn't she arrive home? Was it pre-arranged, a clandestine meeting?' Lee said.

'Well, if she's having an affair and over-slept or decided to leave Richard, that would explain it. I've received the email,' Andrea said, glancing back at the screen and tapping on the keyboard. 'Let's have a look.'

Lee got up and stood next to Andrea's desk. Neither spoke as they watched the car approach Jane Flannagan-Smythe. Andrea rewound the footage and they watched it for a second time, it was less than a minute in length.

'I'm satisfied it's her. The conversation looks amicable, and she seems happy to be getting into the car. But why there? And who is the driver?' Lee asked.

'I'm guessing he doesn't want us to know. A baseball cap isn't the usual attire for one of those functions. He doesn't want to be recognised, does he?' Andrea replied. 'That doesn't bode well.'

'It doesn't look like a long conversation,' Lee observed.

'And there are no hugs or kisses when she gets in. The seat belts are fastened and they're off, it looks almost business-like,' Andrea said, pressing play for a third viewing. Their eyes were glued to the screen, hoping to identify vital information to shed more light on her disappearance.

Andrea exited the screen as the car disappeared out of view. 'Well, there's more than enough there for us to get on with,' she said. 'I'll get a PNC check done on the car registration number.'

'I'll circulate the footage to the team and then go and chat with Mandy, the cleaner. Hopefully, she'll have left the Flannagans' house by now,' Lee said, heading for the door.

*

Jane Flannagan-Smythe had lost track of time. The oppressive darkness and suffocating silence coiled around her, instilling a fear of helplessness. Her mind spun in a loop of continuous regret and self-recrimination: why did she get in the car? It defied every instinct against everything she'd ever been taught, known or experienced. The first words out of the driver's mouth should have rang alarm bells immediately. Richard would never have sent a security detail driver to take her home. Once she had left the function, he wouldn't have given her a second thought. He would have been preoccupied with networking and seeking opportunities for himself.

In her defence, the driver had been compelling. His military-like disposition was no different from that of the security staff she occasionally encountered. He even came across as miffed at having been tasked with the trivial job of taking her home. She simply hadn't seen the danger signals.

Not for the first time, Jane slowly stepped around the small, bleak room, her arms outstretched, fingers brushing against the rough texture of the breeze-block walls. It led back to the wooden door. Once again, she counted her footsteps, six feet by six feet; where the hell was she? Her fists clenched, her knuckles white, she pounded the door. The noise of the bangs echoed in the hollow room. 'Please open the door. I need to talk to you,' she yelled. Her voice was steady and deliberate. She refused to let it waver; she couldn't afford to sound weak. But once again, she was met with deadly silence, which exacerbated the feeling of isolation and fear. She leaned back against the wall, rubbing her hands to soothe the painful throbbing caused by banging on the door. The pain was better than helplessness. At least pain was something.

She closed her eyes, focusing on the slowing rhythm of her breathing. Action—she needed action. Doing something—anything proactive gave her a purpose and motivation. She was determined to get out of this mess unscathed. If it was money he wanted, she had money. She just needed to create opportunities to dig herself out of trouble. Her main focus was to talk to her abductor: who was he? What did he want? Had somebody put him up to this? Questions that continually ruminated, exacerbating her thumping headache.

She slid down the wall into a seated position and pulled her legs towards her, wrapping her arms around her shins. 'You can deal with this, Jane,' she whispered.

Her mind betrayed her, pulling her back to a time, long ago, when she thought she was in imminent danger. The wardrobe. She was crouched there, hidden amongst the clothes, her younger brother trembling in her arms, his soft sobs muffled by her hand. At the same time, she consoled him that everything would be okay as they listened to the sounds of their drunken father's footsteps stomping around the house, banging into things, bellowing threats as to what he would do to them if they didn't appear before him "right this minute".

The memories of the wardrobe were burned into her mind. Now, she discovered she could draw upon them for strength during her current trauma. Just as she had promised her brother that everything would be okay and delivered on that promise, she would now make the same commitment to herself.

The darkness pressed in around her now, too familiar, too oppressive. She wasn't ten anymore, but the fear felt the same: raw and suffocating, allowing her mind to play a cruel trick. She felt like she was back in the wardrobe, but this time alone. Her childhood hadn't been easy following her mother's death. From the age of ten, she'd undertaken an adult role, cooking, cleaning, caring for her younger brother and shielding him from their father's rage. For a while, her father had busied himself with work-related matters but he never got over his wife's death, and fell into a spiral of depression and alcoholism.

Jane had no choice but to grow up fast: learning to anticipate danger, manipulating her father with careful words to maintain a semblance of normality, ensuring food was on the table, cooking and cleaning. Her childhood had been a battlefield, and she'd survived it by becoming resilient and self-sufficient. She'd had no choice.

Her fists were clenched tighter now, her nails digging into the palms of her hands. 'Come on, keep it together, deep breaths. You can deal with this, Jane.'

The deep breaths helped her to relax as best she could. Her focus shifted to survival once again, recalling a book she had read by a kidnap victim who'd been freed after a ransom had been paid. The victim had reportedly chatted to her kidnapper about herself, hoping to form some kind of bond, and prompt her subsequent release. But then Jane started to remember one of his other victims, a young woman who hadn't been so lucky and had been found dead; murdered in cold blood by the evil man who'd captured her.

Her head felt heavy and she bowed forward, her breaths shorter and quicker. 'Let me out of here, you bastard,' she screamed at the top of her voice. 'Now!' Then she jumped to her feet and began pounding on the wooden door, each impact echoing her desperation.

She wouldn't allow herself to be a victim. Never again.

7

Richard glanced at his mirrors one last time before easing his vehicle into the parking lot. The familiar crunch of the gravel under the tyres reverberated through the open window against the stillness of the night. It was a sound that once soothed him but now felt loud and intrusive.

His usual parking spot was empty. It was in the darkest corner, furthest away from the hotel entrance, shadowed by dense woodland gardens. He stopped the car and turned off the lights. For a moment, he just sat there, letting his eyes adjust to the darkness. Slowly, the outline of the ancient oak emerged from the darkness, its thick, gnarled branches stretching into the clear night sky.

The sight stirred something within him, vivid memories, almost tangible. He relived the memory, the wild abandon. Beth's laughter cutting into the dark night as they clumsily stumbled out of the car, hands everywhere, partially undressing each other before having frantic sex against the tree. They hadn't cared about the cold or the rough bark of the tree. The eager fumbling had begun in the car, both overpowered by lust, but the confined surroundings were making things difficult. The tree was the closest location to continue the passion. Checking into the hotel would have taken far too long.

Richard grabbed his phone from the dash and glanced over his messages: nothing. He dropped it on the dash and sat back. Where the hell was she? He picked up the phone and called Jane's number. It was switched off. She never switched her phone off. He placed his palms together and touched his lips with his fingertips.

The screen of his phone lit up, spreading a film of light in the darkness. With a flicker of hope that it was Jane, he snatched the phone. It was Nash. Richard momentarily considered ignoring the call but knew it only delayed the inevitable difficult conversation.

'Ethan, that's spooky. I was just about to call you.'

'Like fuck you were... Don't bullshit me. Update me.'

'The police have interviewed me, then the cheeky bastards searched the house and the grounds.'

'They're obviously good judges of character and can smell a rat, shrewd people,' Nash sneered. 'Any update on Jane?'

'No.'

'It's not looking good, is it? Still, I suppose the media is unaware. That's one good thing. We've not had any enquiries at the press office. We could do without a media circus right now. We've only just recovered from the "Cash for access scandal", what a bloody omnishambles that was. Maybe it's time for you to take time off for family reasons. You know the routine. Protect the reputation of the party and all that. Do the right thing.'

'Christ, Nathan, that's a bit of an overreaction, isn't it? She might be back tomorrow with no scandal for you to worry about.'

'But I do worry about you, Richard. You've made many enemies. Don't be bringing trouble to my door. Get it sorted, or you're gone.' The line went dead.

The headlights from behind swung across the car park, illuminating the inside of his car momentarily and bringing him back to the moment from his troubled thoughts. As Richard had anticipated, Beth's car stopped alongside his. Moments later, his passenger door swung open, and Beth slid into the seat. A strong waft of perfume accompanied the fresh air. The scent of patchouli and vanilla rekindled memories and brought comfort and anticipation to Richard's mind. But this time, there was no lustful abandon and laughter, just dark looming clouds.

'The police have been round to my house. They searched the bloody place from top to bottom, even the gardens. But I've heard nothing since,' Richard announced eagerly, bypassing any greeting.

'This isn't good. I would've expected her to have been back by now. The police seem to be taking it seriously. You've not done something stupid, have you, Richard?' Beth's tone had an unfamiliar distance to it.

'Is that a serious question?' Richard said, clearly irked. 'What are you thinking, Beth? That I've bloody killed her and buried her in the rose bed.'

'You've always said you'd be better off without her, and let's be honest, neither of you really wants to be together.' She looked into the darkness through the passenger window as if wanting to avoid eye contact.

Richard leaned over and brushed her neck, placing his other hand on her thigh. The anxiety and worry began to subside as he edged closer to kiss her, comforted by the intimacy and her perfume.

Beth grabbed his hand and slapped it onto his thigh. 'I've come here to help you think things through, not for a bloody fumble in the car. What's the matter with you?' Richard pulled away from her and placed his head in his hands. 'You need to be straight with me, Richard; what's going on? What are you not telling me?'

'I shouldn't have called you. This is my problem. It's for me to sort out. I'm sorry for burdening you.' Hoping for sympathy, he once again leaned towards her, only to be pushed away.

'Forget it. It's not happening,' Beth spat, glaring at him and straightening her skirt. 'I don't need this hassle, Richard. May I suggest we cool things down for a while if you don't want my help? The last thing you need is a mistress on the scene just as your wife goes missing.'

'What do you think I should do?' Richard asked

'You need to bloody find her, for Christ's sake. Do you really need me to tell you that? Give Hargreaves another call and work something out with him if you suspect he's involved. I feel you're not telling me the full story here, as usual. You're telling me what you want me to know and nothing more. Well, I'm not getting dragged into this any further. I need a break,' and with that, Beth reached for the door handle and stepped out of the car.

Richard sensed fear in her voice and watched as she closed the door and paced back to her own car with a sense of urgency. A dark realisation dawned on him. 'She thinks I've killed Jane,' he muttered to himself. He shot out of the car, a desperate need enveloping him to convince her he wasn't involved in Jane's disappearance and to ensure she didn't share her concerns with anyone else. As he approached the car, Beth pressed down the door lock and put the gear stick into reverse. She didn't hang about to hear what Richard had to say. He slowly ambled back to his car in disbelief at what a mess he'd made of their meeting.

*

Jane's eyes snapped wide open, her heart thudding against her ribs. What was that noise? She sat up, wincing at the sharp ache in her neck, then rubbing it while she strained to listen to the movement outside. It sounded like there was a lone person. How long had she been asleep? Was it just another cruel dream? Her mouth was dry, and her body was heavy with exhaustion. Footsteps... yes, she definitely heard footsteps. The sound was faint but unmistakable. Her pulse started to quicken. 'I need the toilet!' Her words burst out from her without thought, instinct driving her to connect with the person outside. 'Open the door, please. I need the toilet,' shouting even louder this time, trying to sound vulnerable but also insistent. She needed to humanise herself and bond with whoever was out there. It was her best chance, possibly her only chance. The noises of someone moving about outside continued. 'Open this fucking door now,' she yelled at the top of her voice.

The scrape of the metal bolts sliding on the other side of the door sent a jolt through Jane's body. She suddenly wondered if she wanted it to be opened, would it be the start of her worst nightmares? Instinctively, she retreated, stepping back until she touched the surface of the cold, rough wall furthest from the door. A tiny slither of light pierced the darkness, slowly expanding as the door creaked fully open. She squinted and covered her eyes with trembling hands while still trying to watch for imminent danger. A figure filled the doorway, silhouetted against the light, looking towards her. 'Why have you done this?' she whispered.

The man in front of her didn't answer and instead said, 'Follow me,' as he headed away from the door. Jane followed, finding herself in a larger room. She scanned her surroundings immediately: no windows, a high ceiling, and one industrial-looking metal door. She decided it was some kind of industrial building or warehouse. Probably in the middle of nowhere, isolated from civilisation and help. 'There's a toilet behind the studded wall,' he said, nodding to a corner of the room behind them. Jane turned about and headed towards it slowly, her eyes still not fully adjusted to the light. She lifted her dress and sat down on the surprisingly clean toilet. The wall to her right was within touching distance and she quietly knocked on it. It felt solid and cold. An old building? Underground, even? It would explain why there were no windows. To her surprise, she couldn't pee. Maybe she was dehydrated. She stepped out from behind the wall and stopped, facing the man before her. Same baseball cap, same glasses, same beard, same build. It was the guy who abducted her. Every cell in her body wanted to ask: Why? Why me? What do you want? But she waited, not quite sure why, probably through fear or maybe prompting him to talk.

'I don't want to hurt you. I'm waiting for the client's phone call to find out where we go from here.'

Jane detected a hint of a Scottish accent in his matter-of-fact business tone, which seemed to have been lost over time to a generic estuary accent that was hard to place. She was just about to ask why me when the man continued, 'If you do as I say, with no dramas, you'll be okay. This is just business.'

She felt like laughing. It was just business, yeah, right. Maybe for you, not for me. Her head spun, trying to think of the right question while avoiding making him angry. 'Why have you brought me here?' she said, consciously trying not to be confrontational.

'It's not the time for questions. Take this and return to the cell.' He held out a brown paper bag. Jane took the bag and glanced inside: sandwiches and a drink carton.

She was just about to comply but felt compelled to delay the inevitable. 'Please tell me what this is about. You say it's business, but it doesn't feel like that from where I'm standing. Is it about money? I've got money. We can fix a deal that suits us both. You can trust me. Nobody needs to know this ever happened. I don't deserve this. Let's work things through, please,' she said, maintaining eye contact. 'What's your name?'

'John, call me John,' he answered.

Jane guessed it wasn't his real name by his tone, but she sensed empathy in the man's face. She felt her survival tactics were working; she had to get him to bond.

'Get back in the cell now. I don't want to have to drag you back in there. There's no need for that,' he replied in a controlled voice that lacked any flicker of empathy she'd sensed before.

Jane reluctantly returned to the cell. The door banged closed behind her, followed by the sound of sliding bolts. A chill ran down her back and she shivered, struggling to hold back tears. What did he want?

8

DS Lee McCann spotted Mandy straight away. She sat alone in the café by the window, scrolling on her phone. He caught her eye and mimicked drinking from a cup. Mandy shook her head and pointed to the mug on the table in front of her with a polite smile, so Lee ordered himself an Americano and made his way over to join her.

He looked around the place, pulled out a chair, and sat down. He was conscious of the other customers' proximity and pulled his chair closer to Mandy, his back facing the nearest table, occupied by a young guy in a suit.

'We'll have to speak quietly. We don't want people listening,' Lee said, almost whispering. 'The last time we spoke, I got the impression you weren't too keen on Richard.'

'He's a typical politician. I wouldn't trust him as far as I could throw him,' Mandy replied.

'What makes you say that?'

'I'm guessing he's a narcissist. It's all about him and his career. Jane comes second all the time. He treats her like crap unless he needs something, of course.'

'Really?' Lee asked with a look of concern.

'No, not domestic violence or anything like that,' Mandy added quickly, 'just the way he speaks to her and the way he expects her to drop everything at a moment's notice and run around after him.'

'He describes his marriage as strong and loving.'

'Well, he's going to say that, isn't he? I think he's having an affair.'

'What makes you think that?'

'Usual stuff, sneaky phone calls, looking awkward if I walk in on him whilst he's talking.'

'So why does Jane put up with him?'

Mandy shrugged. 'I've often wondered that myself, poor cow. Maybe she likes being the MP's wife, I don't know.'

Lee shifted in his seat, checking again to see if anyone was listening. He was tempted to ask Mandy to sit in his car or go to the station for privacy, but he guessed she preferred the café. It was her choice of venue, a safe place, and therefore, she was more likely to open up. His experience over the years had taught him that. Instead, he continued to cover the routine background questions.

'Do you know who he's having an affair with?' Lee asked, aware that the information was not forthcoming voluntarily.

'Not a clue, nobody I know, for sure. If it were somebody local, word would be out by now.'

'Is there anything else you could tell me to help us find Jane?' he asked, pretty sure she was holding something back. 'There's no problem with breaking confidences in situations like this. The bottom line is that Jane might be in danger.' He paused then, to allow that last word to sink in.

Mandy shook her head. 'I don't think so, but if I think of something or hear anything, I'll call you.'

'Well, that's been useful. Thanks for meeting up. I know it can't be easy opening up about your employers. Are you sure there isn't anything else you think may help us find her?'

Mandy looked out the window and placed her chin in her hand, resting her elbow on the table. She appeared hesitant. Lee patiently waited, maintaining the silence, waiting for her to speak. 'I don't know whether I should tell you this or whether it's even relevant.'

'Well, try me.'

'He's a perv; he can't keep his hands to himself,' Mandy said, still looking out into the street.

Lee leaned into the table, slightly taken aback at such a disclosure. 'He's not done anything to you, has he?'

'I shouldn't have mentioned that. I feel stupid for telling you now.'

'If he has, we can take action for you,' Lee said, moving into victim interview mode.

'I know you can, but leave it. I'm fine.'

'If you're sure. Think it over. We have trained officers who will speak to you about it.'

'I just need a minute to myself. Have you finished?'

'Yes, we've covered everything for now. If you need to speak about anything, give me a call. You've got my number.' He pulled his jacket from the back of his chair and headed for the door, convinced Mandy had more information up her sleeve. Slowly, slowly, he would find out. Rushing in all guns blazing wasn't always the best way with some witnesses: *Slowly, slowly, catchee monkey.*

Mandy watched as Lee walked across the road. She lingered, her fingers drumming softly on the table before finally picking her phone up. Glancing around the café, she typed:

The meeting has finished; all done.

The screen blinked with a single word: *Everything?*

Yes, just as you said.

Mandy waited, but no further message was forthcoming, so she dropped the phone into her handbag. The "no reply" was an anticlimax, and she felt uneasy, wondering where this was heading. Was she doing the right thing, being Hargreaves' eyes and ears? She had an eerie feeling she was being watched, so she covertly glanced around at the other customers before hurrying out of the café.

*

'Right, let's make a start,' Andrea shouted, competing with the noisy chatter in the briefing room. 'Where are we up to with enquiries into the car?' she asked as the room suddenly fell quiet.

Tom, a detective in his fifties who seemed to have been in and around the Serious Crime Squad forever, leant forward in his chair. 'Top and bottom of it, it's a cloned car. I spoke to the registered keeper. He's an accountant from Macclesfield, and he's never been in trouble with the police. He's squeaky clean. He also provided a watertight alibi. His car was parked on his drive. I gave it a good once over. He appeared genuine, so it was unnecessary to seize it as evidence. I'm happy with him and his explanation. To top and tail the action, I've requested CCTV from the golf club he was visiting at the time of the incident to corroborate his alibi.'

Andrea made notes of the update and then looked up at the team. 'CCTV updates?' she asked.

DS Booth was standing by the door. 'We're progressing well. We have sightings of the car on the M6 northbound until it leaves at junction thirty-six and heads west onto the A590.'

'Lake District, interesting destination,' Andrea mused. 'A good place to hide or disappear for a while.'

SILENT BETRAYAL

'He could also be heading to the ferry terminal at Heysham. Maybe he continued to the next junction to put us off the chase? One of our team is making enquiries there tomorrow.'

'Are the ferries to the Isle of Man or Ireland?'

'Both.'

'Okay, will you circulate the car with the Guardia and Manx police?'

DS Booth nodded and scribbled some notes in his casebook.

'DS McCann is interviewing the cleaner, Mandy, at the moment,' Andrea announced. 'If any significant information is forthcoming, we'll let you know. Are there any more updates that were not mentioned in the last briefing?' She scanned the room, conscious of keeping the briefing short to allow the detectives to continue their enquiries. 'No, okay then, let's crack on.'

Andrea returned to her desk and fired up Google Maps. Working out from junction 36 in concentric circles, she studied the most likely locations where the car may have been heading. The Heysham Port call was a good one. She hadn't been aware that ferries still sailed from there. The possibility of the driver taking a diverted route to put the police off the scent was feasible. Scotland also couldn't be ruled out. Andrea sensed the enquiry had the potential to expand across many miles as she considered the possible routes, which in turn would require a lot more resources and dependence on the commitment of other forces. *At least ANPR could prove invaluable in this case,* she thought, finishing on a positive.

She hadn't been back at her office long when Lee tapped on the door and strolled in. He took a seat and updated her about his interview with Mandy, including her revelations of possible sexual offences against her. He continued, 'I don't think she'll make a formal complaint against Richard, but she may have more to tell us at some stage. She seems hesitant; maybe it's a trust thing?'

'I wonder if Jane is aware of her allegations?' Andrea pondered.

'If she is, she might have confronted him; it would explain her wanting out.'

'Or Richard wanting her out; either way, this is no straightforward missing person enquiry.' Andrea went on to update Lee on the cloned vehicle at its last sighting in Cumbria.

'I'm ready for a beer; it's been a long day. Do you fancy one?' Lee asked.

'No, I've arranged a meeting with Samuel to update him. I'll advise him that it's looking like an abduction and ask for more resources. We'll probably need to get the surveillance unit onboard and consider some mobile phone taps.'

'Do you want me to come?'

'No, he's more likely to open up about any political information being held back from us if it's just me. Or maybe he's not been given the full brief. If there's more to this, we need to know now. I'll see you back at mine later.'

9

Richard was slumped at his desk. The study walls felt like they were closing in on him. His arms were tucked together on the desk, with his head resting on them. After tossing and turning for what seemed like an eternity, he'd given up fighting his ruminating mind and the torment of trying to sleep and headed downstairs for a whiskey. He could usually get by on six hours of sleep, but tonight, he longed to shut down his frazzled mind and rest well. But it wasn't happening for him.

The whiskey greased the wheels of his thought processes, allowing him to decide what was required. He needed to gain control of the situation. He'd worked hard to get to where he was in Westminster and wasn't prepared to lose it now.

Locating Jane or establishing what had happened to her was his priority. Only then could he work out a plan. He had to face facts and stop hiding from the obvious truth, certain her disappearance was down to Tony Hargreaves. Richard would be stupid to think otherwise. But the question was, had Hargreaves taken it upon himself to dish out some revenge and blackmail him for money? Or had the wheels of motion finally kicked in with the contract killer? Richard suspected these things took time to research, plan and execute. The fact that he'd since fallen out with Hargreaves was irrelevant. What else could he have expected if the kill hadn't been cancelled? Whatever the outcome, he didn't have the finances to cover either of the scenarios. He relied on Jane and other donors' generosity for the big money.

He looked at the clock; it was still too early to call Tony Hargreaves. Most likely he would still be in bed, next to his wife. Hargreaves' alternative life was in "monied suburbia", where his neighbours had no reason to suspect he was anything other than a straight-down-the-line businessman. Not the side of him that Richard had got to know. His stomach churned at the thought of the conversation. Every instinct screamed at him that it would end badly, but there was no other way around it. He needed to regain control before things spiralled further out of hand.

The memory of that night was clawing at his mind. Drunken conversation about taking out a contract on Jane by the pool table in Hargreaves' basement den. He cringed at the vivid image of the two plastic gangsters setting off on a trajectory way out of their depth, but no matter how Richard tried, he couldn't shut the thoughts away. He banged his fist on the desk, the sound reverberating through the silence of the office. How had he been so bloody naïve? Had Hargreaves really recorded the conversation? Or was he bluffing? Maybe he could cut a deal with the promise of a delayed payment? He'd always managed to manipulate Hargreaves in the past, twisting him around his little finger. Playing on his weaknesses of greed and reputation. Why not now?

The thought of Hargreaves' home life popped back into Richard's mind. Should he fight fire with fire and target his weak spot—his wife? No sooner had the thought arisen than Richard accepted he didn't have the minerals to undertake such a retaliation nor the money to pay for it to be done.

He poured another large whiskey and knocked it back. His anxiety growing, patience not being one of his strengths.

*

Tony Hargreaves waited until his wife had gone shopping for a dress to wear at the charity dinner they were attending that weekend, before picking up the phone. He was in no doubt that the call would turn into a heated, nasty, venomous exchange. He relished the idea of cornering the coward. On a previous occasion, during one of his straighteners, for a fleeting moment he'd thought the MP was actually about to cry like a baby.

The thought of calling and speaking to the worm made him angry. He didn't want his wife to see or even be aware of this side of his personality.

He'd not seen or heard of Richard Flannagan-Smythe for a good while after telling him that he was a fucking piss-stone who shouldn't be fucking about with the Alpha-males. But he also left him in no doubt that he needed to keep looking over his shoulder because revenge was a dish best served cold. Hargreaves knew the power of putting someone in absolute fear for their safety and not knowing when it was coming. His final words to Richard were meant to leave him in no doubt that he would pay the price for what he did or, in these circumstances, didn't do.

He cursed as the dial tone cut off again, then immediately pressed redial. 'Answer the bloody phone, you prick,' he repeated, pacing up and down the lounge—the familiar pang of loathing for the man coursing through him.

*

Richard's head felt heavy as he lifted it off the desk in response to the mobile phone ringing. The thumping sensation in his temples registered immediately. His eyes felt like they'd been glued together as he forced them open. The ringtone filled the room. Where was the bloody thing? He fumbled about the desktop before spotting the illuminated screen of the phone on the floor by the chair leg.

He picked it up and gingerly held it to his ear. 'Hello,' he answered, rubbing his eyes, not having checked the screen to establish the caller's identity.

'The local CID has just visited my house; did you send them?'

Richard recognised the voice immediately, feeling a sense of fear, just like when the bully and his sidekicks sauntered into his dormitory at Prep school years ago. 'No, of course not. Why would I do that?' he stuttered, squinting at the clock in a state of confusion: had he called Hargreaves before falling asleep? What had been said? He had no recollection, it put him on the back foot. He rubbed his neck, wishing he hadn't answered the phone and was still asleep, as Hargreaves' angry voice bounced around in his sore head. He wasn't in a fit state to attempt to lay down the law and take control of the situation.

'We need to talk. Meet me at the bench in the park at two o'clock. Don't be late.'

The line went dead. Richard slid his phone onto the desk and ran his fingers through his hair. He took a sip of the stale water, still there from last night, and dragged himself off to get ready. His mind was already in overdrive. Had he rung Hargreaves? Why the hell had the police been to Hargreaves' house? He felt deflated. Hargreaves had usurped his plan to gain control before he'd even got it off the ground.

He took solace in the shower, the jets of hot water soothing his head, providing a momentary lapse away from the reality of his starring role in another shitshow.

*

Lee McCann was watching Hargreaves' house from a safe distance in the comfort of his car. He held a clipboard against the steering wheel, portraying the role of a salesman so as not to attract attention to himself from nosey neighbours.

He was parked further down the road, using a hedge to provide partial cover to prevent Hargreaves from clocking him, satisfied that Hargreaves' had believed his visit had been *just a routine enquiry*. In truth, however, it was far from routine. Lee had a gut feeling that he didn't like. He'd decided to delay heading back to the station straight away, just in case his visit prompted a knee-jerk reaction from Hargreaves. From his experience, it wasn't unusual for meetings to be arranged hastily after an unexpected call from the police. Lee turned down the volume of the media player and called Andrea.

'How did your interview with Tony Hargreaves go?' Andrea asked, cutting to the chase.

'My gut tells me we're onto something. I think we're heading in the right direction,' Lee confirmed. 'He's a shrewd character. He was trying to get as much information from me as I was from him. It was like a game of poker.'

'Did you come away with the most chips?' Andrea asked, chuckling at her wit.

'I got enough to go on. He was chatting openly about what good friends they were at one time and how that relationship ended abruptly when Richard, a member of the parliamentary planning committee, pulled the rug from under his most ambitious property development, almost sending his business into bankruptcy. It was the one we read about on the internet.'

'Does he still seem angry about it?'

'No, that's what interests me; he forgivingly says it's all water under the bridge now. I'm not buying it. I could smell the bullshit from a mile away. He doesn't look like the forgiving type; more likely the type who wants his pound of flesh in revenge.'

'Did you use your newfound technique for picking up on anxiety leakage from his body?' Andrea teased.

'You can laugh,' Lee replied, suspecting she had patiently waited for the right occasion to take the piss out of him for his newfound knowledge from one of his many favourite podcasts. 'You should follow her on Instagram. She knows her stuff, and it's not witchcraft. It's science. Something we can use to our advantage. Did you know that when a group of women spend much time together in close proximity, their menstrual cycles align with the Alpha female in the group?'

'I have actually heard about that,' Andrea replied. 'I'll give you that one.'

'There's a lot of benefit to trusting your gut feelings and chemistry, as they call it. It's invaluable to me when deployed on undercover assignments. If a situation is taking a dark turn, and you can sense the emotions at play, it can be a lifesaver.'

'There's something in it. You should consider earning some money on the side as a clairvoyant!' Andrea said, failing to curtail her laughter.

'Anyway, you philistine, to answer your question: Yes, I did get the impression that he had the swan effect going on; his calm persona was a shell. He was busy assessing what we knew and what we were after, for sure.'

'Interesting, so you think he could be involved?'

'Yes, I'm in no doubt. I pushed his buttons to trigger an emotive response. I suggested that anyone in their right mind would still be angry, especially after Flannagan-Smythe had given him the nod that the application would sail through the planning process. The truth was leaking from him, but he kept his cool. He doesn't look like the type of guy that would buckle under pressure. He's a formidable guy. He looks like he can handle himself, too. He's built like the proverbial outbuilding. And he was one of your lot a long time ago.'

'One of my lot?'

'He was a Metropolitan police officer years ago. He only served as a PC for four years; he reckons he was fitted up as a scapegoat when an investigation went tits-up. He was disciplined for assault, using excessive force on a suspect, and resigned before he was pushed. He went under a cloud.'

'Well, he's got the motive. Worth some surveillance, I reckon?'

'Probably the best lead we've got right now,' Lee answered, already one step ahead, executing his own quasi-surveillance. I've got to go. Speak later,' he added, noticing the front door at Hargreaves' house open. Lee started his car engine when he saw the man himself getting into his car.

Lee waited until Hargreaves set off and pulled out into traffic, tailing him from two cars behind.

*

Richard had dressed in his default casual incognito clothes for the meeting: a dark blue hoodie, baseball cap, and ripped jeans. The same clothes that maintained his anonymity when he was out and about in London. Truth be told, he wasn't that visible in politics, and nobody would probably recognise him anyway, other than the red-top journalists, maybe.

He took a quieter route from the main path, approached the familiar black metal park bench and looked around, across the lawns and shrubbery, towards the ornamental lake and the café beyond. Everyday life continued peacefully: grandparents and their grandchildren making each other laugh and couples enjoying a coffee together.

They hadn't met here for a long time, but it looked just the same. On previous, more amicable visits, they talked about helping each other to get rich and buying holiday apartments in exotic locations abroad. Hargreaves was planning on building them, in fact. These were happier times, the memories of which helped Richard dissipate his anxiety and fear momentarily. But in a flicker, his mind was reflecting on one of those days, sat on this same bench, when he confidently led Hargreaves to believe that the rubber stamp on his Manchester development was a formality. The memory now held darker connotations for him. The dark clouds swiftly returned. Had he made a promise he couldn't deliver on? Or did he make the promise in good faith? Whichever it was, he could no longer recall.

His mind broke away from the thoughts, his eyes scanning the park, almost like prey in fear, attempting to detect the predator stalking, preparing for the kill. There was no sign of Tony Hargreaves yet, and no familiar faces to be concerned about. The bench was secluded, off the beaten track; the only passers-by were the occasional joggers. He looked over his shoulder, then stood up and began pacing by the shrubbery, out of the sight of unwanted attention. His mind raced through his options: Do I open with an offer of money and get it sorted? Be passive and let Tony be the first to make a move? Or should I threaten him? But running through these options didn't help to make things any clearer.

'Sit down, Richard,' a voice cut through the air like a blade. It was Tony Hargreaves' voice, gruff and commanding: unmistakable. 'You look like an anxious schoolboy waiting outside the head's office.' His words were sinister but laced with mockery as he approached the bench with a deliberate, almost predatory gait. They both sat down, and Hargreaves opened his newspaper with a casualness that belied the tension in the air.

Hargreaves began without looking up from the editorial, his voice deceptively calm, 'Why did CID visit my house today, asking questions about your wife?'

Richard cynically wondered who Hargreaves thought he was, behaving like a spy about to do a dead drop in a le Carre spy thriller. 'You know why, I told you,' Richard replied, trying to keep his voice steady while fiddling with the drawcord of his hoodie. 'She's officially a missing person. The police are obviously going to contact anyone who may be able to assist as a matter of course.'

'Nothing more sinister than that, eh?' Hargreaves' tone was cold, fixing Richard with a stare that sent a chill down his spine. 'I don't trust you. Are you trying to set me up while covering your tracks?'

'Look, Tony, let's stop playing bloody games here. Do you know anything about Jane's disappearance? We need to get this sorted. It's getting out of hand with the police all over it. It's the last thing either of us needs. Where is she?' Richard's voice cracked slightly, betraying his growing desperation.

'I don't know,' Hargreaves said, his eyes now locked on Richard's, unblinking. I've told you.'

Richard jumped up and glared at him, fists clenched. 'Well, why the hell did you want to meet me?'

A slow, menacing smile crept across Hargreaves' face. 'Because I want to warn you, Dicky-boy,' he said, his voice dropping to a sinister whisper, clearly unfazed by Richard's sudden pathetic outburst. 'Pass me your phone,' he demanded almost as an afterthought.

'Why?'

'Just pass me your fucking phone, now. You're not recording this, are you?' It was Tony's turn to glance around, his eyes darting everywhere, checking for police surveillance. Tony took the phone and glanced at the screen, then placed it on the bench between them.

'Are you trying to stitch me up?' he said, his eyes narrowing to slits as he leaned closer into Richard's space.

'No, I don't know where she is. I'm just trying to find her. I'm not trying to stitch anyone up,' Richard stammered.

'Good. I've given the detective an account that he appears happy with, and sent him on his way. I told him what a snake you were for nearly bankrupting me.'

'Not that again; how many times do I need to tell you my hands were tied.'

'They weren't tied tight enough to stop you from taking the backhanders from me.'

'There was nothing I could do to get the application through planning. I tried my best.'

'Shut up and listen,' Hargreaves said impatiently, leaning forward. 'If I hear from the police again, I'll hand over the recordings of you asking me to take out a contract on her.'

'For fuck's sake, Tony, that was beer talk, nothing more,' Richard pleaded.

'Richard,' Hargreaves cut him off, his voice menacing, 'stop fucking me about. It's me you're talking to, not some wet parliamentary select committee who don't know their arses from their elbows. We both know you meant it. You wanted rid of her, and you couldn't sort it out under your own steam, you clown.'

Richard felt dizzy. 'Look, I can't be clearer about this. I don't know where she is, and I think you do. What do you want, money?'

'Can you afford to pay your debt off?' Hargreaves sneered with contempt. 'You nearly bankrupted me. That's a lot of money to pay back. Anyway, I don't need to kidnap your wife. I've got the voice recordings of you asking me to arrange a contract kill, and I've also got photographs of you and your married secretary, Beth.' Richard slumped forward, head in hands, facing the floor. The silence hung over them like the still air before a storm. Hargreaves continued, 'The question is, who do I hand them to? The police, the red tops, or Beth's husband. He's a bit of a brawler by all accounts. He'll probably hunt you down, Dicky-boy, torture you, then throw you in the ship canal.' Hargreaves chuckled darkly.

'What do you want?' Richard mumbled, resigned to defeat.

'Well, that's very nice of you to ask,' Hargreaves replied, his voice oozing with mock politeness. 'Let's start with the first instalment of my compensation and a polite request to keep the fucking police away from my door.'

'What about my wife?'

'Be seeing you, Dicky-boy.' Tony pulled himself up, placed the folded newspaper under his arm with practised elegance, and strolled towards the café.

*

Lee selected a table outside the café and watched Hargreaves sit on a park bench. He was quite a distance away, across the lake. Lee wished he had a pair of binoculars to see more of what Hargreaves was up to. But, just as quickly, he refuted the wish, guessing that someone would probably accuse him of being a paedophile, leching at the kids in the park.

He angled his head as best he could to avoid appearing to be watching Hargreaves, using his peripheral vision. Hargreaves was talking to the male, who was also sitting on the bench. Lee's hunch was correct. This looked like a pre-arranged meeting. He scrutinised the second male, then sat forward in his chair to get a better view. 'You dog,' whispered Lee, realising the second male was Richard Flannagan-Smythe.

The pair seemed to have been talking amicably, but things became more hostile and animated. Lee watched, surprised, as Flannagan-Smythe jumped up, standing over Hargreaves in what he thought was an aggressive stance. Lee took out his phone and photographed them, although he suspected they needed to be closer for the photos to be helpful. *At least it'll provide evidence of the meeting*, he thought, consoling himself.

SILENT BETRAYAL

The waitress appeared by his side, placed his coffee on the table, and left just as quickly. While Lee took his first drink, he watched Hargreaves stand up and walk away from the bench. He was heading for the café and Lee considered slipping away discreetly. He knew the park well and could easily avoid Hargreaves discovering he was there, but he decided otherwise. The thought of another conversation with Hargreaves, on the back of his clandestine meeting with Flannagan-Smythe, was too good an opportunity to miss. He placed his coffee on the table and sat back, watching as he approached.

Hargreaves struggled to hide his surprise when their eyes locked on each other. Lee couldn't work out whether it was an expression of anger or fear, as it was only a flicker. Almost immediately, Hargreaves recomposed himself and smirked as if he had expected to see Lee.

Once in hearing distance, Lee raised his cup as if making a toast. 'The coffee's very nice. You should try it,' he suggested with a smirk.

Hargreaves continued to the table and pulled out the chair opposite. 'Then you won't mind me joining you, will you?' he said confidently, sitting down, his eyes boring into Lee's with menace. His disposition was in total contrast to the earlier meeting at his house. 'So, you've taken to following me around, lurking in the shadows. Seems a bit desperate to me. You know you're following the wrong man, don't you?'

'How did the meeting go?' Lee asked, nonchalantly looking away to take a drink.

'I've met your sort before. Most of them burned themselves out or eventually fucked up and ended up back on the beat or school crossing patrol.'

'Don't knock it,' Lee retorted with a shake of his head. 'Some of the best intelligence comes from walking the streets. Or building sites, the builders are usually more than happy to get one back on their bosses when they can, can't stop them talking.'

Hargreaves let out a low, sinister laugh. 'You don't intimidate me, McCann, especially when you've nothing on me. You can't hurt me. On the other hand, though, people who've crossed me in the past usually live to regret it. You see, your problem is this… the rules restrict you. However, I don't need to play by the rules.'

Lee re-engaged the stare. 'I've heard that before, notably the rules about paying tax. Now, I may not intimidate you, but I guess HMRC will.'

'Well, let's wait and see, shall we? Be safe out there, Lee. It can be a dangerous occupation, policing. I always express my concerns about officer safety to the Chief Constable. I'll be seeing him at his charity night in a few days. Don't you find it's not always what you know but who you know in the world today?'

'I suppose so. I believe in Karma, too. Pass on my regards to the chief. Oh, and by the way, ask him to tell you a funny story about when he turned up for a meeting dressed as a gardener. What a laugh that was,' Lee said, standing up. 'Great to see you, Tony. Catch up again soon. But maybe next time, you'll need a solicitor to keep you company; cells can be very lonely.

10

Jane jolted awake to the cold metallic grinding of the door bolts being slid open. Squinting as the slither of light slowly grew, filling the cell, she instinctively protected her eyes with her hand. 'I've brought you some food,' John's voice came, low and clipped.

She was concerned that he didn't address her by her name; was he maintaining a cold social distance to make killing her easier? She got to her feet and steadied herself against the wall as the blood returned to her numb legs. 'Are you coming or not?' he snapped.

A flicker of rage ignited in Jane's chest, and she almost shouted back, telling him to fuck off, but she bit her lip in fear as she entered the main room, which remained the same as before. Stale. Oppressive. Instead of sitting on her usual upturned bucket, she picked up her sandwich and sat closer to him than before on a wooden pallet. John looked up, barely acknowledging her breach of routine. His eyes, unblinking, locked onto hers as he ate his own sandwich.

'Did you make these?' Jane said, forcing her voice to sound casual, even conversational. 'They're delicious.'

'Just eat it,' he muttered without looking up.

Her pulse quickened, and anger, fear and resentment welled inside her. 'Who is behind this?'

John's eyes narrowed as he lifted his head to look at her. 'I don't know, it's just an assignment.'

That word; assignment. So clinical, so cold. The delivery sent a chill down Jane's spine. The realisation hit home harder than before. She was just a target to be dispatched, not a person being held against her will by him.

'What kind of assignment? Are you going to kill me?' Her voice cracked as she held his gaze, searching for any flicker of humanity.

He didn't answer and took another bite from his sandwich.

'Please, hear me out,' she continued, 'I have no dispute with you. I get it; you're being paid. But I can pay you more. That's why I need to know who's hired you. I'm able to pay more. I have access to funds.' Jane's voice was growing more decisive as her confidence swelled with the desire to survive.

John stopped eating for a moment and replied, 'It's not that easy. I have a professional reputation. Double-crossing a client is a non-starter. The work would dry up instantly. It's a word-of-mouth business, built on trust; references are important.' His delivery was more detached and emotionless than last time, and his words chilled Jane to the core.

She looked at the floor, the swell of fear clawing back at her new lease of confidence. 'How long is this going to go on for? I don't deserve this. I'm a good person.'

John stood abruptly, kicking the wooden bench backwards, its legs scraping the concrete floor. Then, he took a deliberate pace towards her. 'You're asking too many questions. Shut the fuck up,' he demanded, raising his voice for the first time.

Jane's body reacted before her mind could, recoiling in one fluid movement, her back hitting the wall with a dull thud, panic taking over. 'Please don't hurt me. I can pay you,' she gasped, her voice shaking. She felt regret at obviously having pushed him too far. She made eye contact with him again and was flooded with relief when she saw no signs of anger or malice in his eyes. There was a reasonable man in there…somewhere, and she had to connect with him. It was her only way out. She guessed he was simply demanding compliance. But that wasn't an easy expectation in these circumstances, only if compliance was a means to an end. This was by no means over yet. Jane was determined about that.

'It's time to go back to your cell. I have work to do,' John said, his voice calmer but still intimidating in a no-nonsense way.

Jane cursed herself as she entered the cell. Pissing him off and getting thrown back in there as a consequence was a fuck-up. She needed time with him to bond and humanise their relationship, to work towards a positive outcome. She made a snap decision and turned around, catching his eye, working hard to appear vulnerable—a last chance at saving the situation and hoping to bond before the cell door slammed shut.

'I'm sorry to keep asking questions, John, but I'm terrified. Don't you understand? What else can I do to save myself? I don't deserve this. I've never harmed anyone in my life.' Tears started to well in her eyes as she considered reaching out and touching him, before deciding that was a step too far, for now. She felt a tear roll down her cheek as she held eye contact.

'Just step back into the cell,' John instructed, and this time, she definitely detected a hint of empathy in his tone. Her mood suddenly lifted in a microsecond as the cell door closed behind her, followed by the anticipated noise of the bolts sliding into the locked position. A dreaded sound that exacerbated her fears and anxiety.

She slid down the wall, resting on her haunches. 'Well done, girl,' she whispered, reflecting on her last-ditch performance attempting to retrieve something from the situation. *I can do this. I know I can*, she affirmed to herself.

*

John slid the bolt into the housing on the wall and left the basement. He'd never wanted to get into this side of the business. This was for 'H', not him, he was an assassin, not a fucking gaoler. But on this occasion, the money hadn't been received as per the arrangement, which presented a problem that changed things for now.

As he walked up the stairs, he fought his emotional feelings, trying to suppress them. They shouldn't have risen in the first place. Having no emotion was one of the basic tenets of this game. The thought continued to claw at him, with a recognition that it wasn't emotions at play. There was something about this woman, but he couldn't put his finger on it. She had similarities to women he had worked with in the special forces, even though he knew she had no military or similar experience from his comprehensive research. Her career before working for her husband had been in HR management. But what was it? Chemistry? An unexplained respect? He wasn't sure.

John reached the lounge and picked up his encrypted phone; he walked over to the window and selected the recipient while looking across the vast panorama of bleak, desolate moors. There was no sign of human habitation, just how he liked it these days. The nearest farm was miles away, run by a grumpy old bugger who was no trouble or threat to him, someone John suspected was one of those hermit farmers who would rather shoot some city stranger hiking across his land than talk to them.

When John bought this place under a pseudonym, he called on the farmer as part of his reconnaissance to understand his surroundings and identify any threats. He left, satisfied that the threat level was very low, and begrudgingly respected the farmer's audacity after convincing John to agree to let him graze animals on the far side of his land.

H answered the phone. 'Is he still not answering your calls?'

'He answered my last call,' John replied 'but he's shirking any responsibility from paying. He's passing the buck to the target's husband. It's turning into a shit show. I left him in no doubt that he was making a mistake, but he has an arrogance and confidence that will probably bring about his downfall. Have you finished the job in Glasgow?'

'Yes, and the cash is in the account. It went exactly as planned, apart from the deposition site. The building site where I was planning on ditching him in a concrete grave was on a twenty-four-hour shift, fucking floodlights everywhere, probably extra shifts to hit a deadline, so I had to use the docks.'

'That's not what we agreed. What if he resurfaces? You know the script, H. If there's a change of plan, we discuss the options together. There's no I in team... I seem to recall you telling me,' John said, aware he was being scratchy with H and self-conscious that he may lead them to a row.

'There's no chance of him resurfacing. I bound him tight in a tarp for plan A, then fastened it with an old, rusted anchor chain I found. Never to see the light of day again.'

'Unless there's an unconnected police search that finds the body,' John replied, clearly irked at H's modified plan. John trusted H and, on the whole, enjoyed being his business partner. There was no doubt they worked well together. But John had a nagging belief that H's eagerness to get things done could lead to knee-jerk plans and cost them dearly.

'Mate, it's the River Clyde, not a fucking boating lake in a park. Take a chill pill,' H said in his usual straightforward, laid-back, confident manner.

John decided to take H's advice and took the chill pill, changing the subject. 'On your way back, can you visit our client and straighten him out? We need to get this job resolved, too. Our guest says she has money and wants to cut a deal. So, in the worst-case scenario, we could switch targets and remove the problem man in Manchester. We know he's not connected to any major players, so it won't be a problem for us to walk away without getting our fingers burned.'

'It won't come to that. Leave it with me,' H said before hanging up. He had a way of making shitstorm situations sound like it was just a walk in the park. John had every faith in him getting the Yorkshire businessman to see sense.

After the call, John felt relaxed and poured a whiskey before easing back into his favourite rocking chaise lounge chair. He gently rocked using the tiniest momentum from his legs.

His mind started to wander, relaxed by the single malt whiskey. He had been working with H for three years now, and they were an effective team that earned good money. It provided a better lifestyle than his previous VIP security work in the Middle East. He'd grown to hate the place along with the Walter Mitty

Brigade, who were now gaining more influence with the bean counters. Picking up contracts, undercutting the real operators and creating more danger and hassle for everyone. But he was now getting itchy feet again. He took another sip of whiskey and wondered whether it was time for a change. There were plenty of opportunities out there now. Some of his ex-oppos were making decent money with no risk or hardship: reality TV shows, personal development programmes, corporate management development, and even clothing lines for the serious outdoor types. The world was changing, and the ex-special forces operators were in great demand.

*

DS Lee McCann glanced at his watch as he entered the staff canteen at the station. He felt relieved when he spotted Andrea busy chatting with Samuel, not sitting alone, drumming her fingers and waiting for him. The canteen was virtually empty, which seemed the norm these days. At one time, there was a queue at the hot plates and only a few empty seats at the tables. The bosses used to encourage officers to return to the nick for their breaks in days gone by; it was an opportunity to let off steam and vent, away from the public eye, managing the stresses and pressures of the demanding job. Canteen culture was all but gone now. Nowadays, the officers either didn't have time to return to the station and take a break or, if they did have time, they'd be encouraged to take their break in public, therefore maintaining an illusion of the diminishing thin blue line of a police presence. Suffering indigestion in the process, having eaten in a rush was now part of the job description. And that wasn't considering the criticism on social media when an officer would be seen to have the audacity to sit down in a café. *How times have changed*, thought Lee, recalling how talking to people in such places used to be a fundamental part of policing and getting to know what was happening in the community.

He approached the table, confident that Andrea hadn't noticed the time. He pulled out a chair and sat alongside her.

'Nice of you to join us, Lee; I thought you'd decided not to bother,' Andrea said, rolling her eyes. Samuel chuckled politely, shifting uncomfortably in his chair at the humorous barbed comment.

'Well, you know me, I'm not one to disappoint,' Lee said with a smile, deflecting the sarcastic dig with panache.

'See what I have to put up with?' Andrea said, looking at Samuel, raising her arms in mock disdain.

'Anyway, I've got work to discuss; I haven't got the time for such banter and hilarity,' Lee pushed further with a wink.

'What have you got?' Andrea asked, curiosity getting the better of her and bringing the banter to a conclusion.

'Well, I've already updated you about my interview with Tony Hargreaves. I returned to my car and was just about to set off to meet you here when he left his house and got into his car. He didn't look happy, quite pissed off, in fact.' Lee paused, glancing at them both, building up the tension. 'So, I tucked in behind him; he looked like a man on a mission. Sure enough, he met up with Richard Flannagan-Smythe in a quiet little corner of Heaton Park.'

Andrea sat up. 'Excellent, what happened?'

'Flannagan-Smythe was waiting, pacing up and down like a condemned man. Their conversation looked heated. At one stage, Flannagan-Smythe jumped up, towering over Hargreaves. I thought he was about to lay one on Hargreaves' chin. But Hargreaves wasn't fazed. I think he found Flannagan-Smythe's aggression amusing, knowing he didn't have a punch in his armoury. Hargreaves was the one out of the two of them who maintained his composure. It looked like the pressure was on Flannagan.'

'Well, that sheds more light on things; great work, Lee,' Samuel said, sitting back in his chair. 'Good timing, too.'

Lee smiled and nodded at Samuel's kind words while electing not to mention his confrontational conversation with Hargreaves outside the café. That was not for further dissemination, especially to the Head of Serious Crime.

'We were just discussing a surveillance operation when you arrived,' Andrea went on. 'We need to find out what these two are up to. It's probably our best chance of finding Jane at the moment.'

'I've updated the Chief Constable and informed him we're treating this investigation as suspicious and not a routine missing person enquiry. He's guaranteed we'll have access to any force and external resources we need,' Samuel said, with relish.

'I pressed the Chief to lift the sanction on going to the press,' Samuel continued. 'He got back to me and clarified that the powers in Westminster want us to continue low-key for now, but that's subject to continual review and change. So, we can't utilise the media for now,' he said with an expression of bemusement.

Andrea responded, 'Our Intelligence Cell has established points of contact with the Special Branch,

Met Police and the Intelligence Services. They're working closely together to develop the intelligence picture and strategy.'

'We've also got Border Control in the loop to cover the possibility of her being taken to Ireland or the Isle of Man,' Lee added.

Andrea nodded. 'I'm satisfied we're doing all we can,' she said. 'The team are working flat out on sixteen-hour days. We must be due some luck any time now.' She glanced at Lee as if looking for reassurance.

Samuel went to stand up, indicating the meeting was over. 'I'm sure we will,' he said. 'Let's get the surveillance on Flannagan-Smythe and Hargreaves up and running. I'll be shocked if we don't get a positive result.' He then looked at Andrea and added, 'Keep me updated, and I'll see you in the morning.' He only managed about seven paces towards the door before a uniform superintendent accosted him, wanting to discuss the release of his uniform patrols from protecting a serious crime scene in his borough.

'Samuel seems satisfied with the work so far. Did you press him for any more background?' Lee asked.

'I did, he said we know everything he does. But he did say he'd pass anything he gleaned onto us.'

'Do you believe him?'

'Yes, we go back a long way. Trust isn't an issue. I worked for him on the newly formed Armed Crime Task Force back in the days of the media-led Gunchester phenomena, which helped them to sell a lot more newspapers. I was in the CID office when we all had to dive for cover to dodge the incoming bullets of a drive-by shooting show of strength.'

'Are you sure you were there?' Lee asked with a quizzical, mocking expression. 'If all the detectives who've claimed they were there *were* there, they wouldn't have all managed to fit in through the doors.'

'Well, we know for sure you weren't there,' Andrea shot back. 'You were too busy studying for your GCSEs when the real action was going down.'

'I can't argue with that. I know my place. I'll get us a coffee, maybe toast as well,' Lee said with a smirk, standing up.

'Make that cheese on toast,' Andrea called after him. 'A penalty for your cheek, sprog.' She couldn't help but think how good Lee would have fitted into that unit. It was a time of long, busy days. Intelligence-led operations, primarily using informants, which by their nature brought about further shitstorms for the police as they focused on removing the guns and the major players from the streets of Manchester.

As Lee headed to the hot plates, he couldn't help but wonder if Samuel had trusted Andrea with some "Need to Know" information. *Will Andrea trust me with it?* he wondered. There had to be more to this than met the eye. Why didn't Westminster want the press involved, or maybe he was overthinking it? Manipulation of press releases to the masses was nothing new these days.

He stepped up to the counter, looking for any familiar kitchen staff he knew there, but they were all new faces. 'Cheese on toast, a cappuccino and an Americanos, please,' Lee said to the young lad behind the counter while fighting the urge to add a full breakfast to the order for himself, he was very tempted.

'Anything else?' the kitchen assistant asked.

'No... that's fine, thanks,' Lee said, reluctantly, thinking about the gym session he'd got planned after work.

11

Tony Hargreaves parked his car in the driveway, walked to the boot, and grabbed his golf clubs, oblivious to the fact that a police surveillance team had been watching him since he left the house earlier that morning.

He slung the golf bag in the garage and unlocked the front door. His attention was immediately taken by Stella, hovering in the kitchen doorway, beckoning him over dramatically. She looked nervous, almost uneasy.

'What's the matter?' Tony asked, with furrowed eyebrows, sensing something was off.

'One of your friends from the Met is sitting in the lounge,' she whispered, her voice shaky. 'This is the second coffee I'm making him. He was insistent on coming in to wait for you. He wouldn't take no for an answer. I told him he'd find you at the golf club, but he wasn't having any of it. He's a bit scary. He looks like Voldemort on steroids.' Stella grimaced as she retreated further into the kitchen as if seeking protection.

Tony's stomach tightened. He didn't know anyone who vaguely matched that description. He turned on his heels and headed for the lounge, apprehension crawling up his spine. Trying not to look worried in front of his wife.

Pushing the door open, his eyes were immediately drawn to the visitor sitting in the wingback chair at the far end of the room. Stella's description was pretty accurate. The visitor's cold, grey slate eyes immediately locked onto Tony's the moment he entered. They were piercing, devoid of warmth, scanning him like prey.

'Long time no see, Tony. I hope you don't mind me making myself comfortable?' His voice was low, with an intimidating, dangerous edge. His dark, forced smile didn't fool Tony. This was no social visit by a long-lost friend. This person was total bad news, nothing less. And he'd made himself at home in Tony's house, scaring his wife to death in the process. Nobody did that to Tony Hargreaves.

'Are you okay, Tony? You look like you've just bumped into Freddy Krueger... I'm not that bad...well, I suppose as long as you don't try fucking me over.'

Tony didn't recognise the visitor. He felt intimidated, his heart thumping against his ribs, but he tried hard to ensure that none of his unease showed weakness. He was just about to ask who the fuck he was when Stella appeared behind him carrying two coffees on a tray.

'Here you go, guys. Come on, Tony, let me through so I can put these down.' She edged past him and placed the tray on the table, which also contained a bowl of sugar and a couple of teaspoons.

H didn't move, didn't flinch. He smiled a slow, unsettling grin that didn't reach his eyes. 'Sorry, Tony,' he said, the grin growing sharper. 'Am I in your chair?' his expression challenging Tony to do something about it.

The casual dominance of H's tone made Tony bristle, but he stayed silent. As Stella left the room, he sat on the couch furthest away from the man. She closed the door with a click, leaving an unnerving silence.

Tony looked him over again, working his mind hard. Who the hell was this? This shaven-headed lump of muscle and testosterone who appeared to have the hallmarks of a gangster? Then the penny dropped like a hammer... Flannagan-Smythe. Was the heavy here to intimidate him, to make him leave Flannagan-Smythe alone? Or was he here about the contract kill?

'I'm here on behalf of an associate...who isn't exactly happy with you,' H announced, his delivery feeling like a verbal punch to Tony's gut. 'From what I understand, he's delivered on his side of a deal you made with him, and you haven't.'

The visitor's Cockney accent was gritty. It sounded streetwise and menacing. Backed by a confidence that suggested nothing fazed him, especially not the person he was staring at. 'Now, I consider myself as a reasonable man, Tony. But you...' his eyes flickered with something dark, 'maybe not so...you're in a lot of trouble.' He picked up his coffee and stirred it with a spoon, showing a delicacy that was ambivalent to his character.

Tony marvelled over how anyone could make stirring a coffee look so intimidating. His pulse quickened as a bead of sweat ran down his back. He was in no doubt that this was an enforcer up from the smoke to collect a debt. He was also in no doubt that the money he wanted to collect was in connection to the kidnapping of Jane Flannagan-Smythe.

The visitor's lip curled into a sneer. 'My associate tells me you've been avoiding his calls. Is that true, Tony? Not very sincere, is it?'

'No, I've not been ignoring his calls. Why would I?' Tony asked, summoning every Alpha-male mineral in his body, hoping to even things out with his adversary. 'The burner phone he used to contact me was in temporary safe storage. Some other business came up, and I had to hide it quickly. It took me longer than I expected to recover it.' Tony sounded more confident now, his composure returning.

'Unfortunate,' the visitor muttered, eyes narrowing.

'I was just a middleman,' Tony added quickly, his tone urgent, attempting to gain some form of control. 'I just need time to get it sorted for your client.'

H smiled as if everything was now okay, having heard Tony's explanation and that it had all been a trivial misunderstanding. He let a silence hang while his smile slowly disappeared. 'Time...' H's voice was soft now, almost a whisper, but dripping with menace. He leaned back, a dark smirk tugging at his lips. 'Time is something you don't have, Tony.'

Then he paused, the tension in the room thickening. His eyes flicked to the mantlepiece, and he nodded. 'I left you a little gift. It's on the shelf there, next to the photograph of your daughter. How's she doing at Hull University, by the way?'

Tony froze. His eyes darted to the mantelpiece, where a burner phone sat beside the photograph of his daughter. Entering Tony's house was one thing, but implying a threat to his offspring raised this to major league level. He had a sudden impulse to call his daughter immediately to check that she was okay. But to do so would suggest fear on his part. He had to fight the impulse and deal with what was before him.

'Mrs Hargreaves seems very proud of her,' H continued, his voice almost mocking. 'And rightly so, she's on track for a first, isn't she?'

The blood drained from Tony's face. The threat wasn't even thinly veiled. 'There's no need for that,' Tony stammered, his calm façade cracking. 'I'll get you your money. You have my word.' Tony knew that some things didn't justify any risk whatsoever, his daughter being number one. 'I was put in touch with your client through a trusted third party. That person will vouch for me. Your client doesn't need to doubt me.' As the words came out of his mouth, he suddenly realised that the man sitting in his house might actually be the contract killer and not his representative. The thought exacerbated his fear into a panic – was the visitor armed? Was his genuine intention to send a strong message and harm Tony and Stella? Kill them even? Tony glanced around the room. There was nothing he could use to defend himself with. His knife was tucked away in his office.

'The thing is, Tony, my associate, has taken possession of the goods, and you've left him hanging. The interest rate on your debt... well, let's just say it's getting pretty steep. So, you need to move fast.'

'Hey, we're in the same boat here,' Tony said, deciding to go for broke and edge his chances. If nothing else, he was a credible negotiator. Years of experience dealing with building contracts and other situations generally came with the territory of the building game. 'Can we slow this down a bit? The customer who your client is acting on behalf of has gone off the rails, if you know what I mean. I just need to put him back on the rails.'

'Your MP friend – Richard Flannagan-Smythe. Why the mysterious talk? Why not just say his name?'

'Of course, just a habit of mine. The walls have ears and all that,' Tony said, chuckling nervously, seeking a knowing reciprocal nod from his visitor. It didn't happen. There wasn't much reciprocal courtesy happening here.

'You see,' H continued, 'he's not just a customer, is he? He's a close friend of yours. Or he was, until your recent disagreement. Now, I want to keep this simple. I don't want to become involved in your little squabble with your friend over who's paying for our services. You're out of time, Tony, get this fucking sorted. Now.'

Before Tony could reply, H was on his feet and stepping into the hallway. 'Great to catch up. I'll see you for a pint next week, yeah,' he shouted jovially for Stella's benefit. 'Thanks for the brews, Mrs Hargreaves,' he relayed even louder towards the kitchen, his voice casual again. The front door slammed shut behind him, leaving the metal letterbox rattling in its frame.

Stella timidly entered the room. 'Is everything all right, Tony?' she asked, expressing real fear and concern.

'Nothing I can't handle,' he said, placing the burner phone in his pocket. 'Just some unfinished business I'd forgotten about.'

'Are you sure? He looked like a man you shouldn't be messing with,' she said with an air of know-how that she didn't usually possess.

Tony shifted uncomfortably in his seat. He wasn't used to situations like this playing out at home in front of his wife. He was just about to speak when she made an observation.

'You look rattled, Tony. Should I be scared?'

The question pissed him off, maybe because it was a fair question to be asked. He fought back a feeling of rage, wanting to look calm and not inflame the situation any further than needed. This was a new situation for him. Stella had never previously been aware of this aspect of the business, and he needed to think his answer through carefully. There was no margin for error in this scenario.

'Is Jess back at university yet?' he asked, making the question sound as casual as possible.

But she saw right through it. 'You don't think he'd hurt Jess, do you?' Stella asked, her expression now having turned to one of horror.

'No, definitely not,' Tony said, as if the question was absurd. 'But I need to cover all bases.'

'She's got another week in France with Abbie,' she announced, a hint of contentment in her voice as she considered the distance between them.

'Whilst I deal with this, we'll go to the appartment for a short break. It'll give me the time and space to sort things out,' Tony said, his tone sounding more confident. 'Invite Jess and her friend too, and ask them to spend a few days with us when they leave France. It'll give you peace of mind, knowing Jess is safe.'

He took a drink of the coffee that he hadn't touched until now. 'Christ, it's stone cold; stick the kettle on, love,' he said in an effort to restore normality.

Yet his mind was anywhere but normality. Family covered, he now had to progress from defence to attack. He'd taken on bigger challenges than this before and won. Most notably, a notorious group of travellers who moved onto one of his sites a few years back. One of Tony's boys ended up fighting the hardest traveller in a bare-knuckle fight, with bets spiralling out of control. When his boy unexpectedly won the bout, things got messy. Fatalities-type messy. Tony reminisced about the battle and remembered the dead bodies encased in concrete whenever he drove past the completed office block development.

Stella returned to the lounge and placed a mug of steaming hot coffee beside him. 'You were miles away. Penny for your thoughts?'

Tony laughed. 'Nothing for you to worry about. Get packing. It's time for your jollies. We've not been to the appartment for a while,' he said with a carefree, beaming smile, which failed to reach his eyes.

*

H closed the door behind him and strolled to his car. He took no satisfaction from the fear he recognised in the woman's eyes. But that had been brought about by her husband reneging on a deal, not by H. Hopefully, he had done enough to make Tony Hargreaves see sense and make the payment. Therefore avoiding an escalation in hostilities. He chuckled as he recalled the colour draining from Tony's face while he failed miserably to present himself as a made man. He'd met many like him before who couldn't handle the pressure they created for themselves. The car alarm beeped in response to H pressing the key fob. He slid into the leather seat in his four-by-four and pulled away from the kerb. Job done. He'd not even needed to raise his voice or throw the bell-end against the wall. Having been a special forces interrogator for years, this job had presented as child play. 'Call John,' he instructed the hands-free phone system. *Calling John*, the cyborg voice announced dutifully.

'All sorted?' John said, picking up the call.

'Yes, message delivered and understood. I didn't need to select second gear. He looked like a rabbit in the headlights.'

'When will he pay?' John said, always the stickler for detail out of the two of them. It often left H feeling like he was being assessed or micro-managed. He was unsure of which.

'Usual answer,' H replied. 'As soon as he can get the money together. I don't think we'll be waiting long.'

'Okay, I'll be in touch,' John said. The line went dead, the short silence replaced by Thrash metal filling the car at full blast. Looking ahead, drumming the steering wheel, H realised too late that the traffic lights had changed. He cursed at not focusing on his driving and accelerated to ensure it was an amber and not a red. Close but not close enough. He checked his mirror, dreading the flash of a camera.

'No fucking way,' he exclaimed on seeing the police car not far behind him. 'What the hell, what's the odds of the plod being right behind me?' Seeing the blue flashing lights and the patrol car carefully negotiating the red light, he pulled over and wound his window down, ready. He'd dealt with these situations many times before. Usually, passing the attitude test would see him sent on his way with no more than advice and a warning; he could live with that. Operating under the radar was essential to his craft.

The traffic officer appeared at the window. H checked his mirror. The second officer had remained in the driver's seat, no doubt checking the vehicle over the radio. 'Do you know why we stopped you?'

H had learned during his military years never to volunteer or admit to anything until the evidence was presented, and assessed. At which time, present any relevant mitigation. But on this occasion, a positive answer was more likely to grease the wheels and get him on his way. 'Yes, I'm sorry, I left that traffic light a bit late and hit the amber.'

'It was a red, sir. I have it on camera if you'd like to watch it,' the police officer said.

'No need. I'm happy to take your word for it. Like I say, I'm sorry,' H said, holding his hands up in surrender.

'I'll need to see your documents while my colleague runs some PNC checks, but I'm going to just give you a warning on this occasion. You won't be so lucky if you're caught again.'

Once that was completed, the officer got back in the patrol car, allowing H to carry on his journey, He then rang the detective from the Surveillance Unit.

'All done,' the traffic officer said. 'He made our life easy by running a red light. He probably didn't suspect it was a targeted stop. Everything checked out on the PNC. I issued a producer and captured him on my body-cam. I'll email everything to you.'

H checked his mirrors after setting off, but the patrol car was still parked at the roadside. He would have been concerned if it had continued to tail him. He cursed at letting himself down. 'Basics,' he hissed, shaking his head, 'get a fucking grip, man.'

Worse, he needed to inform John of the minor compromise, which was one of their agreed-upon standard operating procedures. That was the worst part, as it gave John the opportunity to take the moral high ground on tradecraft and attention to detail.

'It's me, John, just giving you the heads-up. I was pulled over by the cops, I went through an amber light while we were talking. I don't think there was anything more to it, but obviously wanted to let you know.'

'Was he wearing a camera?'

Here we go, H thought, his grip tightening on the steering wheel. 'Yes, but they don't keep it for long if it's not evidence. Data protection and all that, and it's doubtful that Hargreaves will have made contact with the cops. It should be fine.'

'Are you getting shut of the vehicle?' John asked, not letting him off the hook that easy.

'Yeah, it's time to change it anyway. I'll call you later.'
H scanned the area for a fast-food shop. A burger, fries and coffee would do nicely, right now.

12

'We need to talk, urgently. Meet me at the usual place in an hour,' Tony demanded, his tone uncompromising. His confidence was now riding high again in the absence of his tormenter, H.

'I can't. I'm in Westminster,' Richard replied, unable to hide the sheer relief in his tone, glad to be in London, far away from Hargreaves. He scanned around for any eavesdroppers while walking a lesser-used corridor lined with high stone walls and arched windows that led to the chamber. He needed time to slouch anonymously and rest his eyes on the back benches.

'This can't wait. You've created a shitstorm, and I'm not getting sucked into it. Did you transfer the deposit to the contact's account on the night we discussed a hitman?'

Richard decided to divert to a nearby alcove, which he used often these days to disappear out of sight for ten minutes. It was tucked between two gothic stone arches. He stepped into it and sat on the worn wooden bench. He'd dreaded this call from Hargreaves, his worst fears now being realised. He was struggling to put a sentence together having repressed this memory to the extent that he had managed to forget about paying the deposit until now.

'Well, did you?' Tony hissed, clearly getting impatient.

'Not as such. I got one of my admin team to do it. It wasn't the full amount, just half of the the down payment, as requested,' Richard almost stammered, looking up to the fragmented shards of light from the small stained-glass window as if seeking spiritual guidance from above.

'You fucking clown, by doing that, you activated the contract, and now they've delivered. Why didn't you tell me you'd paid, you fucking moron? No wonder they're angry with you.'

'I was under the impression the payment was a retainer, nothing more,' Richard said, his voice cracking.

'What do you think you were paying for? A fucking lawyer. You've fucked up monumentally this time. You need to get the remainder of the money today, or else you'll be the next corpse to be buried after your wife.'

'What, so you're saying they've got Jane?'

'Well done, Einstein. Are you for real, you fucking imbecile? Who else do you think could have taken Jane? The Benedicta of Solitude? They're not happy, and that's an understatement. You need to speak to them and work out a solution. I'm out. This is a clusterfuck of your own making. Now own it.'

'Have they killed her?'

'How the hell do I know? That's why you need to speak to them and get it sorted before I become impatient and get some of my boys to get *you* sorted.'

Richard by-passed the threat. 'How can I speak to them? I don't even know who they are.'

'Well, lucky for you, an intimidating lump of an enforcer visited me and delivered a burner phone. You need to get back to him now and speak to him, or he'll come looking for you. I was just thankful he was angry with you and not me. He wanted to dismantle you, limb by limb, slowly. He looked like the type of psycho who'd really enjoy doing it. Believe me, you don't want that kind of guy as an enemy. These people don't mess about.'

'I thought you had a contact. Didn't they call you? This is your fault. Are you dealing with amateurs?'

'Yes, a "contact", the clue is in the name. Otherwise known as a middleman or a facilitator. Not fucking daddy daycare to look after a fuckwit like you. These aren't amateurs. You'll be praying they were soon. Get back here and collect the phone, pronto. If I get any more hassle from them, you'll have my boys to worry about, as well.'

Richard was about to protest, but the line went dead. His heart was pounding so fast he couldn't think straight. He held his head, wishing the problem would disappear. The fear he had developed of the hitmen was real. He felt scared… really scared. He sat upright, leaning back into the antique wooden bench, eyes closed, wishing it would swallow him up and transport him to a more peaceful place. He took deep breaths. The air in the alcove was musty, and cooler than the main corridor, with a faint dampness from the ancient stone walls.

'There you are, Richard. Come on, the meeting started without you. What is it with you and this place? I knew I'd find you here.'

Richard opened his eyes and looked up as Beth entered the alcove, slightly breathless. 'I've been looking all over for you,' she said. 'Ethan Nash is seething with you. Why didn't you answer your phone? Are you okay? What's wrong?' She furrowed her eyebrows and added, 'You don't look well, Richard.'

'I'm not. Let's get back to the office,' he said, getting to his feet.

'What about the meeting?'

'Send apologies.'

Beth looked uncomfortable. 'You're not getting it, Richard. Nash has sent me to find you. You need to attend this meeting. You can't run away from this one, and I'm running out of excuses, trying to cover for you. Come on, we need to go now.'

Richard stood up and reluctantly followed Beth like a petulant child. When they reached the conference room, Beth turned around, shook her head in dismay, and then adjusted Richard's tie. 'Pull yourself together,' she said, looking and sounding like she was losing patience with him.

She turned the brass door handle, and they entered the room. The stifling and oppressive atmosphere hit Richard right away. The room was a relic of another age, the air heavy and stale, tinged with the faint scent of polished oak. The centrepiece was a long, imposing oak table. His eyes followed it to the chair at the end, occupied by Ethan Nash, whose eyes were drilling into Richard's with contempt.

'Nice of you to join us, Richard; take a seat,' he said with a menacing, clipped tone.

Richard felt like the opening and the script to follow had been rehearsed. He glanced over to the vacant high-back chairs, not yet taken, upholstered in green leather. Each chair bore the crest of the House of Commons embossed in gold trim, now dulled to a lifeless brass colour.

Nash was flanked by Sir Geoffrey Halesworth, a grizzled back bencher who had survived five leaders, and Marcus Cole, a slick, ambitious MP backed in many circles as a future leader. Richard opted to sit by Cole. That way, he would avoid the sickening keto bad breath of Sir Geoffrey.

SILENT BETRAYAL

'Richard, we need to talk about your performance in the chamber yesterday. Or rather, your lack of it,' Nash said.

Richard suspected this was serious. Nash sounded businesslike, not espousing his usual expletives and sarcastic insults. Richard forced a smile and began fiddling with the top button of his shirt. 'Ah well, Ethan, I admit it wasn't my finest hour—but...'

'It wasn't your finest decade,' Sir Geoffrey interjected dryly, breaking away from a briefing paper he was making a point of reading.

The room fell silent but for Marcus's barely concealed snigger. Richard looked along the towering bookcases that lined one side of the room, shelves crammed with leather-bound volumes, probably never having been read in years. Then, onto the oil paintings of long-forgotten, smug politicians peering down at him from their position on the wall. The room suddenly felt claustrophobic and Richard sensed a feeling of doom as he caught sight of the fading iconic crest on the back of a chair.

Ethan Nash leaned forward, resting his elbows on the table. 'Richard, let me be blunt with you. Your clueless and dithering speech yesterday is the tip of the iceberg. Your colleagues have lost faith in you, never mind the vitriolic pile-on by the opposition. One of their MPs described you as a...' Nash flicked through a pile of papers to locate the quotation, '"wet sock dangling from the party's line".'

Richard sat up straight, his face reddening. 'That's a bit harsh, don't you think? I've always been a loyal party man. The department is right behind me. My speeches—'

'Your speeches,' Marcus cut in with a smirk, 'are so dull they could be marketed as insomnia cures.'

Sir Geoffrey chuckled softly. 'Do you even read your briefing notes, Richard? You often come across as if you don't know what you're talking about. The opposition now sees you as an easy point-scoring sport.'

'I'll have you know that my constituency—'

Nash banged the table with his fist. 'Enough, Richard. This isn't about your constituency... it's about your incompetence. Do you know how many complaints I've batted off about you? From your committee cohort and party colleagues?'

Before Richard could answer, Marcus added fuel to the fire. 'It's common knowledge that you turned up to your last policy meeting pissed. Nobody could get a word in edgeways whilst you were rambling on about a local cheese festival to be held at your constituency.' Marcus shook his head as if saddened by the pathetic disclosure.

'Is there something else you need to tell us about, Richard? Something troubling you, perhaps?' Sir Geoffrey asked, leaning forward, his gaze sharpened.

Richard glared towards Nash, suspecting he had shared the news about Jane with his sidekicks.

'That's enough for now, Sir Geoffrey. Let's be clear, Richard. Things have to change. One way or the other. If you need to take a sabbatical, you only need to ask. That's all for now, fuckity bye.'

Richard was left in no doubt that the knives were out. Sir Geoffrey and Marcus had probably engineered Nash to call the meeting. They probably had someone lined up to take his place already. He took solace in that it looked as if Nash hadn't betrayed his confidence about Jane's disappearance. He stood up, nothing more to say, and headed for the door, feeling shell-shocked, followed closely by Beth.

'Do you think Sir Geoffrey was hinting at our affair, Richard?' Beth asked in a hushed tone as they left the room.

'Well, if he was, he needs to tread carefully,' Richard said. 'There are plenty of rumours circulating about his indiscretions. I might have to mention them in passing to Nash. Not the type of activities to be written off as an error of judgement, believe me. Sometimes you need to fight fire with fire. Let's go to the office,' he added. 'We have things to discuss.'

Beth followed him into the sparse, functional, wooden-panelled office and closed the door behind them. Richard collapsed into the red leather chair behind his oak pedestal desk and looked at Beth. 'I'm being blackmailed.'

Beth tentatively sat opposite him. 'You need to tell the police... Do you know who by?'

'Tony Hargreaves. He wants money in return for Jane being released unharmed,' Richard lied convincingly.

'My god, I know you suspected Hargreaves would want revenge, but I didn't expect he'd go this far. I suspected Jane had walked out on you.'

'We need to travel back to Manchester today. Book the train tickets, Beth. I need to make some calls and try to make Tony see sense. I'm fighting on too many fronts here.'

'Would it not be better if I stayed here and kept an eye on things at this end?' Beth asked, her voice quivering. 'You need me here looking after your interests. You don't need me to tell you discontented voices are planning your downfall.'

Richard registered fear in her eyes, suspecting she was trying to distance herself from the blackmail. 'No, you're coming with me... I need you with me. I can deal with Sir Geoffrey and his cronies another day.'

*

DI Andrea Statham and DS Lee McCann left the Metrolink station and hurriedly walked into the city. They hadn't eaten all day. It had been a tough one of strategy and intelligence meetings at headquarters.

'I just need something filling and a glass of wine to clear my head,' Andrea said.

'Burger and chips will do me fine. Hopefully, there'll be some live music on, too. I'll try and get us that table out of the way near the side of the stage.' They both took the steps quickly before reaching the doorman at the top, who nodded and opened the restaurant door for them.

A charming waitress greeted them and showed them to their table. The restaurant buzzed with customers, reminding Lee of an authentic movie set in a New Orleans bar.

'Great choice, I love it here. What are you having?' he asked, slinging his jacket on the bench seat by his side.

'Andrea picked up the menu and glanced over it. 'You order for us both,' she said, placing the menu on the table and picking up her glass of wine.

The waitress returned and scribbled down the order of a platter of ribs to share and two brisket burgers for mains. Lee noticed Andrea's glass was draining fast and added another two drinks to the order.

'That hit the spot,' she said, placing her glass on the table. 'I think we achieved a lot today. The Surveillance Unit is doing a great job, and the telephone analysis is coming together.'

'Bloody typical that the gangster who visited Tony Hargreaves is a ghost. I can't believe there's no trace of him. Total false identity,' Lee said, shaking his head.

Andrea nodded. 'At least we know what we're up against… Professionals.'

'I think that's what made the spooks sit up and listen,' Lee said before taking a drink. That's a good thing; their covert technical techniques make ours look draconian. They'll be able to access satellite footage, too. It won't be long before they get some results.'

'Let's hope so, we've got photographs of him. The spooks will have access to all sorts of facial identification recognition systems nationwide. And the car he was using was traceable. We'll know who he is before too long and piece together his team,' Andrea said, sounding upbeat.

'There's also no evidence that Jane Flannagan-Smythe has been harmed,' Lee said, raising his eyebrows. 'I'm pretty confident they're pushing for a ransom fee. They wouldn't have had any reason to visit Tony Hargreaves if she was dead already.'

'Unless Hargreaves is the middleman and withholding payment?' Andrea suggested.

'Or he's Flannagan-Smythe's accomplice, but I can't see that. Their dislike for each other is tangible,' Lee said, drawing on his meetings with them.

'Once we've got more intelligence on Hargreaves, we'll get him back in custody for further interviews, but for now, surveillance is our best option.'

'Wow, that looks great,' Lee said, getting a waft of the ribs as the waitress placed them on the table. 'Get stuck in,' he said to Andrea, grabbing his first barbequed rib from the tray.

*

It was dark outside as Andrea and Lee walked down the steps from the restaurant. 'Fancy a nightcap?' Lee asked. 'There's that new place at Deansgate we could try. They have a great selection of cocktails.'

'I need to put my feet up,' Andrea said with a sigh. 'Why don't we get a taxi back to mine? I've got plenty of wine in, or you could make us a cocktail. We could chill out and watch a film.'

'Sounds like a plan. Let's go and grab a taxi.'

Their walk to the taxi rank was interrupted by Lee's mobile, he answered it and selected loud speaker so Andrea could hear too.

'Hi, Lee, it's Dessie from the Force Intelligence Unit. It may be something or nothing, but we've received some intelligence. I guess it originated from the spooks. Richard Flannagan-Smythe was dragged into a meeting today. The communications director raised concerns about his poor performance in the chamber yesterday. He's skating on thin ice, and a suggestion was even made that he should consider taking a sabbatical or even resigning.'

'Sounds like the pressure's getting to him,' Lee replied.

'Maybe,' Dessie said. 'The intelligence log goes on to report that he's unexpectedly left London to head back to Manchester.'

'Why is it unexpected?' Lee asked.

'I'm not sure. It doesn't say why: maybe he had meetings to attend. Who knows?'

'Strange way to behave when you've just had a rollicking about poor performance,' Lee mused aloud.

'That was my line of thought and why I called you at this time of night. Is he heading back up north in response to the enforcer visiting Tony Hargreaves? It would make sense if Hargreaves has been rattled. Maybe there's going to be a meeting?' Dessie suggested.

'Maybe, thanks for letting me know. Give me a call if anything else comes in,' Lee said before placing his phone in his pocket. 'Seems odd, doesn't it?' he said, looking at Andrea.

'It may be what we've been waiting for,' Andrea said. 'It could be a handover of some kind... payment, maybe?'

'Things are looking up. Flannagan-Smythe seems to be losing his cool. We've got them both under surveillance. Let's see what happens,' Lee said, with an air of optimism. 'Bring it on.'

They reached the taxi rank and climbed into the back seat. 'Hopefully, we'll have a busy day tomorrow,' Andrea said as the taxi pulled away from the curb. 'Better go easy on the cocktails.'

13

Richard and Beth paused at the gate at Manchester Piccadilly, where a disinterested man in a fluorescent jacket checked their tickets. Then, they left the platform and entered the station concourse.

'Let's grab a black cab outside. I need to collect a mobile phone from Tony Hargreaves... I'm playing along with his demands for now. Just until I know for sure that Jane's safe,' Richard added as an afterthought for emotional effect, pulling his coat tighter in response to the cold.

'Can't you drop me off first? Or I suppose I could grab my own taxi,' Beth said, checking her watch.

'No, I need you to come back to mine. Two heads are better than one. We need to formulate my response to today's meeting, and I can bounce ideas off you concerning Hargreaves. I need to get this stuff sorted as soon as possible.'

Beth's lips tightened; she was just about to protest when Richard's phone started to ring. He fumbled in his jacket pockets, struggling to locate it. 'Oh Christ, it's Ethan Nash,' he said, looking at the screen with a haunted expression. 'Ethan, how are you?' he said amiably with perhaps too much enthusiasm.

'Where are you?' Ethan demanded. 'You've missed two mandatory meetings today. The boss isn't happy, which means I'm getting it in the neck from him. What are you playing at? Are you pushing my buttons on purpose for a reaction? Are you fucking with me,

Dicky-boy? Did you not tune into the mood music at our meeting?'

Richard laughed nervously. 'No, of course not, why would I want to press your buttons?' he said, looking exasperated and raising the palm of his left hand in a show of bewilderment towards Beth.

'I've sent you an email. Sign and return it. It's your letter of resignation that you are stepping down immediately for personal reasons. For now, I'll hold it back from the media on the pretext that your request is under consideration. You don't help yourself, Richard. Anyone else would have understood the connotations of our meeting this morning and got stuck into their meetings with gusto. But, oh no, not fucking Flannagan-Smythe, he decides to fuck off back to Manchester for a long weekend.'

Richard bowed his head towards the floor. Suddenly irritated by Beth, repeatedly checking her watch with a face like a smacked arse. 'Is that really necessary, Ethan? It was only two meetings. Catching up next week won't be a problem.'

Ethan cut in, 'Absolutely fucking necessary. You're out, persona non grata, sunshine. Comprende, senor? I've spoken to my police contact in Manchester and do not like what I'm being told. I don't think you've been honest with me about Jane, have you? Nor Beth... Oh, have I missed the obvious? Are you two love birds eloping off into the sunset?'

'Of course, I've told you everything. You know as much as I know about Jane,' Richard pleaded, ignoring the snide comment.

'That's not how the police see it. They don't seem convinced. They're onto you... you've nowhere to run now. Well, maybe Argentina, but I'm not sure it'll be Beth's choice of destination.'

Richard's jaw clenched tight, his free hand formed a fist and tapped against the side of his thigh. He looked around for a bench, but there wasn't one nearby. Lost for words, he just about managed to reply, 'Why, how do the police see it, Ethan?'

'Like me, Dicky, they don't think you're telling the truth. What are you hiding from us?'

'Nothing,' Richard said, the only word he could conjure.

'Return the letter, signed with today's date. And stay under your stone until you hear from me.' The line went dead.

Richard turned towards Beth; his shoulders slumped momentarily before stiffening with fury. 'He's told me to resign,' he growled, gripping his mobile phone tightly, his knuckles whitening. 'I've worked damn fucking hard to get here, and he's telling me to resign, just like that. Well, that's a fucking betrayal in my eyes, I don't deserve this.'

Beth stood frozen, speechless, as Richard's anger boiled over. She'd never seen him like this before.

'Resign...discarded like trash. Everything I've worked for...lost, my career ruined in a bloody email,' Richard said, his voice rising with each word.

'Why?' Beth finally asked, as if she was treading on eggshells.

Richard's face twisted with rage, ignoring her. 'Well, I won't be taking this lying down,' he spat. 'Come on, let's get a taxi to mine and get planning. I need to hit this head-on. I'm not going down without a fight.'

Beth took a step back. 'Look, I think it may be better if I give you some space. You have a lot on your plate and need to think things through. I'll call you tomorrow and see how you are after a good night's sleep,' she said, turning towards the exit before Richard had time to reply.

'That's fucking great, Beth, you abandon me as well. You know how to kick a man when he's down,' Richard shouted after her. She didn't look back and continued walking. His shouting was drawing the attention of a couple nearby, who paused, looking shocked at the outburst playing out before them. Richard shot them a glare and shouted, 'What the fuck are you looking at?' then he dashed towards the exit, shouting, 'Beth, wait!' but was too late. The taxi door slammed shut behind her, and she was gone.

He raised his hand and hailed the next black cab in line. His voice tight with tension, he instructed the driver, 'Heaton Park, Sheepfoot Lane entrance,' then began texting Hargreaves, trying but failing miserably to subdue the anger still raging within him.

He passed his credit card to the driver as the taxi stopped. 'It's been declined, mate,' the driver said, passing the card back through the hatch.

Richard returned the card to his wallet before proffering the driver an alternative one. 'Try this,' he said, seething that his expense account credit card had already been cancelled.

'That's gone through fine, mate. Technology, eh?' the driver said as he handed the second card back through the security hatch.

Richard stepped out of the taxi and fastened his coat. He entered the park, walking briskly whilst checking his watch, sticking to the main path, and seeking safety under the street lights. But the dark shadows of the trees and shrubbery made him feel uneasy. His insecurity escalated to fears of Tony Hargreaves having set him up. Was he walking into a trap? An ambush? Was he going to be dumped in the lake? The thoughts jolted him, and he quickened his pace, his eyes darting around, seeking to identify any danger. The shapes in the shadows became more prominent and threatening. He began to question his judgement and wondered whether turning around would be the right thing to do. Or was it now too late? He could hear distant voices, enthusiastic chatter and shouting.

Out of the shadows, a group of teenage males emerged, heading towards him. Their laughter and shouting became louder as they approached, making him feel intimidated, fearing for his safety.

One of them swerved by Richard on a skateboard, far too close for comfort, and he was forced to sidestep to avoid a collision. The rest of the group laughed and sneered, looking back at him as they passed. 'We know where you're going, you fucking paedo,' one of them shouted, receiving rapturous laughter and encouragement from the rest of the group. He increased his pace, resisting the urge to break into a run but lengthening the distance between them.

When he finally reached the bench, he collapsed onto it; his muscles coiled tight with a cocktail of fear and adrenaline. He breathed hard, the anger slowly draining away, replaced by a weary relief that the feral gang hadn't followed him.

The irony wasn't lost on him; this bench, of all places, was now his refuge from the darkness closing in around him. He experienced a wave of relief when he realised the dark figure heading towards him was Tony Hargreaves, not some enforcer hell-bent on extortion.

Hargreaves didn't sit down. He remained standing, towering over Richard, looking down on him. He

SILENT BETRAYAL

thrust out the mobile phone, which Richard dutifully took off him.

'You need to speak to them,' he said with a finality in his tone. 'You're on your own. This is your mess. Don't contact me again.' Hargreaves turned and placed his hands in his pockets, heading back into the darkness from where he emerged.

'This is your mess, just as much as mine,' Richard shouted after him. 'You set it up. You're implicated whether you like it or not.'

Tony turned on his heels and charged back towards Richard. He lunged at him with strong momentum, gripping him tightly around the neck. Richard didn't have time to react, his eyes wide with fear, staring at Tony, just about managing to splutter the words, 'Let go of me.'

'Let fucking go of you? You're lucky I don't fucking kill you here and now,' Tony spat with venom. Richard struggled to break free, pressing down on the bench. He couldn't match Tony's strength.

Tony pushed Richard hard against the back of the bench and stood back, still glaring at him. 'You nearly fucking bankrupted me, and now you want to drag me into this mess? You never learn, do you, you fucking prick. You asked for a contact; I gave you a contact. Now back off...or I'll fucking kill you,' Tony hissed. He pulled back his right arm then landed a punch squarely on Richard's chin before he walked away calmly into the darkness.

Richard felt winded and gently stroked his chin, moving his jaw from side to side, assessing the damage. Shouting after Tony again wasn't an option. He knew it wasn't an idle threat. The dark shadows closed in around him and he sat still, looking at the new burner phone in his hand, unsure what to do next. He'd never felt so alone and helpless. His jaw started to throb painfully, reminding him of his vulnerability.

*

The orange hazard lights momentarily illuminated the car park as Tony unlocked his car. He got into the driver's seat, still breathing heavily, and locked the doors, looking out into the pitch darkness, not that he expected Richard had the balls to come after him. His security actions were more of a habit. Self-preservation. He massaged his right hand, it felt tender and sore, then he smiled, reflecting on his punch, which connected perfectly with Richard's face. It felt cathartic, like he'd righted a wrong, thinking it was nothing less than the coward deserved.

Tony took out his mobile and tapped in the number. The enforcer's familiar cockney accent answered. 'What do you want? I know I said we should go out for a pint, but that was only for your wife's benefit,' H sneered in a blunt, no-nonsense manner.

'I've just met with your client. He's got the burner phone you left at my house. I've advised him to give you a call. That's me done.'

'Steady on, big man, I'll decide when we've done with you. I didn't tell you to give him the phone, did I?' What did you do that for?'

'Because that's me done now. This is his mess, not mine. I want nothing more to do with him. You'll find out soon enough for yourself that he's a prick, a liability, not the type of person I trust or do business with. He's your problem now. Like I say, I'm done. And by the way, he's got no intention of paying you the money,'

Tony added, twisting the knife, hoping to create more grief for Richard. 'Good luck with it,' then he ended the call and placed the phone in his pocket. Job done; it was time to go home. He and his wife needed to be at the airport soon. It was time to make himself scarce and stay out of the way of the cockney enforcer on steroids.

14

Gravity pushed Beth into the seat as the taxi pulled away from Manchester Piccadilly Station. 'Where to?' the driver asked over her shoulder through the open security screen. Beth hadn't noticed the driver was a woman and suddenly felt subconsciously more relaxed. She gave her address and took out her mobile to check for angry messages, but nothing was incoming.

'Have you had a good journey?' the driver asked; she was a good-looking woman in her forties, with a confident manner.

Beth looked up from her phone. 'Not bad, as trains go. I got a seat, which isn't always guaranteed these days, so I can't complain.'

'Anywhere interesting?'

'No, just a meeting in London,' Beth answered, not elaborating further. 'I don't often get a cab with a female driver. How long have you been doing this?'

The driver looked at Beth in the rearview mirror as the taxi stopped at a red light. 'For too long. I used to enjoy it, but there're too many crazies about these days, and that's not counting the drunks. Are you a politician?'

Beth couldn't hide the puzzled look. She was taken aback momentarily, surprised that she'd been recognised from her back-of-house role.

'You've still got your ID lanyard on,' the driver pointed out with a chuckle, seeing her reaction.

Beth laughed and began to remove it from around her neck. 'I wondered what made you think that, so you're not psychic?' They both laughed, comfortable in each other's company.

'So, are you an MP? I've never met an MP,' the driver said.

'No, I work in Richard Flannagan-Smythe's office, just background work, boring stuff.'

'I've heard of him. What's he like?'

Beth was just about to say he's a right prick, but caught herself in the nick of time. 'He works hard; it's like a viper's pit. Not an easy job.' She rechecked her phone, satisfied she'd said enough. Still no angry messages, which made her feel pleasantly surprised, looking forward to getting home and slipping into her casual clothes. The thought of a nice hot bath dissipated when her screen filled with an incoming text: *Call me* from Ethan Nash. Maybe her bath was now delayed, she guessed.

The taxi pulled up. Glancing at the house, she saw the lights were still on behind the curtains. She paid the driver and opened the door, relieved to be back home.

She decided to call Nash before she went inside, just in case Martin hadn't set off on his trip yet. The phone rang for longer than usual, and she hoped he was busy. However, her hopes were dashed. 'Thanks for getting back to me, Beth. Is Richard with you?'

'No,' she answered, wondering whether it was a loaded question.

'Where is he?'

'I don't know. I left him at Piccadilly,' Beth said, feeling guilty as she relived the memory of his meltdown on the concourse. She shuddered, expecting the following question to be about their affair.

'That's good. Richard has been suspended with immediate effect, so don't take his calls. Is that okay with you?'

'Yes, that's not a problem,' Beth replied, surprised at Ethan's diplomacy.

'I appreciate that you've had the run-around today. So, take the morning off and get the train back to Westminster tomorrow afternoon. I need to sit down with you and discuss recent events.'

'Thank you. I'll see you tomorrow,' Beth said, relieved to end the call and finally enter her house.

*

Jane was glad to be out of the dark, suffocating, cell-like room, although the main room wasn't much better. It had a deserted industrial or agricultural feel, where bad things probably happened out of the way of witnesses. It felt cold in more ways than one.

She zipped up the padded fleece John had left her, hoping it was an act of empathy and a sign of bonding. She hadn't said much while they ate their packed lunches earlier, experience having taught her that talking too much irritated him, resulting in a swift, premature return to the solitary, dark, dank cell.

She sensed he was staring at her but didn't look back in his direction. Something told her not to, just a gut feeling. Tinged with fear, she deliberated what he was thinking. How he was going to kill her, or dispose of her body. But she still didn't look up to engage him; she kept her head down, studying her nails, now broken and brittle from surviving in her new surroundings. Maybe he saw a vulnerable young woman before him, who didn't deserve to be treated like this.

'Who do you think hired us to do this to you?' John asked suddenly.

SILENT BETRAYAL

Jane's head jolted up, looking towards him, relieved that the intimidating silence had ended. The question surprised her; the current situation had never been brought up before. She made eye contact, their eyes engaging for longer than usual. Jane ran her hands through her hair, buying time, struggling to understand why he'd asked the question, and wondering how many people he meant by "us".

She decided to begin with an air of naivety and vulnerability and then go from there. 'That's all I've been thinking about since you brought me here. I don't think I've got any enemies that I'm aware of, but I know my husband will have pissed a few people off along the way. He'll have made plenty of enemies. All part of being a politician, I suppose.'

The previous silence had been almost unbearable, and Jane felt a desire to keep talking but wanted John to say more, so she paused and drank from her water bottle to make the pause look natural.

John didn't fill the silent gap; he just raised his eyebrows. Then, he also had a drink and continued watching her intensely.

Jane felt under pressure. Was he playing the same game as she was? It felt like a game of chess or poker. But the stakes were much higher for her than him. Her heart was beating faster, and she suddenly felt giddy. Where was this going? 'Why did you ask me that?' she said, holding his gaze as if pleading for help.

John took another drink and slowly placed the bottle on the floor by his side. 'We have a problem. The person who took out the contract hasn't answered our calls and now doesn't want to pay us.'

She felt dumbfounded. What the hell was going on? It was the last thing she expected him to say to her. A flood of optimism rushed through her body like an adrenaline hit, making her feel revitalised. *Surely, that means I'm safe for now, but what does he do with me? I've seen him. I can identify him. That's not good. He'll see that as a problem.* 'You can let me go. I can pay you. If the police ask me questions, I'll tell them you wore a mask and give a different description. Anything you want,' Jane blurted out, stinking of desperation, giving it her all to seize the opportunity.

John didn't look away. He continued staring at her as if he expected her to provide the answer, running his fingers through his beard, weighing up his following words carefully. When he eventually spoke, his voice was low and calm. 'What if I told you... it was your husband who wanted you dead?'

Jane's world tilted. She jumped to her feet, leaving John looking startled for a moment. She took a few steps in the opposite direction and spun around to face him. 'Are you being serious? Richard has put you up to this?' The muscles in her face tightened and her eyes narrowed as she stared at him in disbelief. The world suddenly didn't feel real. Everything had been tipped upside down.

John slowly nodded his head, eyebrows raised, and his lips pressed firm into an unwavering line of assurance.

'The fucking bastard,' Jane hissed, her voice dripping with venom, pacing up and down, far enough away from John not to be a threat. She then slumped back onto the bench, head in hands, fists clenched, seething. She felt like screaming to release the anger.

John said nothing more. A tense silence hung over the room, extinguishing the earlier optimism she had experienced. She felt overwhelmed with anger and an instinctive urge to kick back at Richard. Why would he want her dead?

'It's not uncommon,' John said. 'They say there's a fine line between love and hate.'

Jane looked up, holding back the tears welling up in her eyes. 'But why? I don't understand.' It was happening again. Her father had abused her and her brother. And now, for the second time, the very person who should be her one protector in this world wanted her dead.

*

Beth had visited the constituency office, and was now relieved to be heading home. The taxi stopped outside her detached, red brick, three-storey Victorian house. Her attention was immediately drawn to a lone male standing at her front door. She felt calmer when she realised that it wasn't Richard. But who was it? She didn't recognise him, and Martin's friends would have known he was away golfing.

'Are you okay?' her new trusted taxi driver asked, looking towards the male. 'You don't need to get out if you don't feel safe.'

'I'm fine, thanks. I don't recognise him, that's all,' Beth replied, averting her stare from the male at her door.

'Well, I won't drive away until you give me a wave, then I know you're okay. That's twenty-six pounds, please.'

Beth handed her three tens, telling her to keep the change, and then got out and approached her front door.

The male took a wallet from his pocket and held it towards her. 'Hi, I'm DS Lee McCann from the CID.

Good timing. Can you spare me twenty minutes? I was hoping to speak to you about a missing person, Jane Flannagan-Smythe.'

Beth nodded. 'I suppose so,' she said, smiling and waving at the taxi driver before retrieving her keys from her handbag. 'I'm sorry, but I've not got long. I've got some urgent reports I need to get done.' Beth led him through the hallway and stopped at the lounge door. 'Grab a seat and I'll make a drink. Is coffee okay?'

'Coffee's great, thank you, black, no sugar,' Lee shouted before browsing through the array of books on the expansive bookcase. He sat on the three-seater sofa, taking in the room while mentally planning his questions.

Beth returned with the drinks shortly after, and sat opposite him in the wingback chair next to the bay window. The room was immaculate and homely.

'I don't know if I can provide you with anything useful,' she said. 'The only thing I know about Jane is what Richard tells me, and I guess you've covered everything with him.'

'No worries, it's just routine stuff. We obviously leave no stone unturned in cases like this and speak to everyone,' Lee said, taking out his notebook and pen. 'How would you describe your relationship with Jane?'

'We don't have one. I see her at party events when she attends with Richard, and even then, it's just passing pleasantries.' Beth's answer was clipped and to the point.

'How would you describe their marriage from your conversations with Richard?'

She shifted in her seat and straightened out her skirt, pausing before giving her answer. 'He doesn't say much about it. Our conversations are usually about work.'

Lee sensed she was uncomfortable and didn't want to expand on much, deciding instead that it was time to put the cat amongst the pigeons. 'Are you and Richard having an affair?'

'Certainly not,' Beth shot back. Her face was reddening and she crossed her legs. 'Why the hell would you think that?'

Lee knew immediately that he was onto something. He'd rattled her cage. He would have expected a calm and measured denial from her, but that was emotional, almost an outburst. 'I know it's an awkward question, but I must cover all bases. Are you aware if Richard is having an affair with anyone else?'

'I haven't got a clue about his sex life. It's got nothing to do with me, and we certainly don't discuss it. I was under the impression Jane had left him. Is there more to it than that? Are you suggesting something bad has happened to her?'

'Until we know she's safe, we can't rule anything out. Her disappearance is totally out of the blue, and therefore causes concern,' Lee said, not holding out much hope that he'd get any more from Beth. He busied himself scribbling notes, providing her with a silence to fill, but she took the opportunity to check her phone for messages.

'Has Richard mentioned that he's experiencing marital problems?' Lee asked.

'No, he rarely talks about Jane. I was under the impression their relationship was fine. I had no reason not to,' Beth answered, back in control.

'Has Richard's behaviour changed of late?' he questioned further, aware that it was a closed question he hoped would pay off with a disclosure rather than a 'no', a risk worth taking in his book under the circumstances.

Beth raised her cup to take a drink. Lee suspected she was buying time, thinking her answer through carefully.

'I wouldn't say I've seen a change in his behaviour, but he is having a hard time with work at the moment. He's certainly under pressure,' she said.

Good answer, Lee reflected. She'd answered the question but told him nothing. But she would be effective, wouldn't she? Saying the right things in her world was the bread and butter of the job.

Lee decided to up the ante again. 'We have received intelligence that suggests you and Richard are having an affair. That's why I asked you the question, and you answered with a denial. Why would someone think that you're involved with him?'

Beth appeared to have reflected on her previous reaction. Unflustered. 'Well,' she began with a slight shrug, 'we work closely together, which sometimes requires travelling to conferences and overnight stays. People love gossip, and I suppose rumours are inevitable. It must be the same in the police or any occupation?'

'Indeed, sorry to labour the point,' Lee said. 'I only do so because, from experience with these types of investigations, everything tends to come out in the end. So, I try to top and tail it at the outset. Sometimes, we can head things off at the pass and be more discreet.' He didn't believe for a moment that an affair would remain beneath the surface.

Beth smiled and went to stand up. 'Is there anything else? I really need to be getting on with my reports.'

Lee stood up and shook his head, walking tentatively into the hallway. 'No, that should suffice for now. Thanks for your time, and if you recall anything that could be helpful, please call me,' he added whilst handing her his business card.

SILENT BETRAYAL

Beth showed him to the door and tried to switch her focus to the upcoming meeting with Ethan Nash, the thought of the affair becoming public knowledge starting to claw at her. She had to protect Martin and her marriage at all costs. While packing her suitcase, she deliberated over who could have told the police, but no one came to mind. Maybe it was an awkward conversation to have with Ethan Nash.

15

DI Andrea Statham and DS Lee McCann arrived at the office after spending all morning at headquarters, where they participated in a strategy meeting chaired by Chief Superintendent Samuel. The Covert Operations, Surveillance, and Intelligence Unit also attended the meeting. The Metropolitan Police and Security Service joined them by conference call. The scale of the operation was growing by the day.

Lee placed the coffee they'd picked up at the drive-thru on the way back to the office on the table. 'I'm surprised the spooks haven't identified the visitor to Tony Hargreaves' house yet,' he said, pouring his Americano from the paper cup to his mug.

'The longer this goes on, I'm even more convinced we're dealing with a skilled professional team. They've covered their tracks very carefully. But still, no ransom demand has been made...why is that?' Andrea asked.

'Maybe it's time to up the ante with Richard Flannagan-Smythe. If no ransom has been demanded, it strengthens the hypothesis that he's in on the conspiracy. It's a straightforward contract kill that results in him receiving a big chunk of inheritance and a new life with his mistress. We know from the financial enquiries that she's loaded. What other motive does he need?'

'It's bloody typical that they had a row and took separate taxis from Piccadilly,' Andrea responded. 'After all that planning and preparation, too. They'd never have suspected an undercover officer was driving the taxi. I'm confident they'd have said something incriminating, especially if things were getting heated between them.' She shook her head in disappointment, albeit not surprised by how it panned out. Luck often conspired against them in these situations; it was nothing new. Getting them in the right taxi was a significant feat in itself.

Lee shrugged and said, 'It's the way it goes, but the undercover officer did a great job trying to get some evidence from Beth. And she's now Beth's go-to taxi in Manchester. So there's still time for her to pull it off. Fair play to her.'

'Let's go and pay Richard another visit later. I can't see him coping too well when we ramp the pressure up. It's safe to say he wasn't rushing back up north for a meeting or handover.'

Lee was about to answer, but Andrea's desk phone started to ring.

'Andrea, is Lee with you?' Samuel asked, skipping the usual pleasantries.

'He is, boss; we're discussing our strategy for approaching Richard Flannagan-Smythe later this afternoon.'

Samuel suggested in what seemed like an ominous tone, 'You'd better stick the phone on loudspeaker. You'll both want to hear this.'

'Okay,' Andrea said, giving Lee a puzzled look. 'You're on loudspeaker now, boss.'

'I've just taken a call from Interpol. They informed me that shortly after arriving at Marbella, Tony Hargreaves fell from a balcony. He was pronounced dead at the scene. Information is sketchy at the moment. His wife has identified him, and the local police are making enquiries. It would appear there are no witnesses to his death at this stage.'

Andrea looked over at Lee, wide-eyed, and he mouthed, 'What the fuck!'

'I didn't see that coming. Is there any indication of whether it's an accident, suicide or a suspicious death?' she asked.

'Like I say, we haven't had much of a briefing yet; no doubt we'll find out soon. I've had the thumbs up from Interpol for us to send a couple of detectives over to act as liaison officers between the two enquiries. Please can you arrange that asap, Andrea?'

'Of course, boss, I'll sort it out now,' she said, her attention drawn to Lee, who whispered, 'I'll go, leave it to me.'

'Speak soon, no doubt. Catch you later,' Samuel said before ending the call.

'You're not going anywhere,' Andrea ordered as Lee stood up. 'You're coming with me to speak to Mr Flannagan-Smythe. Leave your speedos and Hawaiian shirts where they are.'

Lee grimaced mockingly. 'He's not killed himself, and I doubt it's an accident. I only spent a short time with Hargreaves, but I learned enough to know he wouldn't take the suicide option.'

'So,' Andrea began, 'Jane Flannagan-Smythe is still missing, and Tony Hargreaves has been killed. Whoever's behind this means business. Let's send a team out to Spain to start finding some answers.

*

Jane lay stiff on the military cot bed, the thin blanket offering little comfort against the chill in the air. She'd tried to sleep, but the incessant swirl of thoughts in her mind made it impossible. Every creak or movement breaking the silence beyond the solid door felt like a threat. That her time was up, the executioner approaching the door.

Her confidence was growing, but so were the stakes. John was a paid assassin, but the client refused to pay him. If his motivations were purely financial, she could exploit that. If his client wouldn't pay...Jane could, in return for her freedom. This was a massive opportunity that she couldn't let pass her by. But what if she'd miscalculated the situation? One wrong move and she could end up dead, another body left in John's wake, his words replayed, haunting her: *It's business*. The thought gripped her tight, sending a cold chill down her spine.

The initial anger from discovering who the client was had subsided, and a primal survival instinct kicked in. Revenge could wait, one step at a time. There would be an opportunity for that later… If she survived, it wasn't her priority focus for now.

She felt confident that her plan to bond with John was working; he was talking more, shared more information, and let her spend more time out of the cell. There was even a slither of respect from him… or was she misreading the mood? Was he just playing psychological games until the inevitable end game?

She had experience with adversity. She'd handled it well and survived, and she had to once again, because there was no plan B this time.

Her thoughts were interrupted by John's familiar footsteps approaching the door. She stood up, ready, instantly feeling relief in her back. The door swung open, filling the room with light, and she slowly stepped forward into the open space. A rush of adrenaline sped through her veins; John had his back to her. Should she attack him? Was this the best chance she had? Was he dropping his guard? Her heart began to pound fast. But as quickly as the thought had entered her head, she decided against a plan of attack because the odds were most probably against her. He'd overpower her. *Stick to the plan*, she affirmed silently, relieved at her decision rather than acting in haste.

'I've got you a coffee,' John said, sounding like she should be indebted to him.

Jane took the cup and sat on the usual bench, studying the cup for its potential use as a weapon. 'Thanks,' she said, weighing up her best approach to work more on his emotional side. 'Has Richard come up with the money?' she asked, still looking at the coffee mug, dreading hearing the wrong answer, which would mean only one thing.

'No.'

'So, what now?' she asked with palpable relief but expecting a put-down for asking the question.

'He'll see sense soon enough. His associate thought he could call the shots and learned the hard way. Maybe your beloved will get the message that we don't fuck about.'

'Who's his associate?'

John's eyes narrowed as he eyed Jane like a predator. For the first time since she had been kidnapped, she feared she was about to be raped. She'd already clocked him, leering at her breasts. He stepped into her personal space, looking down at her and whispered, 'You're asking too many questions lately.'

She held his stare and stood up, facing formidable intimidation. 'Wouldn't you, in my position? I don't think you'd sit here in silence if the boot were on the

SILENT BETRAYAL

other foot.' The tension in the air was thick enough to choke on. 'I don't want to die...especially from the order of that bastard,' Jane said, her confident demeanour hiding the truth that she was holding things together by a fragile thread of survival instinct.

'You don't need to know the identity of his associate. Finish your coffee; I have things to do,' John said, backing off and returning to his stool.

Jane was awash with relief, her sense heightened with a weird exhilaration at not being attacked. 'I want to do a deal with you,' she said. 'I can pay off his debt for my freedom. Why fuck about with Richard, you know you can no longer trust him. He's a snake; he'll probably try to double-cross you and get the police involved.'

John looked at her questioningly. 'We've already discussed this; it's a non-starter. How do I know I can trust you?'

'You trusted that fucking weasel,' she spat. 'Nobody else I know would. Let me walk away. You'll get paid and never hear from me again. I'll send the police in the opposite direction. I won't have an axe to grind with you; my nemeses is that twat. Seeing his face before I take my revenge is worth the money.'

'Just supposing I agreed to your proposal, you know that if you reneged on the agreement, we have the means to find you and administer retribution, just as we did with your husband's associate?'

Jane's confidence was growing. She was pretty sure John had suppressed a smile in reaction to her feistiness. She guessed he liked that quality in a woman. 'It won't come to that,' she replied, her body rigid with tension.

'How would you pay? The banks would notify the police of any suspicious transactions. Not only that, if

I gave you internet access, the cops would use it to pin down our location here.'

Jane feared now that John was toying with her, but she continued with her efforts to cut a deal. 'I have an estranged brother. He has access to funds, or you could trust me to pay you once I'm released.'

He sneered cynically. 'Really, just let you walk and wait for the money? The police will be taking an interest in your brother already; he may even be a suspect. They're probably looking into his finances right now. He has the motive, being the only sibling and beneficiary of your wealth.'

'You need to trust me,' Jane tried. 'I'm bargaining for my life here. I'm not going to fuck it up. I'll move on. You'll get your money.' A silence hung in the room. She knew she'd given it her best shot, but was it enough? Would he trust her?

John got to his feet and picked up a plastic carrier bag. He tossed it to Jane and she managed to catch it in one hand, relieved that it wasn't heavy.

'There's a tracksuit in there for you,' he said, looking at her elegant dress. 'A bit more practical.'

'Thank you,' Jane said, feeling a warm sensation spreading through her chest to her neck. The kind gesture catching her off guard.

John coughed, uncomfortably. 'Time to go back in the cell. You can try it on in there. It'll go nicely with the fleece.'

Jane fought hard to fight the tears welling up in her eyes, brought on by his sudden act of kindness. She promptly stepped back into the cell, eager to put on the practical, insulated clothing, ignoring the thought of wearing a tracksuit, something she wouldn't normally be seen dead in.

16

DS Lee McCann opened the door. His eyes quickly scanned around the public enquiry counter waiting area, half expecting a no-show. The room was packed full, as usual. Richard Flannagan-Smythe looked uncomfortable, sitting at the far side amongst some of Manchester's finest regulars, who were reluctantly waiting to sign on as a condition of their bail or answering bail to be further interviewed.

Strangely enough, he almost looked relieved to catch Lee's eyes and headed over to join him with a spring in his step. 'Is it always this busy here?' Richard asked.

'This is a quiet day,' Lee replied, opening the door.

Lee stepped back into the corridor, holding the door open, quickly joined by Richard, who almost bumped into him in his haste to leave the rabble. The door slowly closed behind them, leaving the hum of chatter and occasional raised voices.

'Thanks for coming at short notice, Richard,' Lee said, his tone routine sounding.

'Not a problem, as long as you're not arresting me.' Richard laughed at his attempt at humour but failing miserably to hide his angst.

'Not yet, anyway,' Lee answered with a playful wink. 'Follow me, we've got an interview room booked down here. DI Statham is waiting for us.' He couldn't help but notice the dark shadows under Richard's eyes and that he'd not shaved for a few days.

Lee opened the door and beckoned Richard to enter. Then, he followed him inside and closed the door behind them. The room was small and claustrophobic, and the dull light barely illuminated the sterile pale blue walls. It was a stereotypical, neglected police interview room—functional but nothing more.

DI Andrea Statham was sitting on the other side of the desk, but she didn't stand up to greet the newcomers. 'Take a seat, Richard,' she said with a formal *let's get down to business* tone.

Richard's lips were pressed tight and his eyes took in the room, looking everywhere but into Andrea's eyes. He sat down stiffly and crossed his legs while his fingers fidgeted with his shirt buttons.

Lee sat beside him at the end of the table, the sound of his chair scraping against the floor and grating through the silence. Richard forced a smile that didn't hide his anxiety and asked, 'How can I be of assistance?' before adjusting the position on the chair.

Lee couldn't help breaking a smile at Richard's attempts to manage the conversation, with a cynical awareness of what was coming.

Andrea began, 'We need to review your original account with you to ensure our understanding of the circumstances is correct. As investigations progress, inconsistencies and ambiguities arise; addressing them as soon as possible is important to avoid heading down the wrong path.'

'It's routine,' Lee chimed in, playing the good cop, smoothing off the edges of Andrea's formal delivery.

Andrea's gaze sharpened as she leaned forward. 'Are you having an extramarital affair, Richard?' she asked, maintaining an intense stare into his eyes.

Richard shifted nervously in his seat again before recrossing his legs and folding his arms tight over his chest. 'I think I know where you're coming from. And no, I'm not having an affair, but I do have a close friendship with Beth, my advisor. It's not uncommon in Westminster. You're away from home, so working dinners and the like become the norm. You get close to your staff; it's the way it is.' He looked over to Lee as if seeking reassurance for his bullet-proof explanation. Lee nodded.

But Andrea wasn't swayed. 'How does Jane feel about this close working relationship?' she asked. 'Does she suspect you're having an affair?'

Richard's forced smile faltered, and his voice rose defensively. 'She's fine with it. It's work. It's the norm,' he replied. 'No way does she suspect me of having an affair.' His voice was incredulous, as if the suggestion was preposterous, his head tilted to one side, lips parted.

Andrea's eyes bore into his. 'You described your marriage as strong, a happy marriage. Is that the case? I'm beginning to have my doubts,' she said, eyebrows raised in disbelief.

'Of course. Where the hell are you going with this? What are you insinuating?' Richard snapped back, his brows furrowed. He suddenly bolted up from his seat, both hands slamming onto the table as he leaned towards Andrea. 'I don't like where you're heading with this. If you suspect me of something, come out and bloody well say it!' he exclaimed, his right eyelid twitching. 'Am I a bloody suspect now?'

Andrea didn't flinch. 'Sit down, Richard. Save that for the chamber in Westminster. We don't do theatrics here. Just the truth... I'm assessing the facts as to whether your wife has left you, nothing more.' Her voice was now matter-of-fact, feeling further encouraged by Richard's emotional reaction.

He sat back down, folding his arms and legs and occasionally rubbing his twitching eyelid. An oppressive silence briefly blanketed the room, but it seemed longer than it actually was.

Andrea looked over to Lee, sitting further back, more relaxed in her chair. Lee leaned forward, resting his elbows on the table. 'It's come to our attention,' he began, 'that you have met with Tony Hargreaves in Heaton Park. I was somewhat surprised after you informed me of the animosity that existed between you. What was that all about?' His voice was soft, almost conspiratorial and supportive.

Richard's voice stammered as he wiped the sweat from his brow. 'Look, let's be clear. My wife is missing... I'm trying to speak to everyone I can think of to help find her. Even Tony Hargreaves if necessary.'

'And what did Tony say?' Lee asked.

'Nothing, but I guess that's no surprise, is it? I just needed to see the whites of his eyes and ask him some direct questions to watch his reactions. Don't forget that this man has made it clear he seeks to take revenge on me. He blames me for the collapse of his out-of-town residential and retail development. I wanted a heads-up as to whether he had anything to do with Jane's disappearance.'

'He said nothing,' Lee echoed, looking over to Andrea with a confused expression.

'Well, nothing constructive. He was regurgitating his bitterness and bile towards me because of the collapse of his business development, and revelling in my current situation.'

'Do you think he's involved?' Andrea asked in an intrigued, low voice.

'Well, I've no direct evidence, but he's a dodgy bastard who wants payback. He's made that clear, as you're well aware. Who knows? Maybe you should focus the investigation on him. He's more than capable of pulling a stunt like this.'

Lee glanced at Andrea and then back at Richard. 'Tony died yesterday. He fell from a balcony in Marbella and died at the scene.'

The colour drained from Richard's face. 'Tony Hargreaves is dead?' he choked out. His eyes darted between Andrea and Lee, desperately searching for some kind of explanation. 'Was it... Was it an accident?'

Andrea replied, lacking emotion in her voice, 'We don't know yet; it's early days. At this stage it could be suspicious, suicide or an accident. I'm confident we'll establish the facts in due course.'

'Are you sure you're telling us everything, Richard?' Lee asked, his voice warm and reassuring. 'Tell me what's going on, now's your opportunity. I know you have more to tell me. I can help you, but you've got to talk to me. I can't help you otherwise... Jane is missing. Tony Hargreaves is dead...where does that leave you? Are you in imminent danger? Talk to me, Richard.'

Richard looked distressed. He slouched further into the chair, fidgeting with his shirt buttons. 'I've told you everything; I wish I had more to tell you. Believe me, this isn't easy.' He looked defeated—a wounded animal not knowing whether to fight or run.

'I'll get us some drinks,' Lee said, standing up, handing the room to the bad cop.

When he left and the door clicked shut, Andrea leaned forward across the desk, eyes locked onto Richard's, noticing how tired he looked. 'I smell a rat. What's really going on here? Are you being blackmailed? Have the abductors demanded money? Or are you involved in Jane's disappearance? Have things got out of hand? Things don't seem to be stacking up here. Speak to me, Richard, before it's too late.' She then relaxed back into her chair but kept her eyes securely on his.

Richard's heart pounded heavily in his chest. He felt out of his depth, and the walls closed on him. 'I don't have to put up with this; it's insulting that you're trying to intimidate me into making a false confession. You should be out searching for my wife, not trying to intimidate me.' He jumped up from his seat again, this time heading towards the door.

'Sit down, Richard. I'm too tired to entertain your theatrics again. We do need to find Jane, so do you want to help us or not?'

He reached the door, grabbed the handle, and then turned around. His face contorted. 'You should be trying everything to find Jane,' he sneered. 'It doesn't look like you're doing very well. You should be ashamed of yourself. You'll be hearing from my solicitor,' he hissed with newfound pseudo-confidence. He stormed out of the room, almost crashing into Lee and knocking the precariously balanced coffee tray to the floor as he headed to the enquiry counter exit at a determined pace.

Lee stepped into the interview room, eyebrows raised, and placed the coffee on the table. Andrea gave him a knowing look and smiled.

'You've certainly rattled him,' he said, taking a seat and a sip of his coffee. 'Christ, that's hot. That drinks machine is a nightmare; it's never just right, either nuclear hot or lukewarm.' He picked up Richard's coffee and sipped. 'That's better; the milk's cooled it down a little.'

Andrea laughed, watching him. 'You've got coffee issues,' she mocked. 'Saddo.'

'You've no room to talk. You're the pretentious coffee aficionado,' Lee mimicked before flicking a drop of hot liquid at her from the wooden stirrer.

'Stop it now, or I'll pour this over your head,' she said, laughing and raising her cup towards Lee.

'You wouldn't dare!' he said, egging her on, enjoying the flirtatious moment that eased the tension.

In the midst of their banter, there was a knock at the door. A wily, experienced uniform cop entered the room and gave them a knowing look. 'If you two have finished, I've got this room booked for half past,' he said, then stepped back out and closed the door.

Andrea and Lee burst out laughing. 'He must have heard us fooling around,' she said.

'Yes, it'll be all around the nick by tomorrow, with several exaggerated versions,' Lee added.

'Come on, let's go and debrief the interview in my office,' Andrea said, regaining some decorum while collecting her papers.

*

Only four or five stragglers were still working at their computers when Andrea and Lee entered the office, the overhead sensor lights having already clicked off. As they made their way across the far end of the office, Andrea waved her arms about to click them back on again. Tom looked up from his screen. 'How did you get on with Flannagan-Smythe's interview?' he asked, taking his reading glasses off, almost as if he'd been waiting for them to return. 'Did he crack and spill his heart out?'

Andrea sat on the edge of the desk closest to Tom. Lee took a desk chair further away among the other detectives.

'He looks like things are getting on top of him. He's a bit dishevelled, to say the least. He wasn't very convincing when we put the affair to him,' Andrea said, looking over to Lee.

'No, he came up with some cock and bull story about close working relationships. The intelligence is spot on; things aren't rosy in the Flannagan-Smythe household, and he's trying to hide that.'

'How did he react to the news of Hargreaves' death?' Tom asked, leaning forward and resting his arms on the desk.

'For someone who described Hargreaves as an enemy, he looked very concerned,' Andrea replied, eyebrows raised, emphasising the surprising reaction. 'I get the feeling Richard and Tony have been playing with the big boys and got their fingers burned.'

'Yeah, probably fears he's next on the hit list,' Tom replied with a cynical edge. 'Are we locking him up as a suspect?'

'We don't have enough on him yet. He'd go no comment, get bail, and we'd be no better off. Let's see what tomorrow brings,' Andrea said.

'Well, hopefully, we'll have more information on the circumstances of Hargreaves' death tomorrow. Our team are attending an investigation briefing in Malaga with the Cuerpo Nacional de Policia...that's the National Police to you, Tom,' Lee said with a mischievous smirk and a wink.

'Well done, Sergeant, I bet you've been up all night learning that on Duolingo,' Tom hit back, with his trademark deadpan delivery, not missing a beat.

Laughter and mocking crossfire followed. The tone dropping even lower with each shot.

'I'm satisfied we're moving in the right direction and, more importantly, progressing; we just need a break to help speed things up and locate Jane Flannagan Smythe,' Andrea said. The mood of the office sobered instantly at the mention of the victim. No one had lost sight of the priority, reflected in the team's dedication and the long hours. Though humour tended to help them cope with the horrific nature of their work, not the so-called canteen culture... just a coping mechanism.

17

Richard Flannagan-Smythe was pacing the study, his phone held tightly to his ear. He was still angry from his dealings with the police. Who the bloody hell did they think they were? Statham and her sidekick. He felt rough after hitting the whiskey on his return from the police station the night before. Once again, sleep had evaded him, and his mind was a swirl of anxieties, ruminating about the worst-case scenarios that could befall him. How the hell had the enforcer tracked Hargreaves down in Spain and killed him?

The latest recollection to haunt him was calling the number on the burner phone last night. He remembered having cross words with the contract killer, but not much more detail. He was shrouded in a heavy blanket of regret and fear.

'Richard, what do you want?' Beth whispered. 'Martin's here. Can I call you back?'

Anger swelled in Richard's veins; he suspected she was just trying to fob him off. Either that or Nash had instructed her to give him the cold shoulder. He needed her and now he felt isolated and vulnerable. He couldn't handle this alone.

'Why didn't you answer my fucking calls last night?' he growled, his dry mouth making his voice sound gritty.

'Richard, calm down. I was out having dinner with friends. I do have a life beyond Westminster, you know.'

'I needed you. The police were interrogating me at the station. They know we're having an affair. They also told me that Tony Hargreaves is dead. I tried to call him last night, but there was no answer. We need to disappear together until this mess is sorted out.'

Beth's voice sounded shell-shocked. 'I have to go; Martin's coming.' The line went dead.

*

Jane had been sitting with John for over an hour; they'd finished their food some time ago. Usually, John would have been long gone by now, with Jane placed back in the cell.

'I've been mulling over your offer,' he said, looking at Jane.

'And?' she replied, returning his stare with confidence.

'Things have taken a turn, which may have made it more viable,' John said before biting his lip, his stare becoming more intense.

Jane decided against asking what had changed. He would tell her if he wanted her to know. 'So, do we have a deal?' she asked, a knot forming in the pit of her stomach, making her feel slightly nauseous.

John sidestepped the question. 'Your husband made contact last night,' he said before standing up and beginning to pace the room. 'I think he's lost the plot, personally. But he made it clear that he wasn't going to pay.'

Jane felt physically sick and was unsure whether she wanted John to continue. Listening wasn't easy, and she looked down at the floor, unable to raise the energy to say anything.

'He's backtracking, denying any direct involvement in taking out the contract and blaming it on a man who's dead.'

'That sounds like Richard, welcome to my world,' Jane whispered without looking up. But she couldn't hold back her curiosity. 'Who is he blaming it on?'

'A man called Hargreaves. Do you know him? Or should I say, did you know him?'

'Yes,' Jane said, 'they were once friends, then became enemies. So, Hargreaves is the man you talked about yesterday?'

'Indeed, he crossed the wrong people and paid the price with his life, which brings me to the point. Can I trust you? This contract has turned into a bag of shit already. I don't want to make matters worse. The stakes are high in this business, Jane. If we agree on a deal, that's what it is: business. We stick to the agreement no matter what because if you don't...well, just look at Hargreaves.'

'I have no intention of double-crossing you,' Jane said, subduing her voice to hide the growing exhilaration and optimism washing through her body.

'That's good to hear, but things may feel different once you regain your freedom. Feelings of revenge or wanting to seek justice could be overpowering; who knows?'

'You'll never hear from me nor see me again. I can assure you of that,' Jane said, working hard to contain the feelings of hope and excitement, which were building like a pressure valve.

'What about your husband? Won't you want to seek revenge for what he's done to you?'

Jane felt surprised at her lack of anger towards Richard. 'That pathetic bastard,' she spat. 'No, he isn't worth it. Cutting him off from my money will be enough. Money and ambition are all he's bothered about.' Her mind then switched to Hargreaves. Would

Richard meet a similar fate? It would appear he'd crossed these people as well. 'Please believe me, I will stick to the deal. I'm under no illusion here. I know you're a skilled operator in your field of expertise. Why would I want to go into battle with you?' She thought for a moment that she caught John struggling to restrain a smile when she mentioned a battle. Her hope of gaining freedom was growing rapidly as the conversation progressed.

'What about the police?' John asked.

'Not a problem. I can manage them if they come knocking. I have access to top lawyers that will keep them at bay. If we agree on the deal, I'll walk away, and that's it. Being set free is all I want.'

'That's good. Their witness protection programme isn't all it's cracked up to be, especially when they lose interest after the trial, and their boxes are ticked. At that stage, you are no longer of value to them. You've served your purpose.'

'What's the cost of my freedom?'

'It's going to be expensive.'

'My brother can access my trust fund, but I must contact him.'

'One step at a time. I have logistics in place for transfers.'

'So, are you going to let me go?'

'It looks like we have a deal. Make the most of it, Jane. Don't fuck it up. It wouldn't end well for you.'

She stood up and approached John, holding out her hand. They shook on the deal. 'Thank you,' she said before walking to the cell. Enough had been said, and she wanted to rest. The handshake was a conscious effort to imply equality and trust, even on a subliminal level.

*

Richard locked his car and approached the driveway to Hargreaves' modern executive house. Subconsciously, he valued it at just under a million pounds. The front garden was immaculate, not unlike the party garden at the rear, which he'd frequented many times in years past, with its hot tub, gazebo, and outdoor stove.

His mind conjured flashbacks to happier times, and yet his current visit put him on edge with anxiety and fear. He now felt like an intruder...no longer a welcome guest.

He pressed the doorbell and stepped back, glancing around the high-end development at the beautiful houses and cars, sensing nobody was about to answer the door. Fidgeting with his shirt buttons, he approached the lounge window and looked inside. The place looked deserted. A wash of fear enveloped him; maybe the police weren't fucking with his head after all. There was no sign of Tony Hargreaves or his wife, no sign of his car either. The dark clouds of reality hung over him. The police weren't playing mind games after all—this was serious: the thugs had assassinated Tony. Richard suddenly felt exposed, standing out in the open. Was he their next target?

He recalled his last meeting with Tony, realising that with hindsight, Tony looked like a worried man. Richard had misread his demeanour as disdain and loathing directed at himself. But perhaps he had actually misunderstood the situation. Tony was preparing to go into hiding—but they got to him, and if they'd assassinated Tony... he was next on their list, no doubt.

His mind raced back to the phone call to the unknown male, his regret instant and overwhelming. Richard had been calling the shots from the safety of his office. It had been a crazy move; what was he thinking? How he wished he could turn the clock back. He felt physically sick, his stomach churning as panic seized his legs.

Instinctively, he shot a glance over his shoulder; were they following him? Were they watching right now? He needed to get out of there. Should he return cap in hand to the police, and explain how Hargreaves was blackmailing him? It was a tempting option because Hargreaves could no longer argue his case. Or maybe he could call Nash. His mind jolted him back to reality: that would be pointless because if Nash had suspended him, he wouldn't give a toss. Richard returned to his car, his mind ruminating over all the worst-case scenarios it could muster. He needed to run. But where to?

He hadn't even reached fourth gear when the shrill ringtone shattered the silence in the car, blasting from the speakers. He accepted the call, having read Beth's name on the media screen, which brought about a beaming smile, relieved that she'd got back to him. The thought of her ghosting him gnawed at his sanity; facing this alone would be unbearable.

'Beth, we need to get away. Now. We're in danger,' Richard gasped dramatically, barely holding it together, his words tumbling out in a panicked rush. 'I need to protect you,' he added, distorting the circumstances to convince her to run away with him.

'Richard, slow down. Take a breath,' Beth's voice was calm but distant. 'Let's take things one step at a time. What's happened to Tony Hargreaves?' she asked calmly, her tone steady, soothing his troubled mind.

'They've got to him and thrown him off a balcony in Marbella—the people who abducted Jane. We're next. We need to get away, to safety. Now,' Richard ranted. His knuckles whitening as he gripped the steering wheel.

'Richard, you need to go to the police. We can't just run away. Running away isn't going to solve anything. It didn't do Tony Hargreaves any good, did it? Why do you think we're in danger? We haven't done anything wrong, and besides, what about Martin and my job? I can't just up sticks and disappear.'

Her calm logic hit Richard like ice-cold water, and the royal "we" hadn't gone unnoticed either. But his panic grew as he reluctantly accepted that she was trying to distance herself. 'They're not important anymore,' he said, irritation seeping through his voice. 'These people are ruthless, and they're coming for us. The police know about our affair, and they've threatened to tell Martin. So, he's going to find out sooner or later. Your marriage is over, Beth. It's just me and you now. Pack some things and I'll pick you up. We can get through this together, trust me.'

'Why are they coming for you, though? What have you done?' Her voice was sharper now, suspicion creeping in. 'What haven't you told me?' she asked, distancing herself further from Richard's nightmare.

'They want money. Hargreaves hasn't paid them. He's dead and they now want me to pay the ransom. I haven't got that kind of money.' A recollection sprang into his mind from the drunken phone call the night before—telling the male that he wouldn't be getting any money whatsoever and suggesting that he should fuck off. 'We can be together, Beth, start a new life.'

SILENT BETRAYAL

Her silence felt like a knife twisting in his chest. Finally, she spoke, each word a slap of reality. 'Really? From what you're telling me, we'll spend the rest of our lives running, looking over our shoulders.' She paused, then added, 'Go back to the police and tell them everything. They can sort this out; it's what they do. They have a duty to protect you.'

'I told you. I can't go back to the police. I can't trust them. They'll stitch me up. They suspect I'm involved in Jane's disappearance.'

'Are you involved in Jane's disappearance, Richard?' Beth's words were clinical, almost unrecognisable and adversarial. Her usual supportive demeanour was severely lacking, replaced by a tone of distrust.

Suddenly, car horns were blasting in all directions, jolting Richard's attention back to the road, instinctively swerving violently to avoid a collision. He missed the car ahead by inches. His own car bounced onto the grass verge, heading straight towards a lamp post. He shuddered, bracing for the imminent impact. He'd been lucky to have avoided the car, and the lamp post, too, would be a miracle. Survival instincts kicked in, and somehow, he manoeuvred his vehicle between the lamp post and a hedge of conifers before steering the car back onto the road with a thud. He sped off, drenched with relief.

Other cars had stopped, the drivers staring in amazement. 'Fucking hell,' he shouted, high on adrenaline. 'How the hell did I manage that?' then he burst into hysterical laughter. Maybe his luck was changing.

'What the hell's going on, Richard?' Beth's voice was no longer calm. It was cold and palpable. 'Are you having a breakdown?'

'I drove into oncoming traffic. I didn't see the junction. Christ, that was close.' He carried on laughing manically with relief, releasing a cache of nervous energy.

'Richard, listen to me, drive straight to the police station, now. Do not come to my house. I'm going nowhere with you. I mean it.' Her voice was steel now, unyielding.

'I can't, I've told you,' he shouted, his voice cracking. 'I've told you. I can't go to the police station. I can't trust them. They'll pin it all on me.'

'Then I will.' Beth's words landed like the final blow. Her tone was flat, final. No more warmth, just cold, hard truth.

'Beth, Beth, you're not listening to me. You have to listen,' Richard begged before realising it was too late. She'd hung up. Loneliness and vulnerability shrouded him and the car suddenly felt very cold. He was on his own.

18

Beth placed her mobile phone on the table and reached for her coffee. After an initial sip of the now lukewarm drink, she decided to gulp the rest in one go, craving the much-needed caffeine hit.

She felt numb after listening to Richard's rants. It wasn't like him, it was as though he'd become someone else. What the hell had he done? He'd lost the plot, that was for sure. Beth wished she'd never met him, let alone had an affair. He sounded out of control and dangerous, like he was having a nervous breakdown. She concluded there must be more to this nightmare than he had told her, and she was in no doubt that she'd done the right thing by keeping well away from him and giving him the best advice she could.

She looked into the garden. Martin was busy burning chopped branches, oblivious to the situation raging out of control around his wife. The scene before her made her long for normality, for life to be simple again.

A thought flashed before her, stamping all over her daydreaming of normality. Richard wasn't on his way, was he? Surely not; she couldn't have made it any clearer that she was washing her hands of him. She walked to the front door and locked it. Feeling somewhat more secure, she sat in the lounge facing the bay window, with a fear of anticipation, of the sight of his car screeching to a halt outside her house.

At least Martin was in the garden and would hopefully be oblivious to the unwanted caller. Or should she get him out of the way, perhaps ask him to run an errand for her? It was probably too late for that. Beth yearned for Martin's support and protection but couldn't risk Richard making a desperate admission about their affair to him in a last-ditch attempt to force her hand into joining him. The thought knotted tight in her stomach.

Her gaze shifted to the chair opposite, recalling DS Lee McCann sitting there, seeking her assistance to sort out this mess. The thought made her feel safe and comfortable, Lee had made a good impression, and she liked him. Should she call him now? The idea was appealing, and she was tempted. It made her feel safer in the context of this horrible nightmare, but would his involvement lead to the opening of Pandora's box? She couldn't risk that. She needed to take this slowly, one step at a time, keeping lids on things—no knee-jerk reactions.

The next step suddenly formalised clearly in her mind: she needed to call Nash. Why hadn't she thought of that earlier? She walked to the bay window and scanned the quiet Victorian middle-class suburban scene before her. A chill ran down her spine as she imagined an erratic, unpredictable Richard banging on her door and shattering the peacefulness with an embarrassing scene. Christ, she would never be able to face the neighbours again; book club and wine-tasting evenings would be a thing of the past.

She didn't expect the call she was about to make would be easy, but it made sense in the circumstances. She selected Nash from her contacts and touched the green circle.

'Nash, speaking,' he announced, his voice competing with the background noise of a busy pub.

'Sorry to disturb you, Ethan,' Beth began, imagining the scene at the pub, Nash, holding court with his regular clique of pathetic sycophants. 'It's Beth from Richard's team.'

'I know who you are. As if by magic, your name flashed onto my screen when you called,' he mocked in his usual sarcastic, arrogant tone. Beth imagined his gang chuckling alongside him like schoolboys, laughing like a pack of hyenas. She felt a dark pleasure and feeling of satisfaction in guessing that he wouldn't be so cock sure of himself after she'd updated him and ruined his day socialising.

She decided to deliver the message short and sweet for maximum impact and wipe the smirk off his face. 'Richard's gone into meltdown. Tony Hargreaves has been killed, and he thinks he's next.'

'Wait a minute, I need to go outside,' Nash replied, his tone clipped, switching instantly into business mode. Beth smirked, enjoying his reaction, and waited. 'Where is he now?' Nash asked, the background noise gone.

'Not sure. He called me, ranting and raving about going on the run to find a safe place to hide. He sounds paranoid. You know what he's like. This isn't going to end well, for sure.' Her voice sounded smug now, payback for the many times she had been on the receiving end of Nash's sharp tongue.

'If he gets back in touch with you, call me immediately. This stays between me and you, right?'

'Of course,' Beth acknowledged with a fake subservient tone, holding back a chuckle.

'I'm going to release the news of his resignation to the press; damage limitation for the party is the priority now. We need to distance ourselves from him.'

'That should go down well and probably tip him over the edge,' Beth mocked. 'Aren't you going to call him?' She hesitated for a moment, knowing this would only add to Nash's dilemmas. 'It sounds to me like you need to get a grip of him.'

'Thanks, Beth. Without your cutting-edge micromanagement, I don't know how I would have managed for all these years. Keep your phone switched on, and let me know when you have any updates.'

Beth didn't have time to answer because the line went dead. 'A problem shared is a problem halved, thank you, Mr Nash,' she said out loud with glee at passing the monkey.

'Who was that?' Martin asked, having entered the lounge without her noticing.

'Just work, nothing serious,' she replied, counting on Martin having only just arrived and not been party to the entire conversation. She glanced into the street, but there was no sign of Richard. She felt confident he wasn't coming; he'd have been here by now if he was. *He's probably put off by the fear of getting lamped by Martin*, she thought, her mood lifting.

'The gardens done. I'll get a shower, and we can go and grab something to eat,' Martin suggested.

'Good idea, I'll get ready, too,' Beth said, glancing over her shoulder for one last check outside.

*

Jane stole a glance at John from the corner of her eye while slowly savouring the smoky, spiced flavour of her New York deli sandwich. The tension in the air had barely softened since they'd discussed the deal of her paying for her freedom, but the chemistry between them was warmer, the fear factor decreasing with each interaction. Even so, she felt like she was walking on thin ice. She was under no illusion that situations like this could swing instantly because of a wrong move. All that was needed was for Richard to transfer the money, and she was back to square one. There was no room for complacency. She had to keep working on him.

Stockholm syndrome gnawed at the edge of her thoughts. Was that what was happening here? A phenomenon where the hostage develops a psychological bond with their captor? She questioned whether anything had, in fact, changed between her and John or was it all in her head, like some kind of subconscious survival behaviour.

The thought jolted her back to reality. She needed to be laser-focused. She was still watching out for opportunities to overpower John and escape, and was confident that he was working alone here. There had been no sign of anyone else during her capture and incarceration. She couldn't rely on one option…a release that might never happen.

'You look like you're enjoying that,' John said, his tone lighter than it had been, though his eyes remained calculating.

She forced a nod. 'It's not bad. When this is over, and I've paid you, I'll make you a proper one; you'll love it.' She was biding her time, waiting for the right moment to bring up the deal again. Maybe it was now?

'Are you going to assassinate Richard?' she asked, choosing her words carefully, having considered and discounted the word murder, not wanting to push John's buttons the wrong way. In his eyes, he was a paid professional, not a murderer.

'Why do you ask?' he said in contemplation, his eyes narrowing.

'Well, Hargreaves has been hit, he's sorted, and that leaves Richard as the only loose end.'

John stopped eating his sandwich and placed it on the upturned plastic box. 'How would you feel if I said yes?' he asked, observing her for psychological leakage.

'What do you think? He's the reason I'm sitting here. He probably thinks I'm dead already.'

Just when she suspected that John had shut her down, he replied, 'I think you know the answer to your question. He broke the agreement; there's a price to pay. It's nothing personal, but having listened to the prick ranting on the phone, it feels like the right thing to do.'

'I'm not sure if our deal is on yet,' Jane said. *Handshake or no handshake.* 'If it is, once released, I could make contact with him and tell him I forgive. Draw him in for you? Would that help?'

John raised an eyebrow, appearing intrigued but still wary. 'Why would you do that? It implicates you in a conspiracy to murder. Alternatively, you could pay me and walk away into the sunset without spending the rest of your life looking over your shoulder.'

Jane could feel her pulse throbbing in her temples. 'Has nobody ever told you about a woman scorned? Besides, if putting skin in the game and gaining your trust gets me out of here, it's worth the risk. I'm confident you'll ensure the job is done properly with no comebacks. I don't deal with amateurs.' She smiled and winked, putting on her most brazen act to date in the hope of creating a bond. She maintained eye contact whilst taking a bite of her sandwich, warmly satisfied with the pitch of her proposal and how things were progressing.

'And my payment? How does that happen?' John asked.

'Whatever you want, untraceable transfer or I could meet you to hand it over, but I'd need access to my safety deposit box if that were your preference.' She dipped her head slightly and narrowed her eyes, then said, 'You must realise by now that you can trust me? If I survive this, I'll hardly double-cross you and make myself a target again.'

John tilted his head as if considering the proposal more deeply than before. 'And how do you know you can trust *me*? Once I've got the payment, I could still kill you.'

'I don't, but what have I got to lose?' The tension between them crackled like electricity in the air. 'I trust you. You've repeatedly told me this is just business and your employment. I believe you; you're a professional, not a thug. In different circumstances, we would probably be drawn together somehow.' Jane's heart pounded intensely as she spoke the final words. She was totally alive to the fact that she was walking on a tightrope, along the fine line between genuine back-slapping flirtation and John seeing right through her carefully planned smoke and mirrors objective.

Her performance could dictate whether she survived or died. It was a high-octane, winner-takes-all situation, and her confidence was growing.

19

Richard sat perched on the edge of the bed in his room at the motorway services budget hotel. The atmosphere felt cold and damp, so he rummaged through his bag and grabbed a fleece jacket. He glanced at the bottle he'd left by the television last night and grabbed that, too.

Walking to the window, he took a long slug of whiskey straight from the bottle. The warmth of the amber liquid filled his mouth, his hollow friend seeing him right once again. He took another swig as the warm feeling extended to his chest and lingered, blanketing him with much-needed comfort.

The vast parking area of the motorway services area was busy with people and vehicles, their world a picture of normality, while his world was caving in around him. The feeling of anonymity amid the people going about their normal business made him feel safe but lonely at the same time.

He could end this turmoil now if he chose to, and the thought was never far from his mind. It was a viable, peaceful option. The tablets were there, should he require them.

Bottle in hand, he collapsed into the armchair by the window and closed his eyes, trying to calm the raging storm in his mind. His breathing was heavy, and his chest was tight, panic and exhaustion slowly suffocating him.

He told himself to breathe and tried to relax, knowing he needed to rest before deciding what to do next. But the more he tried, the more his unrelenting ruminations continued to fuel the chaos.

His eyes opened, relieving his racing mind, but then he caught his reflection in the mirror: dishevelled hair, unsightly stubble, and dark patches under his eyes. He quickly looked away, shocked at what he'd become, so quickly.

His ears pricked at the sound of footsteps in the corridor outside his room. There were no voices, just the rhythmic tread of feet on the floor. His pulse quickened. *Is this how it ended for Hargreaves?* he speculated. *Will I die the same way?* He held his breath, every nerve attuned to the silence, fearing the person outside had stopped at his door. His hands gripped the arms of the chair in anticipation of the door being kicked in. He'd watched this scene repeatedly play out in the movies, usually at a small, quiet, roadside out-of-town motel. A grisly scene left behind for the poor cleaner to discover. Is this how it would end? He sat waiting almost trancelike—nothing happened.

He walked back over to the bed and collapsed, crashing out, his body heavy with exhaustion and dread, wrapping the duvet around himself like a protective cocoon. The now empty whiskey bottle was cast aside, redundant. His eyes closed and he eventually fell into a restless sleep, tormented by his nightmares and fears.

*

DI Andrea Statham and DS Lee McCann approached the door of the Flannagan-Smythes' mansion with a feeling of familiarity. 'His car isn't here. He must be out somewhere. Maybe that's why she wants to speak to us here,' Andrea said as Lee rang the doorbell.

'Shame, I think he's cracking under the pressure. Another chat might just have done the trick. It's just a matter of time now.'

'Time isn't on our side though, is it?' Andrea lamented.

'Until a body is discovered, I'm working on the premise that Jane's still alive, and we will find her,' Lee said.

'I sure hope so. He's our only source of information now. Tony Hargreaves has taken his knowledge to the grave. Maybe that's the most effective button we can press to get Richard to talk. He must realise he may be next on their hit list.'

Lee grimaced and shifted uncomfortably on his feet. 'Let's see what Mandy has to say, and I'll have another crack at getting him to talk after that,' he said as the front door opened. Mandy leaned out of the doorway and glanced around as if fearing unwelcome parties had followed the detectives to the house.

'Hiya, come in,' she said, heading back into the house.

They followed her to the kitchen and sat in the same seats as on their last visit. 'Where's Richard?' Andrea asked.

Mandy shrugged and began to look worried. 'I don't think he came home last night. Do you think something's happened to him?'

Andrea couldn't hide her tone of annoyance. 'Are you kidding me, Mandy? You've asked us to drop everything and come and see you because he didn't come home last night?'

Mandy's face flushed up. 'No, of course not, you asked where he is, that's all. I told you he didn't come home last night,' she said, puzzled, looking towards Lee for clarity.

'No worries, it's okay,' Lee said, shooting a glance at Andrea. 'Why did you want to see us?'

'I was in the pub last night. A rumour was doing the rounds that Tony Hargreaves had been killed in Spain. Is that right?'

'I don't know about being killed,' Andrea answered. 'It may have been an accident, but yes, Tony Hargreaves has passed away in Spain.'

'Oh my god,' Mandy said, covering her mouth with her hand. 'I thought it was just beer talk, the usual suspects talking the usual crap.'

'Is that why you're worried about Richard?' Lee asked, his tone calm and reassuring.

'Sort of… When Tony came here for the gatherings, we got on together. To be honest, it was a bit more than that. We had a fling,' Mandy said, looking down at the table.

Lee leaned forward, nodding, providing silence for Mandy to continue, convinced she would offer some valuable information or evidence.

She continued, 'Tony sent me an email with a file attached. He said if anything ever happened to him I should give it to the police.'

Lee could barely hide his enthusiasm. 'Do you still have it?'

'Yes, it's on my phone, shall I send it to you?'

Andrea interrupted, 'What's on the file? Have you looked at it?'

'I don't know, I never opened it,' Mandy replied whilst accessing her emails.

'Really,' Andrea said, glancing at Lee in disbelief. 'Why didn't you tell us about this earlier?'

'I'd forgotten about it until I heard he was dead last night, then I remembered. And that's why I called you.

He gave me a password, too, but he told me not to open it and that if I did open it, he would be alerted. Shall I open it now?'

'No, we can't risk the software getting corrupted,' Lee warned quickly before she had a chance to touch it. 'I'll get our tech people to open it forensically; we need to maintain its evidential integrity,' he added. 'I'll need to take your phone so they can access it. It won't take long. I'll return it to you as soon as possible.' Mandy reluctantly slid the smartphone over to him. 'Treat it like a social media detox,' Lee quipped as he placed the phone in his pocket.

'Is there anything else you've not told us, Mandy?' Andrea asked, her stare boring into Mandy's eyes.

'I don't think so. Is there any good news about Jane yet?'

'Not yet, I'm afraid, but this digital audio file might help us to find her,' Andrea said, dropping the intense stare, her voice softening.

'What else can you tell us?' Lee asked. 'Have you got anything else up your sleeve that may help us to find Jane?'

'I wish I had. I'll get in touch again if I come across anything,' Mandy replied, with a hint of relief that the meeting was almost over.

'I'll be in touch,' Lee said. 'I'll need to take a statement from you regarding the audio file.' Lee and Andrea got up to leave, while Mandy looked suddenly lost without her smartphone. It was the first time Lee could recall seeing her without it.

20

Richard was jolted awake by the harsh rasp of his snoring, grating on his throat. His eyes darted around the room in the initial confusion of wondering where the hell he was, but the confusion quickly settled when he recalled checking into the hotel, this time without Beth.

The inside of his mouth felt like sandpaper. He fumbled around to find the neck of the whisky bottle wedged in the folds of the duvet, dropping it in disappointment after realising it was empty. He needed another bottle as soon as possible.

A wave of optimism ran through him as he rubbed his stiff neck and unfolded himself from the duvet. Maybe Beth would return in his hour of need and might have tried to call him. He grabbed his mobile and checked the screen, but there were no missed calls or texts. Dejected, he dropped the phone onto the bed and looked across the car park to the service area facilities.

The logo of a burger restaurant grabbed his attention, and he suddenly felt famished. He couldn't recall the last time he'd eaten, so he decided to shower and freshen up before walking over. He would draw attention to himself if he walked across in his current dishevelled-looking state. The last thing he needed, right now.

He stripped off and ambled over to the bathroom. Turning on the shower was the usual complicated affair, but once he'd got the water running, he held his hand out, waiting for it to warm up.

Just as he was about to step into the shower, the ringtone of his phone began blasting out, killing the silence of the bedroom. He quickly darted back into the room with newfound optimism. If it was Beth, he didn't want to miss her call. Just as he reached out to grab the phone, he stubbed his toe on the corner of the bed. Cursing loudly, he hopped about before sitting down and rubbing it frantically to numb the pain.

He placed the phone to his ear, still wincing, not having glanced at the screen. 'Beth, thanks for ringing. I...'

'It's not Beth, it's me, you fucking idiot.' Richard immediately recognised Nash's acerbic tone. His head dropped as if energy was draining from his body like a fast flowing water leak. He needed Beth, not Nash. His shoulders drooped and he stared at the floor whilst considering ending the call. He wasn't anticipating a convivial chat with Nash; it never was.

'What do you want?' Richard mumbled, trying desperately to get rid of the throbbing pain in his toe. 'I thought you'd thrown me under the bus.'

'A little birdy tells me you're losing your head, Richard. You asked what I want, well, I'll tell you what I fucking want. Do not create any shitstorms for me or the party. Book yourself into a rehabilitation clinic and keep your head down. Can you manage that alone, or do I need to send someone to hold your hand?' Nash's tone was sharp and nasty, totally void of any compassion.

'It's not so simple. Tony Hargreaves manipulated me into a conspiracy to take out a contract on Jane. So that I could access Jane's money and cover his losses on the failed building development. He didn't pay them, so they killed him. I did nothing wrong, but now they're coming after me.'

'Woah, stop right there,' Nash commanded dramatically. 'I don't need to hear this. Don't try and drag me into your squalid shitstorm. Fuck me, Dicky-boy. I know you're an incompetent cretin and a fucking loser, but you've fucked up monumentally this time, haven't you?' Nash started to laugh then said, 'Even I'm blown away by the level of your fucking stupidity this time. So, you failed to tell me everything when Jane disappeared, and now you're feeding me a bullshit half-story. Let's cut to the chase: you got Tony Hargreaves to facilitate Jane's disappearance, and now it's all gone tits up. You want to tell me more, hoping that I'll wave a magic wand. Too late, that ship has sailed.'

'He's framed me. I had nothing to do with it. It's his revenge for the business and retail park deal collapsing. He blames me for that. I'm the victim here,' Richard said, sitting naked and shivering on the bed, pulling the duvet towards him.

'Of course, you are, you deluded fuckwit. People like you are always the victim. It's everyone else's fault, isn't it?' Nash sneered with contempt. 'You've backed me into a corner this time, Dicky-boy, going to the police is my only option. But looking on the positive side, at least you've resigned already.'

'That's right, abandon me just like Beth has done. You're snakes, all of you. Why doesn't anyone believe me?' Richard's voice rose an octave, sounding almost manic. 'Don't go to the police, Ethan, I'm begging you. I need to clear my name. Give me twenty-four hours. That's all I need. Please, Ethan, twenty-four hours.'

'Where are you, Richard? It's probably the correct protocol to tell the cops prior to your arrest. It's best to keep it all diplomatic and low-key,' Nash said, his tone no longer mockingly cynical but businesslike, dealing with the task at hand.

'Now look whose deluded, as if I'm going to tell you that. You'll probably arrange for the Secret Service to take me out like they did with the scientist, and cover it up as death by suicide. No way, do you think I'm totally stupid?'

'Well yes, now you ask, of course I think you're fucking stupid. Have it your way, Richard, but it's probably best to hand yourself in to the cops. Think about it.' Nash's voice began to wane with a sudden lack of interest as if he had other things on his mind. 'You can't walk away from this one, believe me,' he said before ending the call.

Richard lay back on the bed, putting his hands behind his head. The cold, sterile air from the air conditioner made the place feel damp and oppressive. The walls again closed in on him; the feeling of claustrophobia intimidating his senses. He couldn't do time in prison. He'd never survive the regime. He rolled over into the foetal position, tugging in the duvet for comfort. What the hell was he going to do? He wasn't going to the police for sure. But things had just got a whole lot worse. After Nash's call, they'd no doubt commence a manhunt to find him.

*

There was a palpable, upbeat atmosphere in the briefing room. Lee had just finished reading the transcript of the audio voice recording retrieved from Mandy's phone to the detectives. 'Well, that's a game changer,' he said enthusiastically. 'That's definitely evidence beyond reasonable doubt. Richard Flannagan-Smythe clearly conspires to have his wife killed. Tony

Hargreaves knows a man who can and will make the arrangements for the contract kill. Let's get him in custody, team. He's got no way out; he needs to tell us where Jane's being held.'

Andrea stepped forward. 'Richard Flannagan-Smythe is now officially suspect status. He is circulated as a wanted person on PNC and is to be arrested on suspicion of conspiracy to kill. Our priority remains to find his wife, Jane. We will continue to pursue both lines of enquiry robustly. We will be assisted with the manhunt. The Force will be committing all available resources to find him. I'll take this opportunity to thank you for your commitment and hard work, which have got us to this stage. Let's finish the job, bring him in and find Jane.'

Once she'd finished the briefing, the room burst into discussions and chatter about the best way forward to achieve the objective. The enthusiasm and motivation was palpable.

Lee and Andrea returned to Andrea's office as the team got their things together and prepared to move out. 'That's lifted the team. It's the breakthrough we needed. Hopefully, he'll be sitting in a cell sooner than later.'

'It won't be for the lack of trying,' Andrea pointed out, looking at the authority documents approving the covert tactics. 'Hopefully, his mobile phone will ping on a transmission mast and get us a location. We're also monitoring his bank accounts, and his car has an ANPR camera alert.'

Lee nodded. 'The team are focusing on his contacts and associates to locate him. The Security Service and National Crime Agency are interrogating their intelligence systems, and maybe we'll get a facial recognition hit—the net's closing in on him. I'll have a drive out and revisit Beth. She must have a few good ideas of where we'll find him.'

'I'll have to leave soon for the meeting at headquarters,' Andrea said, glancing at her watch. 'I'll catch up with you after the meeting. We can grab something to eat and put our foot on the ball. I have a good feeling that once he's in custody, he'll crack, and we can go on to rescue Jane.'

'Sounds good. Give me a bell if the Spanish police have made any breakthroughs. They must have an update for us by now. We need to know if Tony Hargreaves' visitor is still out there or whether he's sneaked back in the UK.'

'If he's back in the UK, we have competition in finding Richard Flannagan-Smythe,' Andrea added. 'We need to get both of them in custody pronto.'

'It'll be in their best interest to talk and give us Jane's location to mitigate their sentences. Let's get them in,' Lee said, walking over to the whiteboard and studying the places frequented by the subject section, reading between the lines to discover his hide-out.

21

Jane awoke to the familiar sound of John's voice. It was louder than usual, and his tone was quarrelsome. She instinctively shot up from the cot bed and pressed her ear hard to the cold, unforgiving wood of the secure door.

A bolt of fear shot through her veins, her heart racing fast. Was this when she died? Was the executioner here? Why else would someone else have tipped up to this shit hole? John had always worked alone. This wasn't a good sign. The amygdala part of her brain pushed the negative connotations and worst-case scenarios to the forefront of her mind.

The volume of John's voice grew and then dissipated. She guessed he was pacing the room. Then the penny dropped; he must be talking on his mobile phone, and she strained hard to hear what the conversation was about.

'When are you back in the UK?' John asked.

A pause followed; Jane adjusted her position quietly, trying not to alert him she was listening.

'No, I wouldn't risk flying either. Take the boat,' he replied to the unknown person after another pause.

Jane's senses were heightened. She felt convinced this call had direct implications for her future. Whether she lived or died. Maybe it was John's boss? She wished she could hear both sides of the conversation.

A shiver ran down her spine when she suddenly realised it could be Richard arranging to make the payment. She clenched her fist, trying to keep it together, to focus on dealing with the fear and anxiety that was slowly creeping all over her. Her body was rigid and tense. She needed to act.

'Give me a fucking break, H. I don't consider her to be a loose end. I've had the time to analyse her and I'm satisfied she doesn't present a threat to us. It also means we get our money.'

The cold light of reality hit Jane hard between the eyes during the pause. They were discussing whether to kill her or not, and she had an irrational urge to shout out and present her defence. But she thought better of it. No knee-jerk reactions, she affirmed to herself, *Focus on the positives*. A faint glimmer of hope flickered to life inside her as it appeared that John was fighting her corner. There was still hope. He didn't want to kill her. He wanted her money.

Meanwhile, the conversation continued after a long silence, during which the other person was probably pushing the case to kill her.

'Look, H, the biggest threat to us was the builder. You've neutralised him. I'm one hundred per cent confident that once you've dispatched the MP, we're safe.'

During the next pause, Jane became aware of the blood pumping hard in her temples. The feeling of high sensitivity was morphing into nausea. She felt helpless and reliant on John now, wondering if maybe her relentless efforts to bond with him were finally paying off. The quiet manipulation, the shared jokes, the feigned feminine weakness and seeking compassion. Had she done enough? *Please be enough*, she whispered, her voice barely audible.

Did she need to raise the stakes and push the boundary towards intimacy? Or would that ruin her hard work? Would he see straight through her plan to weaken him? She'd noted the name H, and realised that whoever he was, he wanted her dead. Her mind was in overdrive.

Jane's ruminations were interrupted by John's voice. 'Of course, I'll take full responsibility for the decision. When have I ever let you down? Trust me, we need to stick together on this.'

What decision? Jane panicked during the pause.

'No, you know that's not the case. If it were the right decision, I'd shoot her myself. I don't need you to pull the trigger for me, but like I said, we don't need to kill her. Christ, what's up with you? It's the right decision. Are you with me or not?'

She felt dizzy. She could taste the metallic tang of fear whilst listening to one side of a discussion taking place about whether she lived or died, as casually as two friends discussing what to choose from the pizza menu. A warm sensation crept through her body as she considered there was still hope, that John had her back.

'Of course, no worries. Keep me up to speed,' he said, then the place was silent once again.

Jane considered her options regarding whether to admit hearing the conversation, her survival instinct scanning for the best odds. So far, she'd followed her gut feelings, but the pressure now felt intense. Sometimes, it was best to do nothing, she told herself, and that was what her gut was saying now. She changed her focus to calm down and remain positive.

She sat on the edge of the cot bed, regulating her breathing, waiting for the door to open. Then another thought jolted into her mind, *What if John has a gun?* The thought was energy-sapping; she'd never experienced primal fear like this before, but she quickly decided that she wasn't going down without a fight.

*

Andrea left the headquarters briefing room quickly, avoiding eye contact with the other attendees and placed her phone to her ear. Her priority was to update Lee. She felt uplifted and confident about how the meeting had gone. With the resources allocated to the manhunt, it wouldn't be long before Jane was safe and Richard Flannagan-Smythe was behind bars, spending his time reflecting.

'How are you doing?' Lee asked. 'It must have been a quick meeting.'

'It was, just as I like them, down to business,' she replied. 'There was a noticeable absence of bullshit bingo and showboating. Maybe the usual suspects were intimidated by the presence of the spooks. Are you with Beth?'

'No, she's back at Westminster but promised to call me back this evening. Any breakthroughs worthy of mention?'

'Yes, things are looking up at last. Samuel was contacted by the director of communications for Richard's party, a guy called Ethan Nash. He informed us that Richard is on the run, in fear for his life. Richard disclosed to Nash that Hargreaves was responsible for taking out a contract kill on his wife but refused to pay the hitman. He claims Hargreaves was murdered as a result and that Richard is next on their list. He also gave a similar account to his colleague, Beth. Samuel reckons that Nash suspects Richard's involved in the conspiracy but didn't say as such. He's a party man and will have one eye on protecting its reputation.'

'That explains her being called back to London at short notice,' Lee observed. 'They probably want to debrief her before we interview her formally, including the damage limitation and all that.'

'All resources are now directed towards the manhunt for Richard in addition to finding Jane. So, hopefully, he'll be in custody soon. He doesn't seem like the resilient type, does he?' Andrea asked but continued talking before Lee had the chance to answer. 'Also, the Spanish police have done great work with a CCTV investigation. They have the visitor to Hargreaves' house close to the scene before and after his death. Unfortunately, the post-mortem didn't illicit any suspicious findings. The cause of death is consistent with a fall from height. It was the trauma to his head that killed him. No defensive injuries whatsoever, so that doesn't help us much.'

'Our suspect is a big, strong-looking bloke. It wouldn't have taken him much effort to push Hargreaves over the edge,' Lee pointed out. 'Even easier if Hargreaves had been drinking, I guess. He sounds like a professional hitman, good at his craft.'

'He's not that good. We've got him on CCTV near the scene and located the apartment he used as a base. The police are undertaking a forensic examination as we speak. We might even get some of his DNA from the scene. The CCTV footage of the male from the Spanish police matches that of the traffic officer's bodycam footage from when he stopped the car. It's the same man.'

'Excellent, maybe not enough evidence to secure a conviction for Hargreaves' death just yet, but good evidence for the kidnapping and maybe a conspiracy to murder charge,' Lee said, weighing things up.

22

Richard slung his overnight bag over his shoulder and quietly left the hotel, keeping a look out for CCTV cameras, carefully ensuring his back was facing them or that he was looking at the floor. He stepped outside and took a deep breath of welcoming fresh air; it felt invigorating and gave him a much needed pick-me-up. Jane's old car was where he'd left it, in the quietest corner of the car park, furthest away from the hotel entrance—and unwanted attention.

He glanced into the windows of the surrounding parked cars as he passed by, checking for any surveillance operatives. If Nash had been to the police, which Richard was damn sure he would have, he was now probably a wanted man and being hunted down.

He felt a sense of smugness as he walked towards Jane's old car. He'd made a good move, taking it from the lockup. The cops were probably totally unaware that it existed and were checking his SUV, public transport or car rental companies.

He slipped into the driver's seat and slammed the door closed. The car interior was cold and smelled musty.

The few hours of sleep he'd managed to grab had done the trick. He was reinvigorated, and his confidence was slowly returning. Fuck Nash and fuck Beth. He would get out of this mess without them. He tapped the postcode into the Sat Nav with purpose and set off.

SILENT BETRAYAL

*

John sat on his usual makeshift seat, his fingers slowly running through his beard, deep in thought. He leant forward, elbows resting on his knees. The call with H had unsettled him. They'd had their differences of opinion before, but this felt different. Had he allowed himself to get too close to Jane? No, he hadn't, he concluded without hesitation. So why was H so adamant that she should be neutralised? His attention was taken by Jane suddenly shouting and banging on the door.

'John, I need the toilet. Are you there, John?'

'For fuck's sake,' he mumbled. He got to his feet and unlocked the door, stepping aside to let her pass him. He watched as she rushed to the toilet and sat back down again. The toilet flushed, followed by the sound of running water, then she walked over and joined him, sitting on the usual upturned box.

An uneasy silence hung over the room. John watched as Jane looked down towards the floor, her fingers fidgeting. She looked frightened and nervous, more vulnerable than usual. 'It's decision time,' he announced matter-of-factly. His eyes narrowed, studying her carefully. 'My associate has concerns about whether we can trust you. He's questioning my judgement, something he's never done before. So, Jane, can I trust you?' John's eyes were locked on Jane's, noticing raw fear, but he felt no empathy. This was business, and his decision needed to be correct. More than ever, because he was at odds with H on this one.

'What else can I say? Yes, you can trust me. I want to live. Why would I cross you?'

'Don't let me down, Jane. The consequences would be severe, there's nowhere to hide in such situations. Not even the police could protect you. We have a network and contacts in places you wouldn't imagine. Do you understand?'

'Yes,' Jane said, holding John's gaze without flinching.

'You'll be taken from here and dropped off in the city centre. You'll be given a burner phone with only two numbers in the contacts: mine and your husband's. That will be our only means of communication. The phone is encrypted. It's safe. As we discussed, your priority is to buy a pay-as-you-go with cash and arrange for your brother to transfer the money. Don't use the encrypted phone to call him.

'Once that's done, contact your husband and get him to attend at the specified location. Then wait until I call you, is that understood?'

'Yes, I won't let you down,' Jane said, nodding slowly in appreciation.

'We will transport you out of here later this afternoon. You'll be wearing a hood. The location of this place needs to remain a secret. For now, you need to return to the cell.'

'Before I do, John, I just want to thank you. I don't want to die. And I know you've put your neck on the line for me. Please rest assured that I won't let you down. I respect you…' She paused, allowing her words to register.

'It's a financial decision, Jane. That's all it is, nothing more,' he said, maintaining a coldness as he stared into her eyes.

'Even so, thank you. You've saved my life, and I'm indebted to you. I could even be a business asset for you in the future. I need to carve out a new life. I've been walked over too many times. Maybe it's time to stop that from happening to me and others.'

John followed Jane towards the cell and closed the door behind her then headed upstairs to prepare for her release.

Halfway up the stairs, he froze, his breath catching in his throat. A sound, faint but unmistakable, broke the heavy silence. *What was that?* Had he heard something, or was his mind playing tricks? His right hand instinctively slid along his belt until it reached the pistol, his fingers curling around the grip. Reassured it was still in place, he lifted a foot to continue. Another noise followed—this time louder. His pulse quickened. Somebody was in the house.

John pressed his shoulder into the wall for support as he silently edged slowly up the stairs, one cautious step at a time until he reached the kitchen. He glanced to the left—his stomach dropped on seeing the exterior door was open wide. Was he under attack? This didn't bode well; someone must have discovered where he was, even after extensive research had been done to choose the perfect location.

The door frame was suddenly filled by a shadow moving across it, and John's grip on the pistol tightened. Relief and suspicion collided when Harry, the grumpy bugger from the next farm, shuffled into the kitchen.

'What the fuck are you up to, Harry?' he asked, his voice steady but his mind still racing. 'I thought I could hear someone in here.'

'Well, the door was open, and you didn't answer when I knocked, so I came in,' Harry replied casually, his voice annoyingly nonchalant.

Liar—that door was closed, John thought with certainty. He forced a smile, masking his rapid thought process working under the surface. 'To what do I owe the pleasure of your visit,' John asked, his voice edged with forced politeness, while his mind instinctively conducted a risk assessment of what Harry could have seen or heard whilst snooping around the place. John looked towards the door, calculating the angles and considering the timings, reasonably satisfied that Harry couldn't have overheard the conversation in the cellar.

'My chainsaw has packed in. Do you have one I could use to finish the job?'

John decided he needed to cover his tracks, just in case, before answering the question. 'Bloody typical, Harry, the only time you've ever called round is when I'm planning on having a romantic, quiet morning in bed with my lady friend,' he said with a chuckle. He motioned towards the outbuildings. 'Come on, it's in the barn.'

Harry followed him, his eyes darting everywhere when they entered the big, dirt-infested building, checking out the tools and machinery around him.

'Here, take this one,' John said, holding out the chainsaw, guessing he'd never see it again.

'Spot on, that'll be right,' Harry said, taking it before returning to his truck. No need for further conversation.

John followed him out and waved, watching the truck retreat down the drive, replaying every moment, every glance, every sound together with the timeline of how it panned out.

He assessed where Harry had parked and what he may have seen or heard, satisfied he hadn't been compromised. If Harry had stepped down the stairs, John was sure he would have heard them creaking. The grumpy bugger was probably just being nosey.

He returned to the kitchen, this time making sure to lock the door behind him. A gnawing thought crossed his mind: *did H have a point?* Was he getting sloppy with his tradecraft? He shook his head. It was time to get on with the job.

John went to the covert safe in the kitchen, a small space concealed behind a wall cupboard, and removed the silencer attachment for his pistol, confident that he'd wipe away H's nagging doubts about his ability.

*

Richard parked his car on a secluded single-track back road that headed up to Hampsfell through the dense forest. It was an outlying fell on the edge of the Lake District overlooking Grange-over-Sands. He'd hiked it many times in days gone by.

He secured the car and set off on foot down the hill towards the town centre and his holiday let accommodation. He felt safe here. He'd visited often and gone about his business anonymously, the locals disinterested in who he was or what he did for a living.

There were a few pubs and eateries around the centre, a Victorian promenade for exercise, and, most importantly, a low police presence. This was the perfect place where he could pull himself together and plan his next move. It couldn't be that difficult to outwit Mulder and Scully. He chuckled at his comical comparison while imagining Statham and McCann stomping around Greater Manchester, trying to find him, and failing miserably.

He decided to take a slight detour by the local pub, buying himself a pint and then taking a seat overlooking Morecambe Bay, a vast, stunning, peaceful open space that sucked the stresses and pressures of life from you.

He didn't hang around, finishing the pint in four swigs before going to the bar for another. The alcohol immediately began to take the edge off the jaggedness of his troubled mind. He felt much calmer as his confidence returned. His thoughts began to slow down, soothed by the familiar, comforting taste of his real ale.

He took out his burner phone and selected Beth from the contacts. He rationalised that she had probably calmed down by now, so he'd test the water. Why not? He had nothing to lose. Though he knew it would have to be a short call to prevent it from being traced and giving his location away. He couldn't remember how long it took the police to trace calls. *Probably a few minutes was all it took?*

'Richard, where the hell are you?' Beth asked.

'That's not important. I've only got a few minutes. Have you reconsidered what I suggested? We can be together at last.'

'That boat has sailed. Nash went to the police. He told me they have evidence that you and Hargreaves planned to have Jane killed…is it true?'

Richard suddenly had a paranoid thought that the police could be listening to the call. They may even be with her, nudging her to ask the crucial questions. 'No, Hargreaves wanted revenge. Not only by killing Jane but then by framing me and watching me rot in prison. I'm innocent, Beth.' His tone was deflated, as if he was finally accepting that his attempts at them getting together were futile. The high of the alcohol was displaced reluctantly with a spirit-crushing realisation that it was over between him and Beth.

'The police are looking for you, Richard. You need to turn yourself in before this gets out of hand. Do the right thing. Shall I arrange a taxi for you?'

That last question spooked him. He was right. She was helping the police. He glanced at his watch. 'Time's up, Beth. I've got to go...'

'Hang on, Richard. Do you want me to pick you up? I can take you to a police station,' she said, sounding slightly desperate, and Richard imagined the detective she was with giving her an encouraging thumbs up from the sofa and mouthing, *Keep him on the line*.

'Goodbye, Beth,' Richard said with a tone of finality, and ended the call. It was time to pick up a bottle of whiskey from the off-licence, visit the hardware store for essentials, and head back to the accomodation. He was tired and suddenly felt vulnerable again, albeit up for the task ahead of him.

23

DI Andrea Statham pulled into a parking space and looked across to DS Lee McCann as she switched off the engine. 'I'm ready for a coffee. It's your shout, so I'll have a choc chip muffin as well, please,' she said as they stepped out of the car. The café was on a retail park on the city's edge; it wasn't the best, but accessible free parking was convenient.

'I don't mind. With the extra hours I've been working, I can afford it. Especially for a salaried inspector, it can't be easy on your wages,' Lee mocked playfully, knowing it was a bone of contention that always got a reaction from her.

'Don't remind me. Maybe I should slow down, get a cushy nine-to-five job at headquarters, and be home on time every day.'

'That was a bad move when the inspectors voted for ditching the overtime for a salaried fixed wage,' Lee said.

Andrea looked at him with furrowed eyebrows, not sure if he was still taking the piss or being serious. 'The nine-to-five lot outnumbered the operational investigators. It was a good move for them. They rarely did any overtime anyway.'

Inside, Andrea sat at a table in the corner facing the door while Lee went to the counter. She glanced over, watching him. She loved his friendly manner and how easily he got along with people. He was good to be around, and she felt contented sharing these small everyday moments with him. Lee turned around, carrying the tray to the table. 'What are you looking at?' he asked.

'Just checking out your eighties style suit. Obviously not a new one?' She said, supressing a grin.

'No, I've had it a while. It's been in the *need-to-lose-a-bit-of-weight-section* of the wardrobe. I can just about fit in the trousers.' He laughed, fidgeting with his belt. He sipped his Americano and placed the mug on the table. 'That was two hours well spent. There was a lot of CCTV to watch. It's coming along nicely.'

'The CCTV Evidence Team is a Godsend. It's painstaking work pulling the footage together, but their end product never disappoints,' Andrea said.

'Well, they managed to find the last sighting of the abductor and Jane on the A59 near Knaresborough. I'm optimistic the more they find will eventually lead us to her.'

'It might be a case of all roads leading to Whitby, just like the Jason Hamilton investigation,' Andrea said with a frown. 'We tracked him there and missed out on arresting him by minutes, I reckon. What a day that was.'

Lee nodded. 'I remember that day very well. You were so unlucky. Maybe we should check Hamilton's old caravan, where he hid from us. How spooky would that be to find them there?' he said, more in mocking jest than as a viable option.

'I'll stick with my disused farm bet, and there's a hell of a lot of isolated places around the Pennines, Dales, and North Yorkshire moors. Tom's working with… What's his name again, Lee?'

'Alistair Ford,' Lee replied.

'That's him,' Andrea said, nodding, 'the geographical profiler, who's gridding out the area surrounding the last known sighting of the abductor's car. He can then establish the likeliest farms and buildings and prioritise which ones we look at first. I guess the process of elimination will be fairly straightforward. It's a great line of enquiry.'

'Alistair's very good at his job. I was at the initial briefing with him and Tom. I think he's ex-military. I know he's well respected in the field of experts and probably the best practitioner in the UK at the moment. He's also produced some great work on a strategy for potential body deposition sites for us. I'm thankful that the helicopter and satellite searches haven't found any body deposition sites. The images are invaluable for helping us to locate the vehicle and premises where Jane is being held.'

The conversation was interrupted by Lee's ringtone. 'It's Beth, finally returning my call.' He slid the answer button across the screen and said, 'Hi, Beth, thanks for getting back to me. Are you still in London?'

'Hi, Lee, yes, the department is busy following Richard's resignation. I'll probably be down here for a few weeks. But it's better than going to and from Manchester and London, like I've been doing for the last few days. I'm helping the new incumbent get to grips with the portfolio, but she lives in her constituency in Plymouth, which doesn't make things any easier. At least Richard lived up north, same as me.'

'Wow, so Richard's history already. But I suppose there's no room for sentiment in politics,' Lee said diplomatically, holding back his honest opinion of politicians. 'I need to speak to you again. Could you spare me some time if I came down to see you?'

'Yes, that's fine. I'm calling now because I think I might have a good idea where Richard may be.'

'That's great news,' Lee said, sitting up attentively in his seat and beckoning Andrea to hand him a pen.

'He called me. He wants me to meet up with him. While we were talking, I heard the familiar sound of a goods train. It's not a regular one, I think it's connected to the power station at Sellafield. It sounds different from the regular trains. Now, I may be adding one and one and coming up with three, but we used to visit a pub where that train passed by on the west coast line, and, thinking about it, it's the perfect location for him to hide out.'

'Where is the pub?'

'Grange-over-Sands.'

'Where's that?' Lee asked, clicking the pen.

'It's a small town south of the Lake District, overlooking Morecambe Bay.'

Lee hurriedly scribbled down the location. This was a significant breakthrough, the opportunity he was looking for. His mind was racing to the next move. 'Beth, would you be willing to call him back and arrange to meet him? We will support you and make sure you come to no harm. You'd actually be helping him as well as us, because it's in his best interest now to come out of hiding and speak to us.' Lee looked over to Andrea, raising his eyebrows, a sudden wave of optimism enveloping him.

'I offered to pick him up when I spoke to him. Sorry, I didn't manage to get the location. He was very cagey and wasn't on the phone for that long.'

'No worries, you can still call him back,' Lee said enthusiastically.

'It wasn't his usual phone; there was no caller ID,' Beth said. 'He's probably changed phones to make it harder for you to track him down.' Lee scribbled a reminder to get Beth's phone checked by the Technical Investigation Unit, hoping that maybe they could identify Richard's phone. 'Is there anything else you can tell us, Beth?'

'No, but I'll let you know if anything happens,' she said.

'Okay, thanks. I'll get going with this Grange lead and get back to you shortly to arrange a meeting. Thanks, Beth.' Lee ended the call and looked at Andrea with a beaming smile. 'The net's closing in!'

'Let's hope so. If we can get him talking, he may have information about the abductor or where Jane's being held,' Andrea said while retrieving her phone from her bag. 'I'll make some calls and get a surveillance team over to Grange-over-Sands.'

Lee was busy using his maps app to locate the area. 'It's only forty minutes away on the M6, and it's not that big either. If he's there, we should be able to find him.'

'Once I've briefed the Intelligence Unit and got the Surveillance Unit deployed, we can also drive up and look around the pubs and shops. He may have a false sense of security and dropped his guard now that he's out in the sticks.'

'There's no police station there. I guess the patrols operate from Kendal,' Lee said, thinking ahead in case they needed the assistance of local officers.

*

Jane was awoken by the door bolt sliding open. She was surprised that she'd fallen asleep so easily and wondered what time it was. Maybe the realistic possibility of imminent freedom had helped her relax. She rubbed her groggy eyes and stood up, running her fingers through her hair. The door opened slowly, allowing the light to penetrate the room, and she stepped out slowly, still not fully awake but relieved to be leaving the claustrophobic cell.

She followed her usual routine, making her way to the makeshift bathroom. Splashing water onto her face, she washed away the remnants of sleep. The water felt invigorating, clearing her mind and setting her focus on getting out of this place. Then she returned to the main area and sat on her upturned box, picking up the takeaway carton, the delicious smell leaving her in no doubt what was inside. Sure enough when she opened the box, she was delighted to find fish and chips.

She stole a furtive glance at John. He was busy munching on his chips, looking like he had things to mull over, and was quieter than usual. She took the cue and tucked into her own food, savouring the taste and enjoying her favourite moment of the day. She decided she'd wait until he wanted to speak. She'd made her best pitch, and it looked like they had a deal. There was nothing more to say for now.

John wiped over his lips with the back of his hand and took a drink of his coffee, then he inhaled deeply, clasped his hands together and looked at Jane. 'We'll make a move soon,' he said.

She swallowed her food and engaged in eye contact. A swell of euphoria engulfed her instantly. The thought of getting out of this shit hole and being in control of her life was no longer a dream. It was a reality. She held her excitement in check, biting her lips to prevent a substantial beaming smile from spreading across her face. 'Thank you, John. I won't let you down,' were the only words she could muster. The situation felt dreamlike but was accompanied by a primal fear that someone would snatch her good fortune from under her nose and throw her back into the misery of the last few days. The thought of spending another night on the military cot bed in the cell felt like a devastating blow that she couldn't contend with, not now, not being so close to freedom.

'I'll run through what's going to happen. We will leave here in an SUV; the rear windows are one-way glass, and you will be sat in the back seat. For the first part of the journey, you'll be blindfolded. It's operational security, that's all. I don't want this location to be compromised.' He paused and stood up, pacing the room.

Jane nodded like an obedient child. 'Okay.'

'When I tell you, you may remove the hood, but not until then. Do you understand?'

'Yes,' she replied, almost impatiently, just wanting to get the hell out as soon as possible.

'When I tell you we've arrived at the drop-off point, get out of the vehicle and sit on one of the benches for a few minutes to compose yourself. You must be in the right frame of mind. There can be no mistakes.'

She struggled with the monotony of the micromanaged instructions, and felt like suggesting he should just get on with it, but she fought the urge and focused on being acquiescent.

'From there,' he continued, 'I will give you further instructions over the encrypted phone. Stay on the bench until you hear from me. Do you understand?'

'Yes, totally.'

'There's no margin for fuck-ups. You will be under surveillance from my associates at all times. This is your only opportunity to walk away, don't fuck it up. There will be no second chance. Take ten minutes to prepare yourself, and then we'll leave.'

24

It was early afternoon, and Richard Flannagan-Smythe was tucked safely away in his third-floor accomodation refuge. It was a sizeable detached Victorian house, now converted into three holiday let apartments.

He was busy researching ferry crossings from Heysham and other nearby ports on the internet. He sighed and slouched back, rubbing his temples as he slowly concluded that taking a ferry to the Isle of Man or Ireland would be too risky. He was undoubtedly sure the police would have alerts and checks in place at the ports. He placed his phone down, frustrated, and found it hard to concentrate because of the hollow sensation and dull aches in his stomach, which accompanied the hunger pangs.

He walked over to the window, stretched his arms above his head, and took a deep breath. His body had felt stiff and tense for far too long, and he decided to take a hot bath later and have an early night.

Looking out beyond the slate grey rooftops and tall chimneys tailing off down the hill, he took in the panoramic scene of Morecambe Bay. If only they'd back off and leave him alone, it would be peaceful and idyllic here. Beth would love it. He rubbed his head and sunk into the chair by the bay window.

The hunger pangs weren't softening and he was beginning to feel light-headed. Reluctantly, he accepted he would have to take the short walk to the village centre to buy groceries. He was about to stand up when the lightbulb moment struck, totally out of the blue. A feeling of elation and euphoria swelled through him like a wave. 'Why didn't I think of that before?' he said aloud, suddenly seeing the light at the end of the tunnel. His next move was decided upon, and it would prove to be a great move. He clenched his fist and punched the air.

Scoraig was the obvious answer. He'd been there before. It was the perfect place for him to disappear—an off-grid community on a peninsula along the shore of Little Loch Broom in the Scottish Highlands.

His old university friend, Malcolm, whom he'd visited a few years ago, had lived there for years. And better still, Malcolm extended an open offer for Richard to return whenever he fancied taking time out. He smiled at the memory. He needed time out right now, for sure, and it made sense to stay with Malcolm. The location offered him total seclusion. There was no passable road to Scoraig, only a path across rugged terrain, which wasn't for the faint-hearted, especially in winter's bad weather. Richard chuckled at his memory of Malcolm telling him the only proper and safe access was by boat and that it had great benefits. On the rare occasions that the police or other officers of officialdom visited Scoraig, the boat crews forewarned the inhabitants, giving them time to "prepare for the visit". He could build a priest hole as a contingency if things ever came on top for him.

He laughed out loud with relief. Malcolm would welcome him with open arms, and he'd be fine there until the heat died down and the cops rolled back their search. Statham and McCann wouldn't dream of searching there; they'd be bloody clueless, and he would be safe. Feeling invigorated, he grabbed his jacket and was ready to walk to the grocery store.

*

Andrea and Lee got out of the car. Lee looked around, taking in the scenery, while Andrea paid for a ticket at the machine. 'It looks very quaint. Have you been here before?' Lee asked.

'Years ago,' Andrea replied. 'It must have been the late eighties. We used to swim at the lido on the promenade before it closed.' She placed the parking ticket on the dashboard then locked the car. 'Let's have a walk along the promenade. It's as good a place to start as any; there's a good chance we'll find him here if he's seeking to clear his head. Everyone who visits Grange takes a stroll along there.' They left the car park, and checked around the pub, before walking through the tunnel under the railway and onto the Victorian promenade.

'This place is beautiful,' Lee said. 'I can't believe I've never heard of it. It's not rammed with people either.'

'There's a café up near the lido. We can check that out too,' Andrea said, zipping up her against the cold wind blowing in from the Irish Sea.

'It's an interesting place for him to visit. There's nothing linking him here from the intelligence picture. Maybe this is where Jane's being held?' Lee said.

Neither raised the unpalatable possibility that Jane might have been murdered already.

'That would be too good to be true if he led us to her. But I know stranger things have happened,' Andrea replied.

On reaching the café, they glanced inside. 'I suppose it would have been too good to be true, finding him straight away,' Lee said, noting the middle-aged couple sitting in the window, the cafe's only customers.

'Come on,' Andrea beckoned, 'we'll head over the footbridge into the centre. There're plenty of other places for us to find him there.'

*

Richard walked down Laundry Hill with a newfound spring in his step. Things were looking up now, and he couldn't help but smile. Beth would have loved it in Scoraig, connecting with nature, the rugged moorland and sea views. Perfect for her oil painting, too. But it was too late now. Bollocks to her and the others who turned their backs on him. She'd turned her back on him when he needed her, which meant she was removed from his inner circle of trust. She was history now. Persona non grata. Fucking bitch, she was no better than Jane; what was he thinking? Frying pan into the fire.

When he reached the main street, he decided to call at the smaller grocery store with fewer people milling around. It had to be the best option. He filled his basket with pizzas and ready meals before selecting two bottles of red wine and a single malt to celebrate his astounding plan.

He hadn't felt this good for a long while. He slowed his pace and savoured the quaint, peaceful surroundings of the village. He was looking forward to Scoraig; maybe he could work in the local school. Then again, scratch that, he thought, it was a non-starter. He would need references and checks. Working on the boats, however, now that would suit him, and his mind took him to the deck of a fishing boat, taking deep breaths of salty sea air. Navigating the boat through the lashing waves. Life would be idyllic; he could even work on creating a micro-distillery. Malcolm could be his PR man, front of house, dealing with customers and the like. The idea captured his imagination, making him feel enthusiastic. Artisan whiskies were a growing industry. It would make him a significant income. Richard's mind then began to focus on names for his whiskey: *Hideaway Malt, or Red Herring Whiskey*, and he chuckled at the idea.

Suddenly, his world crashed around him. Images of Scoraig and the formulation of sly nods to the law enforcement agencies evaporated instantly.

Surely it can't be, he mused in exasperation, taking another look to ensure he wasn't hallucinating. Survival instincts kicked in as his worst nightmare unfolded before him. He was now sure, one hundred per cent sure. Statham and McCann were walking towards him in the distance, hunting him down. This was a living nightmare. His heart began pounding against his rib cage, adrenaline swamping his system. Panic wasn't far away. He needed to focus on holding things together before he slipped back into the abyss. His eyes darted left and right. He needed to disappear fast. How the hell had they tracked him down to Grange? No way was it a coincidence. Then it dawned on him. They must have traced the phone call he made to Beth and he cursed at how he could have been so bloody stupid.

The answer was in a charity shop window and he opened the door and stepped inside, closing it behind him. They wouldn't look in here for him, would they? He looked around and saw a changing room area at the far end of the shop, separated from the main area by a curtain. He grabbed a shirt from the rail and headed over, nodding to the lone volunteer behind the counter before swishing the curtain closed behind him.

From a nick in the curtain of his temporary sanctuary, he watched the street outside hawk-like. If they walked in, it was all over, and he would never see Scoraig or launch his whiskey distillery. His future would be contained within the walls of prison, a nightmare he struggled to comprehend.

Sure enough, they appeared and stopped outside the shop, Statham and McCann haunting him once again, both looking through the window. Richard slowly stepped back from the crack in the curtain, convinced they'd see him if he didn't. He began taking deep breaths to quell the panic now getting out of control. He leaned against the wall for support and closed his eyes, praying that they'd walk on, allowing him to spirit himself away to Scoraig.

The bell alerting the shop keeper jingled, and the door opened. 'Bastards, the lucky bastards, how did they find me?' he whispered, staying perfectly still, his whole body coiled like a spring. He decided that if they opened the curtain, he needed to run for it, grabbing the coat hanger as a makeshift weapon. He couldn't let them take him into custody. He had to flee at all costs. Surrendering was not an option.

Time had slowed right down. He waited, but nothing was happening. He couldn't hear their annoying voices. What were they doing? Were they toying with him? The sadistic bastards. He wanted to look out, but he couldn't risk being seen. A crazy thought crossed his mind that maybe the whiskey could be called *Cornered Fox*. He shrugged the random thought away, feeling incredulous at what shit his mind could produce when survival was the only priority.

The silence was suddenly filled with the sound of two women talking. Neither sounded like Statham. He figured they mustn't have come into the shop after all, and a wave of hope suddenly lifted his spirits.

SILENT BETRAYAL

Slowly, he edged forward, his eyes razor sharp, focusing through the nick in the curtain and scanning the shop. There was no sign of the two detectives, not even at the window, but he remained in his sanctuary, fear telling him it wasn't safe to step out yet.

The chatter stopped. Had he been wrong and they had slipped into the shop? Were they putting him in a false sense of security? Or requesting backup, maybe? Whispering... he could hear whispering. Should he make a run for it now? He imagined the volunteer pointing out the fitting room to Statham and McCann.

'Are you all right in there?' one of the women called out, interrupting his deliberations.

'Yes, almost done,' he replied, pulling back the curtain and stepping into the shop with trepidation. To his relief, it was just the two women. The second woman must have entered the shop when he heard the bell as the door opened. They both watched him emerge with curiosity.

'I didn't mean to rush you. I was just checking to see if you were okay. You'd been in there a while. Did it fit?'

'What?' Richard replied, heading for the door.

'The shirt. Did it not fit?'

'No, no, it didn't,' Richard called back absent-mindedly over his shoulder before replacing it on the rail and hurriedly leaving the shop.

Looking at her friend, perplexed at the man's strange behaviour, the volunteer shrugged.

'He's probably one of those weirdos you hear about,' the friend said, looking towards the door for reassurance that he wasn't coming back.

Richard paused, using the door recess as cover, and scanned the street; Statham and McCann were just stepping from the pavement, heading towards the entrance of the larger of the two grocery stores further up the road. A massive wave of relief washed over him. He couldn't help but chuckle as the nervous energy dissipated.

'They're bloody useless—I'm not complaining though.' But it had been too close for comfort and he stepped onto the street cautiously, taking off quickly towards Laundry Hill and his apartment.

25

Jane stood perfectly still whilst John slipped the black cotton drill hood over her head. It was an uncomfortable inconvenience she was more than happy to go along with, a means to an end... if it led to her freedom.

As he pulled the cord tighter around her neck, she felt a surge of panic, an overwhelming sense of vulnerability. She was now at his mercy. Was he about to strangle her or, even worse, shoot her? Had the whole plan been a ruse to facilitate a less traumatic execution, maybe to prevent her from going hysterical at the point of the execution? The thought of feeling the cold metal of a pistol against the back of her head made her shiver.

Her mind flipped into overdrive; her head suddenly felt hot inside the hood. Beads of sweat formed above her lip and on her forehead as she feared she was about to have a panic attack. Her mind was racing, encouraging her to kick out and stop what was happening, but she knew he'd overpower her if she tried.

The sound of John's calm voice brought her back into the moment. 'Take your time, don't rush. I'll lead you to the vehicle. I will remove the hood once we've covered sufficient distance from here.'

His words temporarily soothed her, making her believe she was about to be released, and strangely, she trusted him.

'I will place a hand on your shoulder to guide you. Are you ready?'

Jane felt her face flushing with heat and exhaled loudly. 'Yes, I'm ready.'

They began to walk towards the door. Her pace was almost a shuffle, her legs like lead weights following the adrenaline rush. She held out her arms, hoping to avoid walking into something.

'Ten steps ahead. The first one is in front of you,' John informed her. Jane began climbing the stairs and decided to try to remember the journey as best she could. Besides anything else, it would keep her mind busy from the feelings of fear and vulnerability she still had. At the top of the stairs, they proceeded to take a few turns, which led to a corridor. She felt disorientated, and they hadn't even left the building yet.

'Small step down,' John warned. She paused and tentatively stepped outside, instantly recognising loose stone chippings underfoot. For a moment, she fantasised she was walking on the driveway back home, about to enter the safety of her house.

'Stand still,' he instructed, removing his hand from her shoulder. Jane heard a car door being opened. 'Step inside. Sit down and stick to the plan.'

She reached out and felt the fabric of a car seat, then climbed inside and shuffled along the back seat. The car smelled new and familiar, almost comforting.

A voice in her head instructed her to leave DNA traces wherever she could, so she rubbed her hands hard against the seat fabric and dragged her fingernails over it. The door slammed shut behind her. The seat felt comfortable, and she guessed it was a high-end brand, perhaps an SUV because of the height she experienced while climbing into the back. She prayed that life was returning to normality and focused on slowing her breathing down. The sweat on her face was itching, but she decided against trying to relieve it. *Don't touch the hood*, she decided, *don't piss him off. It could be worse. I could be trussed up in the boat*, she thought in an attempt to ease the fear.

The front car door opened and then shut with a loud bang almost immediately, making her jump. She sensed that John had climbed into the driver's seat but couldn't be sure until her heightened sense of hearing recognised the sound of him adjusting the position of his seat. The familiarity of being inside a car was helping her to feel calmer. To occupy her mind, she scanned her body, beginning with her feet, focusing on easing the tension in her muscles and relaxing as best she could.

The engine started, and the momentum pushed her back into the seat as the car moved off rapidly. He wasn't hanging about, the tyres spinning on the loose stones. Jane tried memorising their route while gravity tossed her about in the back.

*

Andrea and Lee stepped from the pavement under the cover of a shop canopy. Lee immediately spun around, looking down the main street towards the charity shop from behind the cover. 'He's still there,' he said, his eyes fixed rigid. 'He looks like a meerkat peeping out from the shop doorway.' Lee laughed to ease the tension. 'Shall we call the arrest teams in or follow him?'

'I'm going to let him run for a while longer,' Andrea decided out loud, taking her phone from her handbag. 'It's worth the risk. It's unlikely we'll lose him in such a small place. He might just lead us to Jane. He must have a place here.'

'I'm with you. There's no guarantee he'll talk if we arrest him right now,' Lee said without turning around, his eyes still fixed on the charity shop.

Andrea placed her phone to her ear. 'We have eyes on the suspect,' she said calmly. He's just entered a charity shop opposite a church on Kents Bank Road. I've decided not to arrest him immediately. Can you get a surveillance team to him? We'll follow and see if he leads us to Jane.'

'Yes, no problem. Let's keep this line open while we get into position,' the surveillance team leader replied. Andrea could hear him relay the information to the other team members over his radio.

'He's out of the shop. Having a good look around. He's off, walking away from us,' Lee said.

'Suspect is out of the shop,' Andrea repeated into the phone.

'Right, into Laundry Hill,' Lee said concisely.

'Right, into Laundry Hill,' Andrea repeated.

'He's out of sight now,' Lee said, still watching.

'We've lost "eyes on" the suspect. Last seen turning into Laundry Hill heading away from the centre. How far away is your team?' she asked with a hint of anxiety in her voice, fearing they may lose him.

'Almost there,' came back the reply, barely audible above the surveillance team's frantic radio chatter crackling away in the background.

Time was standing still for Andrea. She couldn't afford to lose him and felt the pressure building. It didn't bear thinking about. This was her best lead yet to find Jane. If Richard had slipped away... well, the consequences were dire. She began pacing along the front of the shop display, her phone glued to her ear. 'Have your units got eyes on yet?' she asked, her anxiety rising as the seconds ticked by.

'Stand by,' answered the team leader, who was juggling several radio channels and Andrea's phone.

'Don't worry, they'll have him back under observations any time now,' Lee said, breaking the silence while not taking his eyes from the main street, just in case the target reappeared.

The detective on Andrea's phone suddenly broke the silence, saying, 'Suspect at Laundry Hill now onto Fernleigh Road. Stand by.'

'Thank Christ for that,' Andrea said, the tension instantly draining from her shoulders. 'Let's see where he's off to.'

'Suspect entering residential premises on the same road,' came the following update from her phone.

'He's gone into a residential premises, using the side door. He let himself in with a key. 'Lee, what do you reckon? Shall we go straight in after him?' Andrea asked quickly, bouncing the idea as two minds were better than one, but quietly knowing her chosen course of action already.

'Let's give him five minutes. I reckon we've spooked him, and he's on the move. I doubt he'll sit there waiting for us to find him. Besides, it's unlikely that Jane is being held there. It's not isolated enough, it's too populated.'

'But if she is there...' Andrea said before making her decision. She spoke into the phone. 'Do not approach suspect yet. Form a covert containment of the premises and stand by.'

'Roger, will do. Awaiting your next order,' the surveillance team leader said—his words heaping the responsibility in spades onto Andrea's shoulders.

She looked at her wristwatch. 'If there's no movement in five minutes, we're putting the door in.'

'For what it's worth, I think that's the right decision. We'll be okay,' Lee said, aware of the ramifications if the target got away from under their noses.

'Famous last words,' Andrea said.

26

Richard placed his hands on his knees as he reached the top of the third flight of stairs. His heart was pounding as he attempted to regain his breath. A mixture of euphoria and exhaustion was a heavy hit. Even so, he felt better than he had done ten minutes ago.

He went into the bedroom and threw his few possessions into his holdall. He had to keep moving. The cops had managed to track him to Grange-over-Sands and only missed him by the skin of his teeth in the town centre. He needed a proper bolt hole out of the way to ensure they wouldn't find him, and he knew just the place to hide before setting off to Scoraig during rush hour when he could blend anonymously into the heavy peak traffic.

He headed back down the stairs and left the flat, his eyes darting around the close vicinity for signs of any police officers. Keeping to the shadows, he headed out of the residential area and into the dense woodland of Hampsfell. He'd climbed this hill many times before and knew the paths like the back of his hand. He slowed as the ascent steepened, feeling safer under the cover of the tree canopy, and paced himself to manage the steep incline more effectively.

The pathways were deserted except for the odd walkers here and there—nothing unusual. Nature's surroundings helped him cope with the stress of the situation and he began to feel slightly calmer, his pace slowing with each step, allowing him to regulate his breathing. He was satisfied that he came across as a walker and wasn't drawing any unwanted attention to himself. More importantly, he felt assured that the police weren't following him.

Head down and focused, Richard continued up the hill, taking an occasional breather to regain his energy, and allowing himself to scan for any pursuers. After about thirty minutes, the hospice at the top of the fell came into view over the horizon. It was a sturdy stone hut built by the vicar of Cartmel in the mid-eighteenth century to shelter weary travellers and walkers. He carefully navigated the limestone pavement as he approached the building, a contented, smug smile spreading across his face in appreciation of reaching the hospice. *They won't have a bloody clue about this place*, he gloated. He stepped over the chain link surround and glanced inside to check if anyone was about; it was empty. So far, so good. He began to climb the narrow stone staircase, holding the metal rail tightly, and stepped onto the flat roof viewing point. The three-hundred-and-sixty-degree view was spectacular. He took a few deep breaths as he looked over the Lake District Fells and the expansive water of Morecambe Bay and for a moment, he forgot that he was being hunted down and instead enjoyed the wide-open space. A feeling of welcome calm enveloped him, and the stress slowly dissipated as thoughts of his new life in Scoraig manifested once more. It wouldn't be dissimilar to his current position. Now feeling safe, he suddenly laughed out loud at himself and how he'd come up with the *Cornered Fox Whiskey* at the most inappropriate time possible. Maybe that name was meant to be?

Rejuvenated and more confident, he climbed down the stairs and entered the hospice room. Nothing had changed since his visits years ago: a stone fireplace and stone seating. He sat down, mulling over the inscription above the door: "Rest and be Thankful". Things were looking up for him. He felt good, and a spiritual connection resonated within the four walls. He'd done well evading the detectives, and his quick thinking had prevented his capture.

He closed his eyes and sat back, enjoying the warm feeling generated by his self-adulation. Then, he continued to read the spiritual inscriptions and quotes on the walls.

*

Andrea looked at Lee with a welcome expression of relief on hearing the update that Richard had left the flat. She got straight onto her mobile. 'Enter the flat as soon as possible. We don't need a warrant. I'm satisfied there are reasonable grounds to suspect a risk to life. Update me straight away, please.'

'You made the right decision,' Lee said. 'You may be criticised for not going in as he entered the flat, but I doubt she's there anyway. If he's heading off into the woods, that's where she'll be.'

Andrea smiled. 'Thanks, Lee. Or she could be in Yorkshire, the last sighting of the abductor's car was the A59, don't forget. This job will never change; you're damned if you do, and damned if you don't. It's the nature of the beast, unfortunately.'

Lee looked around, satisfied no one was nearby, and hugged her. Andrea's phone rang, forcing her to break away, eager to take the call. 'It's a negative, Ma'am. No one is present, and there is no sign of anyone being held here. All the same, we'll undertake a thorough search. I've passed the address details to the Intelligence Unit so they can do some digging about the owners of this place and establish any links with Flannagan-Smythe.'

'Thanks, mate. Keep me updated.' She ended the call and looked at Lee. 'As expected, she's not there, and it doesn't look like she has been there on first impressions. But we'll undertake a thorough search and forensic examination, then we know either way for sure.'

'I'm more of a mind that he doesn't know where she is, and he's just on the run, trying to save his skin. Hargreaves' death will have put the wind up him. In his mind, he's next. You saw his reaction when we informed him of the death during his interview. The surveillance teams are on his heels. Let's see where he takes them.'

'Do you fancy a drink while we have the chance?' Andrea asked. 'I'm getting the feeling it's going to be a long day. Hopefully, the surveillance teams will have a positive update for us soon.'

Lee agreed and they stopped at a quaint café a few doors further on, a dark green awning hanging over the window with a sign saying *Ellie's Bistro*. They sat at a table in the window and a young waitress who'd been hovering took their order and returned to the counter. Andrea's phone began to ring almost immediately.

'Here we go, fingers crossed. We must be due a lucky break,' she said before answering.

Lee watched as the surveillance team briefed her, looking for a reaction to whether the news was good or bad. He concluded that it was neither and drank his coffee while he waited to hear the update.

Andrea placed her mobile on the table. 'He's sitting in a stone shed on the top of Hampsfell, the hill that overlooks Grange,' she informed him with a puzzled expression.

'Perhaps he's waiting for a helicopter!' Lee said, laughing. 'He thought he was safe in the apartment, and then he saw us in the village. Now he's running for the hills…literally.'

'Don't mock, I've seen it happen in Bond films,' Andrea said sardonically. 'Either that or he thinks he's John Rambo.'

'*You struck first blood*, Andrea,' Lee growled, failing miserably with an attempted impression of Rambo.

'It's a catch twenty-two, now. If we bring him in and he makes no comment, it won't help us find Jane,' Andrea said, thinking out loud, moving on from the banter.

'But that's good leverage for us if we can convince him the court will look favourably on such assistance. It may tip him over the edge to open up.'

'I'll give Samuel a call,' she added. 'The spooks have gone quiet all of a sudden. Let's see if he can chase them up for any intelligence they're holding back on.'

27

'You can take the hood off now,' John said, breaking the silence. 'Feel around the bottom edge. There's a plastic release mechanism. Just press it.'

Jane shoved the hood into her pocket, aware of the DNA traces it may contain, and breathed in a gulp of cool, fresh air, feeling instant relief. She took a deep breath, glad of the air that wafted across her face instantly. 'That's better,' was the best she could muster. She instinctively began running her fingers through her hair, tidying up her appearance, seeking normality.

'Pass it to me,' John said, holding his left hand towards her.

Reluctantly, she pulled it from her pocket and handed it over.

The road they were travelling along was a main route lined by forestry. For a moment, she gazed out of the window, soaking up the view and appreciating nature's vast open space.

'We'll be there in half an hour. Stick to the plan, and you'll be fine,' John said.

Jane was aware of his eyes in the rearview mirror, studying her. She smiled back warmly. 'Don't you trust me yet, John? Believe it or not, I respect you. I quite like you. Why the hell would I cross you? We're doing business, right? We'd make a great team.' Then she began fretting that she'd laid on the charm offensive too thickly, too quickly.

John's eyes darted back to the mirror. Jane wondered if she'd caught him off guard and that he hadn't expected such a disclosure.

'You're fucking presumptuous, aren't you?' he said with a smile and hint of laughter.

She instantly liked the tone of his reply, and she smiled. 'I grew up the hard way, the school of hard knocks. I learned pretty quickly that the past is best left in the past. It's pointless ruminating on it. Like you said, it's business, nothing personal. In fact, you've been pretty good to me, given the circumstances.' But her mind was oblivious to her sentiment and flashed back to the past. Her abusive father, her treacherous husband, and now John's mugshot had joined their ranks, standing alongside them. *All the fucking same, all of them*, she mused. She waited quietly, but he didn't answer, his eyes remaining fixed on the road ahead.

She decided that she'd said enough for now and returned her gaze to outside of the window. A warm feeling washed over her; confidence and control of her destiny were slowly returning. Freedom wasn't far away now. She continued to gaze at the trees as they passed by, reminded of the mental wellness they provided in many ways. Fractals: intricate, self-repeating patterns in trees, leaves, and other plants proven to promote relaxation, reduce stress and improve overall mental wellbeing. Jane had read that the human brain was naturally attuned to fractals. It certainly felt like she was attuned to them now. She daydreamed about setting up in a house in the sticks once she sorted out this mess.

The rhythmic clicking of the vehicle indicator broke her thoughts. She looked ahead and saw the road sign: M6 South. John manoeuvred onto the slip road and joined the motorway. She looked at the occupants of the other cars as they passed them, going about their everyday routine lives whilst she was being held hostage in plain sight. The thought did occur to her to signal for help, but she instantly dismissed it. They probably couldn't see her through the tinted privacy glass, anyway. The best chance of freedom was to stick with her current plan. No knee-jerk decisions, she reminded herself. 'Where are we heading to, John?' she asked, almost sounding like a partner out for a Sunday drive with her husband.

'Lancaster,' he replied, glancing in the mirror. 'Have you thought about what you'll do with yourself after this?' he continued, clumsily trying to change the subject.

Jane took the question as a positive indicator that she was going to be walking away from this situation, provided she paid, of course. 'Not yet, probably, crash at my brother's place for a while. I haven't seen him for years. What about you? Is your next target lined up for you?'

'Usual stuff,' he replied.

She guessed he wasn't for opening up and didn't bother asking anything else. Gazing out of the window, watching normality around her, felt good. Her mind switched to Richard. Was she really going to lure him to his death? She didn't feel any emotions at the question and instead felt the cold hollowness that had shrouded the relationship for some years. Her current predicament exacerbated the feeling of nonchalance. She was sitting in this car because he wanted her dead. She owed him no loyalty. What goes around comes around, she self-affirmed with conviction. Things were about to change.

'Right, we're almost there. Get your mindset sorted. Let's get this done, then you can move on with your life.'

SILENT BETRAYAL

John's instruction brought her back into the moment. She recognised her surroundings; they'd reached Lancaster. She'd been here before.

John stopped the car in Dalton Square in the heart of the city. A vibrant green open space was populated by flowerbeds and a grand bronze statue of Queen Victoria, overlooked by the Edwardian, Baroque-style town hall and other Georgian and Victorian architecture. A perfect place to blend into, unnoticed.

'Get out here. Take a seat, as we discussed, and ground yourself. I'll call you shortly,' he said.

Jane flicked the door handle and stepped outside. She leaned into the car. 'One last thing. How are you going to kill Richard?'

'Good question, I should have prepared you for that. Once he's in an open space, I'll take the shot. So decide whether you want to avoid seeing it happen or not,' John said, matter-of-factly.

She nodded while pushing the car door closed behind her. The shock of suddenly being alone in this beautiful, open space was almost overwhelming. She heard the throaty engine of John's car accelerating away, but she didn't look back. She headed into the square and sat on a black metal bench, where she watched people walking by momentarily, savouring the joy of being free, or almost free. She still had things to do yet to ensure her liberty.

She reached for the bottle of water from her handbag and took a drink. Looking around, she felt the urge to run. But where to? The police? It was a tempting option, but the dark shadow of fear hung over her that she would spend the rest of her life looking over her shoulder. She was in no doubt that John and his associate would find her. She had to see this through. There was no other viable option.

The burner phone ringing grabbed her attention. She fumbled through the contents of her handbag, located the phone, and answered it.

'Put the call into Richard now. Arrange for him to meet at the Priory Church garden, just behind the castle. Get him down here as soon as you can. Let's get this done. You got it?'

'Yes,' Jane replied, relieved that things were underway.

'Good. Call me back when it's sorted,' John replied before abruptly ending the call.

28

Richard heard several voices from just outside the stone hut. He glanced at his watch. It was almost time for him to leave anyway, so it didn't matter if they also wanted to shelter there. The traffic would be building up nicely towards rush hour, just as he'd planned, allowing him to continue his journey hidden and sheltered in a high volume of motorway traffic. He stood up and walked away just as two hikers ascended the steps to the roof. He hadn't got far when the burner phone vibrated in his pocket, its sharp tone slicing through the peaceful silence. His heart stopped for a beat, then took off again racing. It had to be the killer. What did he want? He answered with trembling fingers.

'Richard, it's me,' Jane's voice whispered, raw with fear.

For a moment, the world closed in around him. It couldn't be. She was supposed to be dead.

Silence swelled between them, thick and suffocating.

'Richard? Can you hear me?' Jane's panic surged, her voice quivering.

'I...' He forced his voice to work, masking the shock with a performance of concern. 'Jane? Where are you? Thank God, you've called me. I've been worried sick! I've been searching high and low for you!' The words felt foreign, almost catching in his throat.

'I was taken hostage,' she said, her voice dropping to a hush. 'I haven't got much time. You need to listen carefully. After the fundraiser, they grabbed me. But I managed to escape... I think I'm safe now. Can you pick me up, or should I go to the police? What should I do, Richard?'

The mention of the police snapped him back into control. His mind now raced at a hundred miles an hour. If she was alive, there was an opportunity here—a high risk, fragile thread of an opportunity. If he could get to her first and manipulate her trust, he could get access to cash. He could turn this to his advantage. With the cash he could pay the debt and get the contract killer to back off. Then tell Jane he needed to get her to a safe place... Scoraig. Things were suddenly looking even better. He inhaled deeply, forcing calm into his voice.

'Where are you, Jane?' he said, his tone oozing concern.

'I'm at the church gardens in Lancaster. Near the castle. I think I'm safe here, for now. How soon can you get here? They'll come looking for me soon. I need to get out of here.' She almost tumbled over her words.

'An hour. At most. Jane, I...' He allowed his voice to falter, injecting a note of anguish. 'I'm so sorry. This... this is all my fault. Tony Hargreaves—he's behind this. He wanted to ruin me, and now the police think I'm involved. Nash fired me. Everything's falling apart...'

'I know,' Jane said quickly, cutting him off.' There was a sharp edge to her desperation. 'The kidnapper told me everything. Just get here, Richard. I can help you. We'll figure this out together.'

'I'm on my way,' he said, his voice steady now, carrying all the weight of a concerned husband. But beneath the surface his thoughts churned, cold and calculating.

He ended the call and stared at the phone for a long moment. Jane was alive. She'd escaped. And now, the situation presented an opportunity. But also, danger... the contract killer was still in the equation, no doubt hunting her down at this very moment. *Maybe I should call the killer,* he thought, rubbing his forehead. *Make the payment, then head to Scoraig.* Then he suddenly realised he couldn't...Jane has the money, and the contract killers burner phone. How had she managed to get hold of that? Had the killer been with her when she made the call? Was it a set up? He could handle that, he assured himself. Approach the situation with extreme caution, and stay in public view...he needed the money.

Then he suddenly noticed the two hikers hovering nearby.

Lancaster was not on the way to Scoraig, but luckily, it wasn't far away. No problem. Jane could access her money, and Richard was confident he could sort this mess out. He had a newly found spring in his step as he headed to his car. Access to funds was the one aspect of his new life he hadn't sorted, but now it was fixed. Together with *Cornered Fox Whiskey*, he'd be fine.

*

Andrea pulled her car into the tree-lined track alongside the white van and opened the window. The surveillance operative team leader, known as "Postman" smiled. 'I think you're going to like this update, Ma'am.'

She glanced at Lee, her eyebrows raised. 'You never fail to deliver. Perhaps you should change your callsign to the postman.' She laughed in anticipation of the good news. 'Come on, Lee. It sounds like this is worth getting out of the car for.' They both walked around to the van. The side door slid open, and they carefully climbed into the back, followed by the team leader.

'The target left the shelter a few minutes ago. Two of our guys, operating as a couple of hikers, got close to him just as he answered a phone call. Our impression is that he was talking to the hostage and arranged to meet her. Slip these headphones on, and you can listen to what he said on the audio file.' The detective sitting at the surveillance workstation handed Lee and Andrea a pair of headphones each.

The van went quiet while they listened intently. Andrea was the first to remove the headphones, followed quickly by Lee. 'I agree, I didn't expect that,' she said, turning to Lee.

'It seems unusual, have thet released her?' Lee said with puzzled expression.

'Or she's escaped,' Andrea suggested.

Lee nodded and said, 'Whatever the case, it's a great lead. If he leads us to Jane, it's a perfect result. Great work by your lads. Top job, Postman,' he added to the team leader.

'Thanks, they did well to get so close to him. I'm just waiting for the next update. It should be coming through any time now,' he replied. 'I guess he's making his way to a vehicle. It makes sense.'

The four of them settled down in the surveillance team command van. The workstation operator sorted out coffees from the boiler and handed them out.

'Cheers, all mod cons in here, I see,' Lee said with an appreciative grin. 'Have you got any biscuits?'

'Got to get your priorities right. It's no use being stuck in here for hours with no hot drinks. We'll leave the champagne on ice until the hostage is released,' Postman replied. 'As for biscuits, we thought you were bringing them.'

The workstation operator raised her hand, beckoning for silence, and adjusted her headset. She was totally focused on the incoming communication, quietly watched by the others. After a short conversation, she looked around. 'He's just got into a car parked halfway up the fell. He's set off further up the hill, which then drops down into Cartmel, but there is an option to double back into Grange, we can't rule that out yet. I'll get teams to cover both eventualities.' Update delivered, she returned to her desk and began coordinating the teams over the radio.

'Cartmel makes sense. He's probably avoiding Grange now at all costs, especially if someone has let him know we've searched the flat,' Postman suggested.

'I'll step outside and call our teams with the updates,' Andrea said. 'We all need to be ready to tuck in behind the surveillance operation, ready to strike when he arrives at his rendezvous.' She then slid the van door open and stepped out.

Silence fell over the van as Lee texted Richard's car details to the intelligence team for further research. The radio broke into life, and the detective at the workstation sprang into action, directing the units and logging their activities. Once finished, she turned around. 'As we expected, he's sticking to the back roads. We have him covered. The teams have followed him through Cartmel, and he's heading east towards the A roads. His route is consistent with heading to the M6 while avoiding Grange.'

'Right, we'd better join the party. Catch you later, Lee,' Postman said, heading back to his seat in the front of the van. Lee took the cue and joined Andrea in their car.

'The teams are up to speed now. I've just looked on Google Maps. There's a discreet layby near the A590.

We can sit up there and then tag behind the surveillance at a safe distance when we know where he's heading.'

'Sounds good,' Lee said, starting the engine. 'Let's go and find Jane.' An air of optimism filled the car, and they both felt good about how things were panning out.

*

Jane placed the burner phone back in her handbag and stretched her legs by walking up to the Queen Victoria Monument. As she was running through her conversation with Richard, she smiled at the fact he hadn't even asked how she was physically or mentally, or if she was safe. It was still all about him. Some things never changed. *The fucking coward probably won't even show up*, she mused. But weirdly, she didn't care anymore. He'd been a bastard with her for years now, and the tosser had even wanted her dead.

Jane felt like she had turned a corner in her life. She felt stronger and more empowered than ever. It was payback time. *Whatever doesn't kill you makes you stronger*, she pondered and right now, that sounded spot on.

The burner phone ringtone bellowed out from inside her bag like music to her ears. She was beginning to feel impatient and wanted to get on with it. It was John, as expected. 'He's on his way, should be here in about an hour,' Jane said matter-of-factly, mirroring John from his conversation in the car.

'Good work,' he said. 'Any concerns arising from the conversation?'

'No, he's all yours. It's payback time,' Jane said, her tone cold and detached.

'I didn't mean that. Did he mention where he was coming from or if the police were sniffing around him?

It's a possibility they may be following him. Did you pick up on anything like that?'

She suddenly felt she'd let him down and should have asked more questions. 'No, he was just being the same old self-centred bastard as always.'

John laughed. 'Well, we can raise a toast when he's been dispatched. Go to the castle area, grab a coffee, and be ready. I'll be in touch.'

'Hang on a minute. What if he doesn't show up?' she asked, dreading a journey back to her cell.

'It would be no great deal. You access the cash, pay me, and I'll sort Richard out sometime later,' John said.

'I still want to be there when he dies,' Jane spat out, almost involuntarily, from deep within her subconscious. 'I want to watch him pay.'

'That's not important for now. One thing at a time, eh? But for the record, I think he will turn up. From what you've told me, if for no other reason than the financial benefit.'

'We'll see,' Jane said, taking the lead and ending the call. A feral disposition had taken over from the fear of death, her focus now razor-sharp. This was a new beginning. A new Jane—with a totally new outlook on life.

29

Jane reached the church gardens and selected a bench in the specified area. She could see why he'd chosen this location—it was quiet and off the beaten track. There was no one else in the vicinity. She soaked in the peaceful surroundings, shaded by old Yew and Oak trees. Her eyes were drawn to the view of the city and hills in the distance, though the tranquillity and beauty of the place clashed horribly with her reason for being there.

She cursed at hearing the ringtone of the burner phone again. 'You're in position early. I told you to hang back until you heard from me. There's a greater chance of drawing attention the longer you're in there,' John said, sounding pissed off.

Jane began looking around to see him. She couldn't be arsed apologising. She just wanted to get things done and get out of there. He no longer held the blanket of fear over her and if push came to shove, she'd take him on. One thing was for sure—she wasn't being taken hostage again.

'You won't see me. I'm out of the way for now. It allows me to see him arrive and clock any cops if he's being tailed. Hold tight, and I'll give you two ringtones when he's approaching. Stick to the drill.'

She continued to look around, identifying areas of cover or escape routes. *Where is John?* she deliberated, checking out the high ground, needing to avoid being in the crossfire at all costs. But she felt confident he wouldn't target her intentionally. He wanted cash, just like the other bastard who was on his way. She glanced at her watch. He shouldn't be long now.

*

Richard was making good time on his journey. The traffic on the M6 South was congested but still moving along at a reasonable speed. Though the extra miles were a risk he could have done without. He should have been heading north to the safety of Scoraig, but having access to Jane's finances would be a game-changer. He could convince her that paying them off to save her was in her best interests.

Then, he would try to get her to buy property in the Highlands, feigning it was for her own protection. She would see him as her saviour and would never know otherwise—Hargreaves was dead, and dead men tell no tales. The cliché made him smile; he'd done well. He'd evaded the cops and was about to start a new life up in Scotland. Jane had always wanted to live out in the countryside, and now she could.

Richard indicated and drove onto the slip road, signed for Lancaster. Checking his rearview mirror, he was satisfied that Statham and McCann weren't following him. They were probably still walking around the shops in Grange-over-Sands. As he approached the city centre, the traffic slowed and became snarled in the congestion of the irritating one-way system. Finally, he reached the car park at the railway station and parked in a secluded corner. He remained in the driver's seat, watching the entrance. Nobody was following him. It was safe. He was running rings around the Keystone Cops. And for now, he just looked like another commuter, running late for his train.

He headed towards the castle, a dark foreboding passing over him as he looked through the main portcullis entrance which led to the former HMP Lancaster, now a well-visited penal museum.

The former cell windows caught his eye and sent a shiver of fear through him at the thought of incarceration. Glad to leave the sight behind, he continued briskly and walked alongside the towering castle walls to the path that led to the church gardens. At first glance, his eyes scanning everywhere, he couldn't see Jane. Then the penny dropped. It was a set-up. He'd walked into a trap. How bloody naïve and stupid had he been? He looked around in a panic; he needed to escape.

No sooner than he had decided to run for it, he saw her and changed his mind. She was sitting on a bench under a tree, talking on a mobile. He quickly raised his hand, waving to get her attention. Then confusion and fear swelled up again and took over. He watched, open-mouthed, as she stood up and looked straight through him. And instead of acknowledging him, she darted away in the opposite direction.

*

The phone had continued bellowing out beyond the expected two rings. Jane answered it and heard John's voice before she could speak. 'Get out of there, now. The police are following him.' Then the line went dead. She looked across the gardens and saw Richard waving.

As she turned around and ran into the shadows, a cynical thought crossed her mind about how pathetic he looked. She prayed that John would still get to him before the police did. He had to pay for what he'd done.

SILENT BETRAYAL

The path took her through some trees to a lane, lined by high stone walls and shadowed by the trees. She glanced over her shoulder, relieved that she wasn't being chased. Her ears strained, hoping to hear gunshots. But she heard nothing. Was the lucky bastard now in custody?

Why am I running? she asked herself. She was the victim, after all, and she could surrender herself to the safety of the police. In response to the thought, John's words replayed in her head: *"The police can't guarantee your safety. We will still be able to get to you."* Surrender was ruled out immediately. She'd stick to her plan. No knee-jerk decisions—remember—stay focused.

*

DI Andrea Statham and DS Lee McCann broke away from the surveillance and strike teams, advancing towards Richard Flannagan-Smythe, confident they had him covered. They carried on and took the higher ground. 'That's Jane Flannagan-Smythe, I'm sure it is,' Andrea said breathlessly. 'Look over by the church. She's running away.'

'Christ, you're right, it is her,' Lee said. 'Why is she running away? It doesn't make sense.'

Andrea didn't answer and grabbed her radio instead. 'DI Statham: Urgent,' she called. 'I have eyes on the hostage near to the church. Arrest the target, I'm going after the victim.'

Lee wasn't hanging around. He was sprinting towards Jane, Andrea following closely behind, confused as to why she was running away. Maybe she was in shock or completely overcome by fear, which wouldn't be unusual in these circumstances.

Lee reached the side road first and saw Jane ahead of him. 'Jane, we're the police. It's okay. We're here to help you,' he shouted while closing the gap on her. 'You're safe now. You can stop running!'

Jane stopped and slowly stepped to the side of the road where she sat down, her back against the stone wall for support, her head in her hands. This wasn't what she had wanted. Her mind was racing, trying to work out how best to handle the situation. She'd simply not envisaged this happening. Lee approached her and squatted down alongside her. 'It's okay, Jane. You're safe now. Everything's going to be fine.'

She wasn't as convinced as the cop sat beside her but knew she had to perform the victim role or else they'd suspect something wasn't right. 'I think they were going to kill us both,' she mumbled. 'They made me call Richard and get him to meet us here. They're here somewhere.'

'Don't worry, Richard's safe. Nobody has been killed. What do they look like, Jane? Can you describe them to me?'

Andrea approached them with her radio held towards her ear. 'Roger, understood,' she said into it. 'The target is in custody.' Then she, too, crouched down close to Jane. 'I need to ask you an important question, Jane. The people who kidnapped you, are they nearby?'

'Did you say the target is in custody? Have you caught them?' Jane asked, looking up at Andrea.

Andrea had to think fast on her feet. It was too early to disclose Richard's suspected involvement. That was for later in the interview process. 'No, we haven't, I wasn't talking about the criminals. I was talking about Richard—he's safe.'

'Do you know where they are, Jane?' Lee asked.

'No, I'm sorry, I'm not much use, am I?' she said, still staring at the floor, head in hands.

'Do you know the location where you were held? Is it near here?'

'No, I'm really sorry. I can't think straight. I think I'm in shock,' Jane said, buying time to formulate a plan B. 'They told me they needed to speak to Richard and asked me to call him to arrange a meeting here. They said he needed to know I was alive. When he arrived, I panicked and took my chance to escape.' She was repeating herself for effect now, still not looking up.

'Do you know the identity of the kidnapper?' Andrea asked.

'No, sorry.'

'You don't need to be sorry, Jane. I've just got to cover all bases, that's all.' Andrea gave Lee a look of disappointment. 'Is there anything you can tell us right now that may help us to catch the people who took you? Where's the phone you used? This might be our only chance, we need to move fast.'

'No, I don't have a clue where they are or where I was held, they've got the phone, sorry I wish I knew more.'

Andrea looked at Lee, shaking her head. 'If you feel up to it, we'd like to take you to a place of safety. Once there, we would like to take your clothing for forensic examination and take some swab samples from you to see if we can gather evidence,' Lee said. 'I know it's going to be difficult but it's going to be our best chance to help us catch whoever did this to you.'

'Richard said it was Tony Hargreaves who set it up,' Jane replied in her best shell-shocked tone. 'In revenge for Richard messing up his business deal.'

'Can you stand up, Jane? Once you've rested and you feel up to it, we'll take an account of what you've been through. Does that sound okay?'

'Yes, that's fine. I'd just like to get on with it. I want to go home and sleep as soon as I can.'

The unmarked police people carrier pulled up alongside them. Lee carefully helped Jane to her feet and assisted her inside the vehicle, conscious of protecting any forensic evidence.

Andrea climbed into the front alongside the driver. 'Let's go,' she said, her relief at knowing Jane was safe replaced by her formulation of her next steps to get her justice.

She grabbed her mobile phone, it was time to update Samuel.

30

Statham and McCann had just finished meeting with DS Zak Kershaw, a suspect interview adviser. They were now putting their finishing touches on the interview strategy.

'I guess he'll make no comment on all the questions we put to him,' Andrea said.

'I'm not too sure about that. I reckon he'll try and pass the blame onto the dead man, Tony Hargreaves. That's more like his style,' Lee replied.

'The voice recording is compelling evidence. Even his solicitor will agree with that. I can foresee a guilty plea coming, followed by mitigating circumstances of mental health problems, maybe a plea on the grounds of diminished responsibility. I don't see any way out for him. I don't think he'll fancy the prospect of a trial at Crown Court.'

Andrea's phone began to ring. 'It's Ian Fraser from the victim support unit, excellent. Hopefully, he has an update for us,' she said, before taking the call. 'How's it going, Ian?'

'Very well, she's coping fine considering what she's been through. Her disposition is very calm and controlled. She just wants to get home and have some time to herself. She has declined counselling and other support for now but may be interested in engaging at a later date. We've conducted the forensic procedure: clothing was seized, and swabs were taken as we agreed. And we've completed the first video interview to cover the areas that may require fast-track actions.'

'That's great timing. Has she said anything further that will be useful for the interview? We're heading down to the custody suite to interview him shortly.'

'The main headlines are that she only had day-to-day contact with one offender,' Ian confirmed. 'Her description of him is very vague, as she says she wore a hood whenever she was in his presence. There was a fixed routine: when she heard the bell ring, she placed a hood on her head as instructed to protect the suspect's identity. She wasn't subjected to any violence or sexual contact. In fact, she doesn't recall being touched at all. In her view, he was very professional and businesslike in the way he dealt with her.'

'That's a relief. Is she sure that she wasn't drugged at any time?'

'Yes, she's sure. But we've taken blood samples, so we'll have a better picture when the results are back from the lab. You'll like the next bit. The offender informed her that her husband had taken out a contract for her to be killed and that Tony Hargreaves was the middleman, as we suspected.'

'That corroborates the voice recording between her husband and Hargreaves,' Andrea said. 'Did you have time to talk about where she was being held?'

'Jane said she can't be one hundred per cent sure, but the offender let slip something about Preston. She recollects the sound of a crowd shouting. Maybe she was being held near the football ground. Jane thinks the journey in the white van would have taken thirty minutes or so, so maybe it was Preston.'

'And how did she end up at the church in Lancaster?'

'The offender told her that her husband and Hargreaves had refused to pay for his services,' Ian replied. 'He used Jane to call Richard and lure him in by telling him she'd escaped. She was then told to wait in the church gardens, with a threat that she was being watched. Richard Flannagan-Smythe went for it hook, line and sinker and went to the church graveyard next to the old prison. Quite an ironic location given where he's heading.'

'Right, that should do us for now. Thanks for the update. Are you knocking on to the second interview with Jane?'

'Yes, she's just having a break. We'll delve more into the offender and location when she's ready. I wouldn't hold your breath though. She doesn't appear to recollect much at this stage. Maybe something will return to her over the coming days. One last thing, if you have no objections, I've agreed for her brother to pick her up after the next interview. She wants to stay with him for a few days. I'll ensure the person-at-risk assessments are sorted out.'

'Thanks, Ian. Text me if she discloses anything we need to know for the interview.' Andrea ended the call and dropped the mobile into her bag.

'Did you get the gist of that?' she asked Lee.

'Yes, thank God she's safe, and it looks like it could have been a lot worse. Let's go and get her husband bang to rights,' Lee said collecting his papers together and preparing to leave.

*

The secure door bolt clicked as Andrea and Lee were buzzed into the custody suite. They approached the sergeant at the counter, who was busy booking a scrawny young lad with plenty of lip and attitude into custody.

He broke away for a second, looking towards Andrea and Lee—totally unfazed by the petulant whining miscreant standing before him. The custody sergeant was a hulk of a man with a quiet diplomatic disposition which made him appear all the more sinister. 'Your suspect is ready for the interview. He's met with his brief,' he said, pointing to a solicitor sitting in the waiting area, a goldfish bowl-like construction built around nineteen eighty-four following the introduction of the Police and Criminal Evidence Act. The solicitor, Giles Montford, a stick-thin, bespectacled man in his forties, was busying himself with a sheaf of legal papers.

The young lad appeared bored of the interruption and continued gobbing off to the other custody office staff. 'I don't want the duty. I also want that solicitor,' he said, pointing to the waiting area. 'The posh one.'

Lee approached the waiting area and opened the door. 'I'm DS Lee McCann, and this is DI Andrea Statham. We're ready to interview your client if you'd like to follow us.'

The three of them went to the interview room, passing the noisy cell corridor, nonplussed by the bangs of a prisoner kicking the hell out of his cell door and various others shouting demands, threats and insults. It was just another day in the custody office, nothing to see here.

The detention officer accompanying Richard Flannagan-Smythe met them as they reached the interview room. 'Thank you, we'll take it from here,' Andrea said to the smartly presented detention officer. He nodded and headed back towards the main custody area, the keys attached to his belt clinking as they rattled against each other.

Lee held a hand towards the interview room, beckoning Richard to enter. Giles Montford followed him and Lee noticed his highly polished shoes and observed that they were something you don't see often these days.

Richard's appearance contrasted his solicitor's attire. He wore dark blue chino trousers and a lighter blue Oxford shirt, which looked like it hadn't been ironed. His blond hair was all over the place, matching his disposition. He selected the same chair he used on the first occasion he was interviewed and leaned forward, resting his forearms on his thighs while looking towards the floor. His brief sat alongside him, instantly sorting out his yellow-paged legal pad and other notes.

Andrea sat opposite Montford and got a waft of his woody scented aftershave. She didn't recognise the brand but guessed it was expensive. She caught his eye and politely smiled, which he reciprocated. This was no back street criminal lawyer, no doubt well-connected and experienced in representing members of parliament who had made an error of judgement and found themselves in contact with the law.

The brief placed his papers and pen on the table, his demeanour poised and composed. He interlocked his fingers and rested them on the table. Holding a gaze towards Andrea, he spoke diplomatically and calmly. 'Thank you for the disclosure, Inspector. My client is prepared to be interviewed. Please carry on.'

Andrea suspected that getting in first with his opening gambit was a cheap ploy to project his authority and to reassure Richard that he was on top of his game. 'Thank you. That's very kind of you,' Andrea said, unable to help herself. 'In that case, we will switch the audio recording on and commence the interview,' nodding at Lee to do the honours.

Once the loud buzzing sound from the recorder had stopped, much to everyone's relief, Andrea began the introductions and read the script outlining the interview process before cautioning Richard and explaining his rights.

The brief replied by outlining his role and his expectations during the interview. This time, Andrea noticed there was no amicable gaze. It had been replaced by his game face and an adversarial disposition. The gloves were off.

She began the interview by summarising Richard's salient points from his last interview and the circumstances leading to his arrest. Giles Montford didn't look up from his legal pad. He remained focused on listening and scribbling notes.

Andrea continued a non-challenging line of questions, during which Richard gave a *"no comment"* answer to all questions asked.

Montford looked at his watch dramatically and made a suggestion. 'Look, let's be clear. My client will not be answering any questions. How long is this going to go on for? He must be due a rest period by now?'

'I wouldn't want your client not to have the opportunity to have his say about the allegations, Mr Montford,' Andrea replied. 'In the interests of fairness, I will continue to provide that opportunity to him. After all, it's not you but Richard who has everything to lose here. This is a very serious offence for which a custodial sentence would be likely in the event of a guilty verdict.'

Richard glanced at Montford with a bewildered look. Montford didn't return the glance but looked puzzled.

'Come on, Inspector, you've not even charged my client. Talk of a custodial sentence is a bit premature, isn't it? Scare tactics won't wash with us. I expect my client to be granted bail shortly, not remanded into custody.'

Richard didn't look as convinced, and Andrea saw fear in his eyes. 'Let's not speculate further, but I will continue my questions,' she said. 'Richard, you previously stated you have a strong and loving marriage with Jane. Do you still stand by that?'

'No comment,' he replied.

'We have several witness statements from the party fundraiser that describe you being abusive to Jane. Do you recall being abusive?'

'No comment.'

'Not only did the witnesses describe your behaviour on that occasion, but they went on to say it was nothing new. He *"treated her like a doormat"* was one observation made. They allege it was not uncommon to witness you being abusive and humiliating Jane. Are they right, Richard?'

'No comment.'

'It certainly paints the picture of a troubled, failing marriage, doesn't it? We provided a copy of a log in your disclosure package. I have another copy here for your convenience.' Andrea slid the document across the table to him. 'This document contains a list of times and dates when you met Tony Hargreaves. You previously told us that you and Hargreaves had fallen out and don't bother with each other. In fact, you said the fallout was acrimonious, and he detested you because of a failed development plan. Why did you meet him on these occasions?'

'No comment.'

'Maybe that's why he ensured the police were handed a voice recording of a conversation between the two of you in the event of his death.' Andrea's eyes were locked onto Richard's for a moment before he looked away. She stared at him and watched with satisfaction as the colour drained from his face.

'I will play you the recording now, Richard. I also have a transcript of the conversation, should you wish to read it,' Andrea said, nodding to Lee before sliding the transcript across the table.

Lee opened the audio file on his laptop and pressed play. Tension hung over the room, filling the momentary, uncomfortable silence.

'I'm being serious, Tony. Don't fuck me about. Can you give me access to a hitman?'

'Yes, I can. But are you sure you want to go down that road? It doesn't always end well. Why not just divorce her?'

'I want her dead. No ifs, no buts. Money isn't a problem. I'll be rich when she dies. She's holding me back. She's a fucking embarrassment. Besides, I've got a younger model lined up to take her place.'

Andrea scrutinised Richard while he listened. She could have sworn that he physically cringed at his "younger model" comment. She would openly admit that she cherished the moment as Karma was served.

Lee pressed pause. 'That's just a small segment of the conversation. There's much more. But it paints the picture, doesn't it,' he said. 'Do you recognise the two parties from the recording?'

'No comment,' Richard said, wringing his hands together, distressed at the odds stacking up against him. A defeated and tormented man.

'Is that you talking on the recording, Richard?' Andrea asked.

'No comment,' he returned, almost inaudibly in a deflated, beaten tone. 'I've had enough. I want a break.' He looked at his solicitor.

Andrea noticed his bloodshot eyes and lack of composure. She guessed the recording had tipped him over the edge, and he was struggling to hold it together. 'Okay. Let's take a break,' she agreed, observing him from the corner of her eye. Richard hadn't made eye contact with her throughout the interview. Now, he had a thousand-yard stare. Staring into the abyss.

'For the purpose of the recording, we are now ending the interview and I will switch off the machine,' Lee said.

31

Andrea and Lee handed Richard over to the custody of the detention officer. 'This way,' he said to Richard, walking towards the cell corridor.

Giles Montford hung back, then turned to face Andrea. 'Well, I think that covers everything. I take it there will be no further interviews?' he asked.

Andrea suspected that for Richard, the penny had dropped. His fear was palpable. He looked like a man expecting the worst and one more interview might provide the opportunity for him to come clean.

'We'll have one more interview after this break, that should do it,' she said.

'Great, that means another wait in that wretched room,' Montford said, checking his watch. 'Shall we keep the break short? Ten minutes?'

'Yes, that's fine by us. Ask the custody sergeant to call us when you've finished your consultation,' Lee said before he and Andrea left the custody office and returned to the major incident room for a final review of the evidence they'd put forward for a charging decision.

Montford caught the eye of the detention officer returning from the cell corridor. 'Could I speak to my client, please?'

'Of course,' the officer said, then turned about and returned to the cell from where he'd just secured Richard, followed by the brief. 'Just press the buzzer when you want me to let you out of the cell.'

'Don't you have a consultation room? The cell is hardly the best place,' Montford enquired, in an attempt to avoid facing the stale stench of the claustrophobic box.

'All taken, I'm afraid. You could wait until one is free if you like?'

'Definitely not, I don't want to prolong my visit any longer than I need to, let's get on with it.'

Montford entered the cell to find Richard lying on the bench in the fetal position. 'Christ, don't they clean these places?' he said, in response to the entrenched smell of body odour and God knows what else. 'This is more rancid than the so-called waiting area.' He brushed a section of the bench with his hand before sitting down.

Richard lethargically pulled himself up into a seated position. 'Is that it now, Giles? Do you think they will press charges?'

'You're certainly up against it. You always have the option of pleading guilty at the next interview. The court would look favourably on an early guilty plea.'

'If I plead guilty, can you get me bail?' Richard asked, more in hope than expectation.

'I'll try my best,' Giles Montford replied unconvincingly.

Richard got up and slowly paced the cell while rubbing his temples. 'So, you've no tricks up your sleeve to get me off this then? I'm fucked, am I?' he asked in response to the lacklustre, even disinterested disposition of his brief.

'Not quite. If and when they charge you, we get another chance. We will review the evidence and disclosure schedules and see what we can find. We may find a technicality in the evidence or procedural issues that haven't been followed. That is if Eden Nash doesn't pull the plug on the party financing your defence.' Montford took a document from his briefcase. 'He wants you to sign this Non-Disclosure Agreement. I've read through it, and it's just routine. Just a quick signature, please.' He passed the NDA over along with a classy-looking Montblanc pen.

Richard returned to the bench and signed the document without reading it. He felt deflated and alone, accepting that his future would be decided by a bureaucratic process that was just about to begin. Then a flicker of hope crossed his mind: maybe his family or associates were connected to the judge, or Nash could influence which judge would be presiding at the trial.

Montford returned the document to his briefcase and stood up. 'I'll speak with the interviewing officers and find out their intentions. See you shortly,' he said, pressing the buzzer by the cell door with the slightest contact.

The detention officer responded swiftly and opened the door. 'Tell them I want to speak to Jane,' Richard shouted towards the closing door as his brief exited the cell.

'Shall I pass his request on to the custody sergeant?' the detention officer asked.

'No point,' Montford replied. 'I can tell you the answer now—No.'

Once Montford had left the cell, Richard placed his head in his hands. 'What the fuck have I done,' he sobbed in self-pity. Not for the first time in his life, he felt abandoned and alone. At times like this, Jane would put an arm around him and lift him back up.

Worse, he had never felt so helpless, no longer in control of life. The fear of prison made him feel sick with worry, and he continued sobbing as the reality took hold. He was out of his depth and no doubt heading to prison.

*

Andrea and Lee had completed their plan for the interview and were just finishing their coffees when the phone rang. The custody officer spoke in his usual monotone, routine manner. 'Your suspect is ready for the next interview. His brief has just returned from their consultation.'

'Okay, we'll make our way back down. See you in a few minutes,' Andrea replied.

'Oh, he has also requested to speak to his wife. He wants to apologise, apparently,' the officer added.

'Well, that's not happening. She's a prosecution witness,' Andrea said, surprised at the request.

'That's what I told the brief. If you don't ask, you don't get, I suppose. See you in a bit.'

When Andrea and Lee entered the custody office, Richard, Giles Montford, and the detention officer were waiting by the interview room door.

'He's been crying,' Andrea whispered to Lee as they approached, checking out his heavy, bloodshot eyes. The detention officer nodded to Lee and returned to his duties in the cell area.

Lee carefully watched Richard as he opened the door and gestured for them to enter. The four of them took their seats, and a sombre silence engulfed the room. Lee activated the recording machine, and the strident buzzing noise momentarily broke the silence. Richard looked oblivious, staring at the floor. He was a defeated man, drained of spirit and fight.

The buzzing sound stopped and Lee began: 'Richard, we have received an update from the officers supporting Jane and who are taking her statement of evidence. Under the circumstances, she is bearing up well, you'll be pleased to hear.'

'I want to see her,' Richard said, lifting his gaze from the floor towards his brief. 'This has all got out of hand. I want to apologise and make sure she's okay.'

Montford jumped in before Andrea or Lee had the chance. 'Richard, I've explained that you can't see her right now. Let's focus on the matter at hand. We can cross that bridge later.'

'Jane is now a prosecution witness, Richard,' Andrea added, observing what she believed was genuine remorse leaking from Richard for the first time. 'She's experienced a horrendous situation, having been kidnapped and held against her will, and is cooperating with the police in providing a statement of complaint.' Andrea left it there to allow the significance of her words to sink in.

'Jane has given us a thorough account of your relationship together. It's not the strong marriage you described to us. Is it, Richard?' Lee said.

'No comment,' he replied quietly, his head bowed towards the floor again.

'The hostage taker told Jane that Tony Hargreaves had hired him on your behalf,' Lee said, followed by a pause. 'He further stated that both of you had reneged on the payment. Is that why you and Tony were arguing in the park?'

'No comment.' Richard's voice was trembling, almost inaudible.

Andrea noticed he was rocking back and forth ever so slightly in his chair and wringing his hands. She waited

SILENT BETRAYAL

while watching the tears welling in his bloodshot eyes. Then she spoke in a calm, soothing tone. 'Richard, why did you conspire with Tony Hargreaves to have Jane killed?'

'I don't fucking know, do I? I was under a lot of pressure.' Everyone in the room appeared shocked and surprised at the reply, having been expecting another mumbled *"No comment"*.

Andrea glanced at Lee with a *Where the fuck did that come from?* expression.

Lee raised his eyebrows nonchalantly as if it had just been a matter of time until Richard's pressure valve burst.

'Richard, my advice is not to comment,' Giles Montford barked, jolting up from his laid-back position, letting his calm and composed persona slip for the first time during the interview process.

'It's too late for no comment. I'm fucked. I just want to see Jane and tell her I'm sorry.'

'I'd like to take a break to consult with my client. He is quite clearly suffering from a mental impairment, obviously brought on by exhaustion and trauma. He will withdraw his last comments in due course.' Montford said, sounding agitated now, his eyes darting from Lee to Andrea as if they were to blame.

He glared at Richard as he stood up. 'Come on, Richard, that's enough for now.' Looking back at Andrea, he added, 'I'd like my client to be examined by a doctor. He is not in a fit state for any further interviews. It's clear to see that his mental capacity has been diminishing throughout this process. The man needs to see a doctor. You have neglected his wellbeing to push him for an admission.'

'There'll be no need for further interviews,' Andrea said coldly. 'Richard has admitted his guilt. I will consult with the Crown Prosecution Service and seek to charge him with conspiracy to kill and put him before the court at the earliest opportunity. Bail is out of the question—Before you ask.'

32

DS Fraser led Jane Flannagan-Smythe from the video interview suite down the short corridor to the witness lounge. A room furnished with comfortable sofas and chairs to create a relaxing oasis within the police station for victims, rather than a sterile police setting, like the staff canteen.

'Help yourself to a coffee from the machine, Jane. I'll go and find out where the interviewing officers are up to with Richard. I recommend the Mocha, it's very nice.'

She reciprocated with a warm, tired smile. It had been a long day, and she was flagging. While selecting an Americano at the drinks machine, she came to a decision. If DS Fraser didn't thank her for her patience today and send her on her way any time soon, she would decide for him and insist on leaving. Once her coffee was served, she selected another cup and pressed the Mocha option.

Jane placed both cups on the table and sat back on the comfy sofa, sinking back into a comfortable position. She lifted the Americano and took a sip. Her hands cupped the drink as her mind scanned the day's events. Her thoughts shifted quickly to John; up to now, she'd assumed he must have withdrawn to safety from his vantage point. The police hadn't mentioned making an arrest, which they would have done in the circumstances, wouldn't they? Of course, they would. They would require her to pick him out on an identification parade. She guessed he'd be angry that Richard got arrested and evaded his demise. Her thoughts were interrupted by DS Fraser returning to the room.

'I've poured you a Mocha,' she said, nodding to the table before her. 'I'm a creature of habit and stuck to my favourite.'

'Thanks, Jane,' he said, sitting in the armchair beside the sofa. 'I've just spoken with the interviewing officers. It's good news and bad, I'm afraid. Good in that he has admitted to conspiring to have you killed, but bad in that someone close to you, whom you trusted, betrayed you so callously. I can only guess how difficult it must be for you to deal with this.'

'I've always known he's capable of anything. Especially if it works to his advantage,' Jane said before sipping her drink. 'Why did he want to kill me?' She hadn't consciously wanted to ask the question, the words just seeped out, maybe down to the tiredness.

'It's unclear yet, and he didn't give a reason.'

'He probably wanted to run away with one of the staffers he was fucking. And with my money in his pocket, too,' Jane suggested with no trace of emotion, just a hint of satisfaction that he'd failed in his quest.

'We have an on-call specialist counsellor that could help you. Shall I call her? She could be here in less than half an hour. Other victims who've spoken to her have been happy with the result and been able to move forward.'

'No, thank you,' Jane replied. 'I'm the resilient type. I just need to get a good sleep. I've got plenty of friends I can call on, and my brother, too. We'll probably stay together for a few days.' She had no intention of calling her brother. But giving the impression that she had a caring family around her was what the police probably wanted to hear. Allowing them to back off and give her some space, instead of fretting about their responsibility and duty of care. 'I'm lucky, I suppose. I'll get going if that's okay?'

'Are you sure, Jane?' DS Fraser asked with a look of concern.

'Yes, I'll be fine. Seriously. I'm made of tough stuff.'

'Okay, I'll get your belongings for you. I won't be a minute.' He got up from the chair, leaving his drink untouched.

'While you're doing that, could you call me a taxi, please? I'll arrange to meet my brother at home, I just need to chill out.'

Lee nodded and left the room. The thought of returning home for Jane and spending some peaceful time alone lifted her spirits, and she felt a resurgence of energy. She had unfinished business to attend to and wondered where next to go with John.

DS Fraser returned with a twine-coloured tote bag she'd never seen before. 'Forensics haven't finished with your rucksack yet. Your personal effects, which aren't being examined, are inside this bag.'

She took the bag and stood up, ready to leave but trying not to look too eager.

'You've got my number. Ring me anytime you feel the need to speak. The offer of a counsellor is always open, too. I've put the pay-as-you-go mobile in your bag. My number is in the contacts. I'll return your mobile phone to you as soon as possible. I've arranged for patrols to pay extra attention to your house, and for a panic alarm to be fitted first thing in the morning.'

As Jane exited the police station annexe building, her taxi pulled up in the car park. She jumped into the back of the cab, gave her address, and closed her eyes.

*

John had managed to easily slip away from the castle grounds following his contingency plan. As he had predicted, the police were blinkered in their approach, focused on Richard Flannagan-Smythe and his wife. But in fairness, they probably didn't have any intelligence to suggest he was there. Their objective would clearly have been to rescue Jane. John was back in his vehicle within minutes and heading north on the M6 back to the farm.

He appraised the situation and how it had panned out whilst maintaining a steady seventy miles per hour in the inside lane. Now was not the time to attract the attention of the police motorway patrols.

He'd made a split-second decision not to take the shot. Had it been the right decision? Probably. The target was partially hidden in cover, with a police arrest team moving in fast. Taking a police officer out besides the target would have spelt disaster. Would that have happened?—maybe not, but why take the risk? He wasn't despondent; he had contacts and assets everywhere. Richard was safe for now. But a revised plan would be implemented soon.

His mind switched to Jane. Had she managed to get away? Or had the police managed to catch up with her? He guessed the latter. The plainclothes officer, sprinting behind her, was closing in fast before John lost his line of sight of them.

Would she renege on their deal and ask to go on the witness protection programme? John doubted it, he trusted her. He wouldn't call her yet; her situation was currently unknown. Explaining the incoming call to the police was an additional burden for her, which she could do without. So he decided he would wait until she made contact.

Before heading back to the farm, he stopped at a layby on the higher ground on the other side of the valley. The view across the moors included the farm and the surrounding area. He grabbed his military-grade binoculars, a memento from his special forces days, and climbed out of the SUV. The binoculars provided him with a detailed view of the land's layout.

After several sweeps, he was satisfied that no intruders or specialist surveillance officers were embedded in the landscape watching the farm—not that he expected any. His tradecraft was second to none, and he effectively covered his tracks. Then he got back into his vehicle and drove to the farm. The roads were deserted, and there were no signs of law enforcement agencies mooching about.

He followed his standard operating procedures at the farmhouse, checking the trip wires and tamper indicators. Everything looked fine; no new tyre tracks or footprints were visible on the ground. It was second nature to him; the coast was clear of external threats.

Inside, he commenced the forensic clean-up to ensure there was no trace of Jane ever having been there. He shrugged off a strange gnawing feeling that he was missing her already, albeit reluctantly conceding there was something about her he liked. He pushed the thoughts away by busying himself and scrubbing the bathroom furniture beside the cell with bleach. Experience told him it was now a waiting game. He was in no doubt that Jane would make contact at some stage. Hopefully, sooner than later. He was also confident that the police had only delayed the demise of Richard; he was still in the crosshairs, living on borrowed time.

Work done, John retired to his favourite room in the attic, poured a single malt and sat, looking out over the idyllic spectacular view of the Yorkshire countryside. He noticed a solitary roe deer tentatively stepping out from the forest and grabbed his binoculars to take a closer look, admiring the old buck as he rubbed his antlers against the trees and shrubs, marking his territory — an acquaintance he'd monitored since buying the farm. After the buck disappeared back into the forest, John placed the binoculars on the table beside him and picked up his book, then he settled down to read, feeling relaxed and confident that he would hear from Jane soon.

Just as he was a few pages into the book, his mobile phone sprang into life, killing the peaceful silence. He reached over, grabbed it and glanced at the screen. It wasn't the caller he was expecting.

'H, how are you doing? Are you back in the UK yet?'

'If only. There's law enforcement everywhere. Somehow, they've located the flat I was using. They've been there for a good few hours,' H said, trying not to sound concerned.

'Is the flat clean?' John asked hurriedly, aware of the possible serious ramifications. Ensuring no DNA or other incriminating evidence was left behind was standard operating procedures for them. It could prove catastrophic for H. But John chose not to spell it out, they both knew the score. Even though H had rinsed him about not seeing Jane as a loose end, to be eliminated.

'Yes, I sorted that before I left,' H said. 'I don't think they'll produce any positive forensic evidence hits. The problem is, I guess they have me on CCTV footage, so they'll know who they're looking for.' He paused, then added, 'I probably need to change my appearance.'

'What are you considering? A crash diet?' John said, sniggering.

'Either that or a tummy tuck and hair extensions,' H replied.

'They could match that up with their footage from when the police stopped you in Manchester.' John knew he could go for the jugular if he chose to. H clearly hadn't been on the top of his game. 'Why don't you go inland and keep your head down for a week or two? Enjoy some R and R. Then maybe pick up a ride back from Holland or France?' John suggested, confident there was now a manhunt on both sides of the channel looking for H.

'I might do. I'll check out the local fishermen first and see if I can sort some transport from the local port.' There was a pause. John let it ride, waiting for the inevitable question he guessed was coming. 'Have you sorted your house guest yet?' John sensed conflict and tension in H's tone. He wasn't going to back down on this one. He felt irked that H was making such a big deal about it.

'There's been a delay. But don't worry, I'm on top of it,' he answered calmly.

'You've not slotted her, have you? Has she fucking escaped?' H said, the pitch of his voice rising with each word.

John ran his fingers through his beard then stood up and walked closer to the window. 'Everything's fine,' he began before explaining how the events at the church gardens transpired.

'So, has she contacted you yet?' H asked, a smug tone in his voice.

'No, I thought it was her calling when you rang. She will.'

'For fuck's sake, John. What were you thinking? You know this isn't how we operate. What are you going to do when she doesn't make contact?'

'She will make contact. I'm in no doubt. It was like she had an epiphany whilst she was being held here. It felt like she'd shrugged off the doormat wife image and was hell-bent on taking her revenge. A woman scorned and all that. She could be a future asset for us. We've always thought a female operative would be good for us.' His confidence didn't go unnoticed. 'She's got something about her—the right attitude,' he continued. 'And besides, you've got enough on your plate, avoiding the dragnet that's out to catch you. Your photograph will be disseminated to law enforcement agencies right across Europe.'

'You worry me sometimes, mate. That's a big step to take. She's obviously made a good impression on you—'

John interrupted, 'Before you ask. No, I haven't fucked her. Give me some credit, please.'

'My stance remains the same, she's a loose end, and I'd rather not take the risk. Our agreed protocols also back up my argument. Remember, John, it's how we operate. Don't leave things to chance. Head them off at the pass. Think it through, mate. I'm happy to sort it out when I get back.' Then, changing the subject, H asked, 'What about the MP?'

'I'm not sure yet. Like I said, he was arrested. I'll do some digging and find out what's happening with him. He's low-risk; he's never seen us and has no other links to us. We can hit him anytime. I'll initiate contact with our sources in the prison service. There's no worries on that score.'

'Fair enough. Keep me up to speed.'

SILENT BETRAYAL

'You too, don't compromise yourself by rushing back. It sounds like they're throwing a lot of resources towards catching you,' John said, hopeful of more time to get things sorted before H's return. Then, they could put it all behind them and get on with the next assignment.

'Okay, speak soon,' H said before hanging up.

John returned to his chair and took a sip of his whiskey. A low mist was forming across the fields as dusk approached. He felt relaxed and confident. H hadn't unsettled his belief in Jane. He had no nagging doubts about Jane whatsoever. And now H would be occupied putting his own house in order.

But what if he gets arrested? the question shot across John's mind, preventing him from switching off, and losing himself in the pages of his book. *H won't talk,* he satisfied himself. If he did, John would have contingency plans in place to deal with it.

33

Jane paid the cab driver and walked along the driveway towards the house. Its outline, lit by the full moon, felt welcoming. She was instantly filled with a warm, comfortable feeling radiating throughout her body. The crunching of the stones underfoot provided a comforting familiarity. Once inside the house, she headed through the darkness to the kitchen and flicked the lights on, surprised at the place's pristine state. Her mind played tricks, anticipating Richard's booming voice shouting, *"Is that you, Jane?"*

She undid her trousers and retrieved the burner phone from her underwear. The phone had been pressing against her skin for the last few hours and had caused it to feel tender and sore. She poured a large glass of prosecco and headed to the lounge, almost in disbelief that she was back home, experiencing a surreal aura. It felt almost like an anti-climax, having been dreaming about this moment for the last few days. Now it was here, it all seemed so normal and run-of-the-mill.

A thought flashed into her head: *Does John know my address? Of course he does,* her mind answered right away. But would he risk turning up at her house with the potential of police surveillance a reality? Probably not. She felt like closing her eyes and sleeping but knew she had to hang on until she'd made the call. She sat silently, just listening to her breath while calmness enveloped her.

SILENT BETRAYAL

Jane selected the sole contact in the address book and pressed the green button. After four rings, the call was answered.

'Hello,' John answered, his voice now familiar.

'Hi, John, sorry, this is the first opportunity I've had to call you. I've just left the police station.'

'Where are you?'

'At home.'

'Alone?'

'Yes,' Jane replied, unsure whether giving up her location and the fact she was by herself was a good move. Maybe she should have said the cleaner was with her, staying over to give her some support.

'You sound tired,' John said. 'What's been happening?'

'My clothing and stuff have been taken for forensic examination, and I've been interviewed about everything that happened since leaving the hotel.' Jane went on to give him a summary of her time with the police.

He listened carefully for signs that raised suspicion that the police were with her or perhaps monitoring the call remotely. The questions she asked and the answers she gave would give an indication, along with unnatural pauses and her tone of voice. 'What did you tell them in the interviews?'

'I implicated Richard as best I could to keep it real. I used what Tony Hargreaves said about the contract they took out on me. The detectives pricked their ears up at that.'

'What about me?'

'Misinformation. As we agreed. I got the impression they had no investigative leads on you, just some grainy CCTV footage of you in the driver's seat from when you picked me up. It could have been anybody.'

'Would it be possible to identify me from the footage?'

'I didn't see it, but I'm guessing not from the way they talked about it. They sounded frustrated.'

'We need to sort out the payment. I'm not far away. I will be at your house in twenty minutes.'

Jane was about to protest that she needed to go to bed, but the line went dead. 'For fuck's sake,' she cursed. Then she headed to the kitchen, needing caffeine to help her stay awake.

While waiting for the kettle to boil, her tired mind began to ruminate. Why was John risking coming to the house? It didn't seem like something he would do or need to do in the circumstances, and the police might have set up surveillance in case the abductors *did* come back for her. Was he coming to kill her? Had that been his intention all along? She opened the kitchen drawer and selected the sharpest knife she possessed, placing it into her jacket pocket.

She then raced to her bedroom, grabbed the pepper spray canister from her dressing table drawer, and returned to the kitchen. The kettle had boiled, but she changed her mind and poured another glass of wine instead.

While drinking, she glanced around the room, then moved the knife block into the pantry, out of sight, before concealing the individual knives strategically around the kitchen. Her mind was going into survival overdrive. She decided that the kitchen island must be between them at all times. Or would she be better off calling the police before he arrived?

She could easily hide and evade him while the police were making their way to the address. Or should she change her plan entirely and try to seduce him, which would place him in a vulnerable position? It wouldn't be difficult to do that. Physically, she was attracted to him, and it *was* an option which would create further possibilities. A kitchen knife discreetly placed under a pillow? She remained standing at the kitchen island, sipping her wine. Her thoughts were in overdrive, considering options, while images of her white bedsheets covered in blood drifted into her mind. Nobody would be looking for him. Or maybe his friend H would be. He saw Jane as a loose end to be neutralised, anyway.

*

John returned to his seat with his laptop. He clicked on the surveillance app, and four live camera feeds instantly appeared on his screen. He sipped his whiskey, watching for any police activity at Jane's house. Experience told him they would set up a protective cordon outside. They wouldn't risk letting him get too close to her if she'd tipped them off as a result of his call. He had no intention of going to Jane's house tonight. But he had set things in place to help him ascertain whether she'd double crossed him or that the police had a protective containment around her. If so, he would draw them out. He needed to be prepared for the following day, for his plan to proceed successfully.

As the minutes ticked by, nothing changed. There was no movement on the grounds or around the house's exterior and no activity outside the road other than the expected passing traffic.

Thirty minutes later, John's trust in Jane was confirmed. He was satisfied that there was no police activity whatsoever.

The headlights of a car then appeared at the entrance to the drive, on time, just as he'd planned.

The car slowly headed towards the house and parked up. The driver exited the vehicle carrying an insulated pizza bag and knocked on the door. John watched as Jane appeared and took in the two pizza boxes, then the driver returned to his car before heading towards the exit. John smiled at the thought of the police breaking their cover and jumping all over the poor, unsuspecting pizza delivery guy, having assumed he might be involved with the abductors. Part of him wished they'd been staking out the gardens. It would have been a good watch.

As a final check, he activated the previous movement sensor trips and viewed the historic footage. Just as Jane had described, her cab stopped at the gates. She got out and approached the house, which was in total darkness. A moment later, the lights went on in the kitchen, and she appeared to be alone.

John reached for his burner phone and called her, satisfied that all was well.

*

Jane was standing at the kitchen window, looking out along the driveway. She'd placed the two pizza boxes with a scribbled note, *"Keep these warm – John"* on the worktop alongside her. She checked her watch again. It was now forty minutes since they'd ended their phone call. *He should be here by now,* she reasoned. She ran her hand over her jacket pockets, feeling for the concealed weapons. Why wasn't he there? Had the police picked him up? Was the house under surveillance?

The ringtone on the burner phone suddenly kicked in, breaking the silence and making her jump. She grabbed the phone and answered.

'Change of plan, Jane. I've had a drink and can't risk driving. It's making the stupid mistakes that get you nicked,' John lied, covering his tracks of never having intended to be there sharing the pizza. 'We can discuss the plan over the phone now while you enjoy the pizzas. I guessed you were probably hungry after the day you've had.'

'Okay, thanks for the pizza. But it's a shame I'm too tired to eat it,' Jane said, lifting the lid of one of the boxes and taking a peek at the contents. 'So, what's the plan?'

'I want you to take the two o'clock train into Manchester. Go straight to your safety deposit box and collect the cash.'

'I'm going to pay you in Krugerrands if that's okay? They're what my father stashed away years ago. Untraceable, I guess. Probably an unofficial payment from his time working in Africa.'

'Krugerrands are fine,' John said, sounding somewhat surprised. 'I'll direct you further over the burner phone to the handover location.'

'What then?' she enquired.

'You walk away.'

'Are you sure, John. What about Richard? I want my revenge, don't forget. I want to be part of it.'

'Leave that to me. It'll get sorted. I assure you.'

'How? He's probably looking at jail time.'

'Then I'll have a reception committee waiting for him on the wing. I told you that I have contacts and associates everywhere. There's no hiding from Johnny.'

'Shall I keep the burner phone after the payment? I may be useful to you in the future,' Jane said, purposefully not describing further how she could be useful.

'Yes, keep the burner phone until Richard's been despatched,' he replied. 'I'll let you know when that's been completed.'

'Can I go to bed now?' she asked, stifling a yawn.

'One last thing. You will be watched tomorrow from the moment you leave the house. If I suspect the police are following you, I will call you. Likewise, if you get a gut feeling that something isn't right, call me, and we'll review the situation.'

'See you tomorrow. I'm looking forward to it in a strange way,' Jane said, ending the call before he could reply. She wanted him to feel at ease and relaxed with her, and in no doubt that he could trust her, which would hopefully make him more complacent.

34

Andrea and Lee sat opposite Samuel in his office. They'd been summoned by text before setting off from home and instructed to head straight to his office.

'You could have given us more notice, boss. We could have set off earlier. The traffic is a nightmare at this time of morning,' Andrea said, placing her coffee on the edge of his desk.

'It always is these days. It's no longer *a* rush hour. It's probably *three* hours. Anyway, you're here now, and the investigation is progressing well. Great work by you and your team. Please pass on my thanks to them.'

'Will do, boss. What's the update from Spain?' Andrea asked, more interested in results than hollow back-slapping for the troops.

'Our suspect for the Tony Hargreaves murder has been arrested,' Samuel said, with a beaming smile of satisfaction.

'Result!' Andrea exclaimed, glancing at Lee.

'This just gets better. How did they get him?' Lee asked, leaning forward in his chair.

'He was mooching around the port, looking for transport back to the UK. Unlucky for him, the Spanish police had the area locked down. He'd walked straight into the middle of a surveillance operation on a drug smuggling gang, cops everywhere.' Samuel was shaking his head in disbelief. 'It couldn't have been easier for them. They all had the wanted image of his face on their phones. So they knew who he was straight away. I bet they couldn't believe their luck.'

'Has he been interviewed yet?' Lee asked.

'Not yet. He's probably still at the hospital getting stitched up. The surveillance teams called in uniform support so they didn't need to break cover and compromise their operation. Once uniform arrived, our suspect decided to take them on in a bid to escape. By all accounts, he almost got away after inflicting some nasty injuries in the process and hospitalising several police officers, but they finally overpowered him. He was a bit of a handful, to say the least.'

'I'm not surprised. He's a man mountain and an evil-looking bastard,' Andrea said.

'As wide as he is tall with muscle, I'm glad I wasn't going toe-to-toe with him,' Lee said grimly.

'Well, he's got it to do now,' Samuel assured. 'He'll be going straight to jail for assaulting the police officers on grievous bodily harm charges alone, never mind the murder charge. They don't mess about over there: do not pass go, straight to jail.'

'Did they update you on the murder investigation?' Andrea asked.

Samuel nodded and gave them the low-down: 'The evidence is stacking up against him. He's not having much luck, our enforcer. They have good CCTV evidence from near his flat, at a bar where he met the victim, and onwards to the holiday apartments—a very tight time frame, too, which puts him at the scene at the right time.

'A holidaymaker reported hearing an argument raging outside her apartment. Looking out her window, she saw a man matching his description push another man over the balcony's edge. The evidence against him is stacking up nicely.'

'A lot will depend on the deceased's wife picking him out on an identification parade. The statement she gave you, Lee, about this guy threatening her husband at their house is good supporting evidence, he's stuffed, bang to rights. I think they also have decent forensic evidence from his flat.'

'How did the enforcer catch up with Hargreaves so quickly in Spain?' Lee asked.

'Don't forget we're dealing with professional assassins here, Lee. I'm in no doubt they undertook impeccable research. They probably knew about his apartment. It was a straightforward job for them once he booked the flight and headed to the airport.'

'What a way to go,' Lee said, shaking his head. 'Which floor did he fall from?'

'Fourth floor. The witness said it was all over in a flash. Hargreaves was whipped off his feet in a rugby-like tackle and disappeared over the edge instantly. The offender then walked away as calmly as you like.'

'Not a man you'd want to upset... I'll request that our detectives work alongside the Spanish police on the interviews. In fact, it may assist them if one of our team is the lead interviewer,' Andrea said as an afterthought. 'It sounds like we have leverage to get him to talk to us about Jane's abduction, too.'

'It's all looking good from where I'm sitting. Richard Flannagan-Smythe charged and up before the court, any time now,' Lee said, looking at his watch. 'He'll be remanded into custody, and Jane Flannagan-Smythe is safe.'

'Let's now focus on where she was being held and by whom,' Andrea suggested. 'Unfortunately, her description of him isn't very good, and our video footage isn't the best. But the CCTV trawls are still tracking the locations of the vehicle. We may locate him getting in or out of his car before the event. It's happened before.'

'The geographical profiler is pulling things together nicely,' Lee pointed out. 'Our teams have been visiting the potential premises he's highlighted so far. I'd like to do more interviews with Jane about where she was held. The two lines of enquiry together might speed things up for us.'

*

Richard was escorted back to his cell after his brief appearance before the stipendiary magistrate in court. The door slammed shut behind him as he sat on the bench, where a stale cheese sandwich, a packet of crisps, and an insipid-looking cup of tea in a Styrofoam cup had been left for him.

He sipped the tea, immediately spitting the cold, tasteless liquid back into the cup. He zoned out from the shouting and sounds of doors being slammed shut in the corridor and lay on the cold, hard bed, covered by a thin foam, blue PVC-covered mattress.

The speed of the court appearance had surprised him and he'd felt insignificant during the procedure. He felt like a nobody. No one there appeared to give a shit about him. He was just one of many wrongdoers being processed before the court that morning. Part of the machine. His only involvement had been to answer his name and date of birth. He'd listened intently to the prosecution lawyer outlining the case to the court, followed by a local solicitor, deputising for his brief. He stated he had nothing further to add but to remind the court that his client had cooperated with the police throughout the investigation. Richard observed that it

SILENT BETRAYAL

had fallen on deaf ears. Nobody seemed to give a fuck either way. Maybe the lawyer felt compelled to say something. *Who knows*, Richard reflected.

Montford was probably back in London already, meeting Nash in one of the restaurants at the House of Commons. Richard suspected the knives would have been sharpened already, and the backstabbing would be in full swing. One-time colleagues and friends would denounce how they had always suspected he was weird and untrustworthy. The potential candidates jostling to take over his safe seat would be in hyperdrive, falling over themselves to ingratiate with Nash, who had probably already decided who the next chosen one was to be.

Richard couldn't settle and struggled to quieten his mind. He sat up, placing his head in his hands, elbows resting on his thighs. He was experiencing a brain fog thick with gnawing regret and self-pity.

The loneliness in the cell mirrored the void in his soul. The woman he had once sworn to love and protect had almost been killed at his request, and now his mind was on a mission to remind him of all the good things she had done for him. A kick in the bollocks would have been preferable, just to get the torture over with quickly.

But his mind wandered back to the good days that he and Jane had shared before sharply veering to the memory of him conspiring about her demise with that bastard, Tony Hargreaves. What had he done? Why? Blinded by political ambition and his own ego? Jane had always supported him, always been there for him—and this was how he repaid her. He tried to take solace and find peace in the fact that she had survived the ordeal, she was still alive and hopefully safe. Yet his thoughts remained fractured, his head spinning, with no comforting bottle of scotch to steady him. Restless, he stood and began pacing the cell, desperate for some distraction from his racing mind.

The distraction came quickly, in the form of the jarring sound of keys rattling in the door shattering his solitude, dragging him out of the endless loop of regret and self-recrimination.

'Time to go, Richard. You're off to prison,' the detention officer announced in his usual calm, non-conflictual manner.

Even though he knew it was coming, the words hit like a punch to the gut. He was about to join the exclusive, dishonourable club of ex-parliamentarians doing time in prison. Some of them had even found ways to spin it to their advantage after being released—writing books, appearing on television, and basking in post-incarceration notoriety. But that thought brought no comfort. He had hit rock-bottom. He was a broken man.

A wave of fear rolled over him, smothering the guilt and self-pity that had consumed him moments before. A stretch in prison loomed ahead—a harsh, brutal world where survival would be his only focus.

The detention officer was joined at the cell door by a scruffy-looking security guard. 'I'm escorting you to the prison,' he said.

The guard stepped forward and clipped handcuffs onto Richard's trembling wrists. Cold sweat broke out across his skin as panic clawed its way up his chest. His legs felt unsteady, threatening to buckle beneath him. 'I need to speak to my solicitor,' he demanded, his voice edged with desperation.

'It's a bit late for that,' the guard replied indifferently. 'The screws at reception might let you make a call—depends how busy they are, I suppose.'

The guard's nonchalant tone infuriated Richard, whose crisis felt insurmountable. 'Look, if you don't let me call now, I'll file an official complaint against you,' Richard snapped, glaring at him.

The guard snorted, unimpressed. 'Go ahead, mate. I'll add it to the pile,' he said with a shrug, leading Richard from the cell.

At the custody desk, Richard was handed a pen to sign for his belongings, though the custody sergeant was engrossed in a phone call, multi-tasking, barely acknowledging him.

The guard grabbed the clear polythene bag containing Richard's property and tugged him toward the exit. But he resisted. 'I want to make a phone call,' he demanded, this time addressing the custody sergeant directly.

The sergeant placed his hand over the phone's receiver briefly. 'You'll have the chance to make a call when you get there,' he said dismissively before resuming his conversation.

The guard pulled him forward with a firm grip, leading him into the secure yard where the prison van waited. Richard clumsily stepped into the rear of the van, awkwardly manoeuvring to account for the handcuffs binding him to the guard. The guard opened a small compartment—the "sweat box"—and motioned for Richard to step inside.

Once the cuffs were removed, he sat on the hard bench, facing the narrow doorway. The door slammed shut in his face, with a finality that reverberated through his chest. Alone in the confined space, the familiar cycle began anew: his mind racing, his regrets mounting, his fear of the unknown swallowing everything else. He could hear the echo of heavy footsteps, sharp voices, and the clang of more doors shutting as other prisoners were loaded into the truck. The fear was inescapable.

*

On arrival at the prison, Richard was the first prisoner to be escorted from the vehicle. He was led straight to a tall counter behind which prison officers busied themselves in a world of routine and regulations. He had never felt fear and intimidation like it. The stark reality of being alone and vulnerable was etched across his face.

'Cheer up, it could be a lot worse,' the well-built, muscular prison officer said from behind the counter. 'But then again, maybe not.' He laughed, looking over to a colleague who joined in, chuckling at the wisecrack.

Richard answered question after question while noticing the other prisoners being led into the room and processed through the same induction. The noise in the room was getting louder, the other prisoners gobbing off at each other and also at the prison officers.

He heard a voice from behind him. 'He's definitely a fucking nonce; he's going to get a pasting the first chance I get.' Richard felt frozen with fear. He was out of his depth here, and he knew it. 'Oi, you fucking nonce, look at me when I'm talking about you,' the lag shouted, to the amusement of his cronies, who all burst out laughing.

Richard turned towards him. 'I'm not a fucking nonce. Just leave me alone and let me do my time,' he said, not doing himself any favours, to which he received a rapturous round of laughter and further insults and threats from the cons.

One of the cronies shouted out, 'Fuckin' hell, leave him alone, he's going to start crying.'

'Take 374727 straight up to the wing, VIP section, Tony. Let's get him banged up and out of the way for now,' the prison officer shouted to a colleague.

'This way,' the other officer instructed.

Richard followed him, trying to hide in his shadow for protection. They walked past a cleaning work party in the corridor and one of the lags stopped mopping and glared at him, then burst out laughing. 'What's your name, sweetheart?' he called after Richard. The other lags burst into fits of laughter, while Richard struggled to hide his fear. He couldn't bear to look at them or say anything in return.

Relieved to have left the reception area behind, he followed the officer along two corridors and through several barred gates to a cast iron staircase.

'It's a bit different to the House of Commons, I guess?' he said with a chuckle as he commenced climbing the metal staircase, wheezing as he went.

Richard seized the opportunity to hopefully bond and develop a trusted ally. 'It has its similarities too; I guess you can't trust anyone here either,' he said, his voice quivering.

The officer laughed. 'I suppose that's true. You'll be wishing you voted for more prison officer numbers soon. The cons think they run this place because there's so few of us.'

Richard didn't miss the danger implied by the officer's words and kept his head down as they passed by other prisoners on the wing.

'This is your cell. There's a welcome pack on the bed. If you're lucky, you'll have the cell to yourself tonight. Do as you're told, keep your head down and don't upset anybody.'

Richard stepped into the cell, and the door slammed closed behind him. His eyes scanned the small area: bunkbeds, sink, stainless steel toilet behind a vanity shield, and a barred window. The smell of body odour and stale sweat filled the air. He sat on the lower bunk and looked through his welcome pack: induction book, tobacco and papers, toothbrush, toothpaste and soap. Feeling fearful and depressed, he went about making his bed with a single sheet and orange blanket that had seen better days. He then laid back and closed his eyes, feeling strangely thankful that the cell door was locked.

35

Jane awoke early from an undisturbed, peaceful sleep. She'd created a cocoon with the duvet and was reluctant to leave its warmth behind, delaying getting up for a bit longer. This was in contrast to the military cot bed in the damp, claustrophobic cell. She closed her eyes, appreciating the comfort and warmth of her surroundings. She was on the brink of falling asleep when she heard a noise from downstairs. Her ears pricked up, straining to confirm that she hadn't imagined the noises. The familiar sound of the front door being closed sent a shiver of fear through her body. Someone had definitely just entered the house, was the nightmare about to continue?

She leapt out of bed, grabbed the discarded clothes from the night before, and hurriedly dressed as the noise of someone moving around downstairs continued. Frantically, she scurried around the bedroom, her eyes darting around. She needed her mobile, but it was nowhere to be seen.

Jane took the kitchen knife from her jacket pocket. Pointing outwards from her outstretched arm, she edged slowly through the door and onto the landing. Her breathing was becoming rapid, and her heart was racing. The sound of someone moving around continued, now emanating from the kitchen. Slowly, one careful step at a time, she descended the stairs, keeping a firm grip on the rail, her eyes remaining fixed on the kitchen door. Confused when she heard the unexpected sound of the kettle boiling, she yelled out, 'Who's there?'

There was a momentary pause before Mandy appeared at the kitchen door. 'Jane! Thank God you're okay,' she said, with her stare fixed on the knife in Jane's hand, a look of apprehension swiftly turning to fear.

Jane hastily pocketed it in her jacket. 'What the hell are you doing, Mandy? You scared me to death.'

Mandy approached and hugged her. 'I'm so glad to see you,' she said. 'I don't know what to say. Are you okay?'

Jane broke away from the embrace. 'I'm fine now. But what are you doing here?' Survival thoughts were rapidly flashing through her mind. Had Mandy been involved in the abduction? Was she Richard's bit on the side? What was she up to? Jane scanned her for weapons or signs of leakage from her behaviour. Was she a threat?

'The kettle's on. You look like you could use a coffee,' Mandy said, backing off into the kitchen, closely followed by Jane.

'Mandy, what are you doing here? You've not answered me yet.'

'Jane, you're scaring me,' she replied. 'I'm your cleaner, for fuck's sake. DS Lee McCann told me to carry on looking after the place. What do you think I'm doing here?' She then placed two mugs of coffee on the kitchen island.

Jane suddenly felt engulfed by a feeling of calmness and relaxation. Her shoulders drooped as the tension drained from her muscles. There was no threat here, she decided. But she recognised a change in herself. She was thinking and seeing things differently, and her outlook had changed. 'Sorry, Mandy, you caught me by surprise, that's all. I've been under a lot of pressure. I just grabbed the knife because I was scared, that's all.'

'Don't worry about it. We can talk if you like?' she said, struggling to hide her eagerness to discover what had happened.

'Some other time, but not now,' Jane said, knowing that whatever she said would be common knowledge around the local pub by last orders tonight.

Mandy appeared to understood the mood music and grabbed her coffee. 'I understand. I'll give you some space, but I'm here if you need me,' she said with a smile. 'It's great to have you back safe and well. I'll crack on with the hoovering,' she said, as she left the room.

Jane checked her watch; it was time to get ready. After her mammoth sleep, she didn't have much time to prepare for the day ahead. She grabbed some gardening gloves and headed towards the back door, pausing momentarily, listening, to ensure Mandy was hoovering in the lounge, and not overlooking the garden. Outside, she walked over to a quiet overgrown corner of the garden and carefully approached a six foot tall plant. The purple spotted stem and delicate leaves spelled danger. Doing her best to ignore the rank, acrid smell of the plant, she carefully selected several brown tiny oval capsules, that contained seeds, and a few leaves from the branches. Delicately, she placed them into a small plastic bag, task completed, she returned to the kitchen to complete the final touches.

*

Richard hadn't managed to get much sleep. Initially, the noise on the landing kept him awake, and then the shouting from cell to cell continued well into the night until an oppressive silence swept over the place.

The security light outside the window shone brightly, casting a strip of light across the cell. By then, he had already given up trying to sleep as he tossed and turned on the hard, uncomfortable mattress.

He lay still, staring at the peeling grey paint on the ceiling. How the hell had it come to this? The guilt gnawed at his brain relentlessly as he obsessed about Jane, only to be overpowered by the fear and uncertainty of what lay ahead for him.

Banging doors and shouting from beyond his cell on the landing resumed from last night, the volume growing all the time. The place was coming to life again. He had an upset stomach, dry mouth, and a dull headache was now pounding at his temples. He listened as a key was placed into the door, and the lock was undone. His heart started to race as he felt restless but frozen at the same time.

A man mountain of a prison officer looked into his cell, his face and demeanour lacking any compassion or emotion. He had probably been hardened over many years on the prison wing and was now institutionalised, part of the system.

His bald head and muscular build made him look all the more intimidating. A lot of the screws looked like the cons, but in the wrong uniform. 'This is Bob. He will be your peer mentor while you accustom yourself to life inside. Listen carefully to what he tells you. It's a bit different here from what you're used to at Westminster, although there are some similarities: the food here is subsidised, too,' the prisoner officer said in an automated fashion before turning about and leaving the doorway.

An old skinny lag with unruly, wiry grey hair stepped into the cell slowly, not taking his eyes off Richard for a moment. The lag leaned back against the steel wash basin, still staring at Richard. 'You look fucking petrified,' he said with a sneer. 'Don't go out on the landing looking like that. If they see a sign of weakness, they'll exploit it. You need to get a grip on yourself.'

Richard nodded his head, then wiped his hands vigorously over his face. 'It's just the shock of all this, that's all. I'm tired. I haven't slept for days.'

The lag shook his head. 'You need to get yourself on seg. You've pissed off some influential enemies. You're not safe here. Word of your arrival was passed on to the boys who run this wing. They're proper nasty bastards.'

Richards's stomach cramped, and he felt like throwing up, his palms were sweating, and his heart began beating fast against his chest again. 'You're my mentor. Aren't you supposed to help me?'

The lag burst out laughing. 'What the fuck am I supposed to do? Anyway, I'm a listener, not a fucking mentor. That title's just corporate bullshit. They just want to know if you're likely to top yourself. They're trying to cut the number of suicides—an edict from the governor. Too many deaths don't look good on the annual report. Anyway, I've told you. Get yourself on seg before it's too late. That's the best advice I can give you.'

'How do I do that?'

'Tell one of the screws that you want to go rule forty-five. Tell them you've been threatened and you're in fear for your life. They will get the safer custody team to sort it out and move you.'

'Can you not ask them as you know the threat? Surely, they'll take it more seriously if it comes from you?'

The lag started laughing again. 'This isn't fucking Eton, you clown. You really are fucking clueless, aren't you? I've done all I can for you already. Don't even think of telling anyone what I've told you, got it?'

'Yes, I understand,' Richard said, nodding.

'Off you go then, go and find a prison officer.'

Richard got up. He'd never felt fear like this in his life. His legs trembled and felt like jelly as he slowly edged closer to the cell door. He looked over his shoulder at the listener, sitting on the bottom bunk, reading the newspaper he'd taken out of his back pocket.

Stepping onto the landing, the cacophony of noise almost overwhelmed him. It was an immediate sensory overload. Laughter, arguing and shouting competed with the banging of doors. His eyes darted around the wing, looking for a prison officer among the sea of light blue T-shirts and grey woollen sweaters of cons milling around the wing.

When he realised there were no officers around, he felt panicked and isolated. It looked like mob rule. The listener was right, this place was his worst nightmare, he thought, as the prison officer's words replayed in his head: *"The cons think they run this place."*

A young, cocky-looking inmate with a swagger was approaching his cell. Richard stepped back into the doorway, trying his best to be innocuous. The inmate clocked on, a broad, beaming smile crossing his face. Richard smiled back, not recognising the menace in the smile.

'Oi, Nozzer, there's some fresh meat for you here. Go easy on him, won't you?' The inmate shouted across the safety netting to the other side of the wing. Richard froze as he became the focus of the prisoners nearby; some looked over, laughing, adding further insults and abuse, and others just stared. The lag who instigated his torment continued on his way, towel in hand, seeming to be enjoying his shit housing and the discomfort he'd caused to the newcomer.

Richard guessed he was going to the shower room, a place that he would avoid at all costs. He'd heard the horrific stories of what happened there and wasn't risking a visit. As the taunts and threats being shouted in his direction died down, he continued looking for a prison officer. Still, he couldn't see one, and he reluctantly decided he'd have to go further afield to find one. Now he was in no doubt that he had to get off this wing, pronto. He turned to his left and slowly headed towards the stairway. *Surely, there'd be an officer there.* He didn't look inside as he passed open cell doors, and avoided eye contact with anyone.

A sixth sense suddenly shrouded him; it felt like danger was imminent. The movement of the prison inmates appeared orchestrated. No one was anywhere near his personal space, but a baying mob was congregating ahead of him.

The sheer sensory overload overwhelmed him: the bright lighting, the insipid grey colour of the peeling paint on the wall, the safety nets strung across the void, and the iron bars at the end of the wing. All hostile, he was abandoned and alone.

A thought flashed across his mind that he should go back to the cell, slam the door shut, and buy some time until he could get himself moved onto seg. But when he turned around, he was confronted by a gang of prisoners approaching him purposefully. The one at the front looked hyper, as if he was high on something; focused like he was on a mission. Richard resigned himself to what was coming. There was nowhere to hide. He had to take his chances and run for the nearest cell door and lock himself inside. It was his only option.

He turned around and sprinted, fuelled by adrenaline and feral fear. He reached the next cell and darted inside. 'You've got to help me,' he yelled at the two occupants, fear reeking from every pore. He grabbed the door and slammed it shut, leaning his back against it.

'What the fuck are you doing?' shouted one of the occupants. 'Get out of my fucking pad, now.' Then he pulled Richard away from the door and pulled it wide open. Immediately, a mob of cons swarmed into the cell, headed by the psycho-looking guy who'd chased him down.

The psycho inmate shoulder-charged Richard against the wall. He hit the wall with force and slid down to a crouched position, feeling winded and disorientated.

Other inmates swarmed around him, filling the cell. Kicks and punches rained down on him as they climbed over each other to get a piece of the action. He tried covering his head for protection, but the blows were relentless. Richard screamed in response, but the noise of the mob shouting and jostling for the best positions to land their blows drowned out the screams.

Through blurred eyes, he saw blood on his arms, lots of blood, scary amounts of blood. The pack of hyenas suddenly withdrew, dispersing from the cell to around the wing. A baying crowd of onlookers remained shouting abuse at him from outside, but he couldn't hear the detail: his ears were ringing, and his whole body was traumatised in pain.

The occupant was bent down, shouting into Richards's face. 'Look what they've done to my pad. This is your fucking fault.'

SILENT BETRAYAL

Richard pulled his arms away from his head and stared at them, blood everywhere. Where was it coming from? The baying crowd was becoming more hostile, their faces contorted, stunned, horrified, and shocked.

Richard noticed bright red blood pumping rhythmically from his neck from the corner of his eye. It looked surreal, spurting against the cold grey wall. He raised a hand to his neck and immediately felt the gaping wound. He pressed against it hard, looking towards the crowd for help but none was forthcoming, until the alarm sounded.

The crowds began to disperse, being pushed aside by prison officers rushing to his aid. Shouts of *"Lock it down"* and *"Get behind your doors, now"* rang out above the ongoing melee.

The feeling of fear and terror dissipated as Richard slipped fully to the floor in a heap. He felt lightheaded and tired but no longer scared. The volume of the noise receded as a prison officer crouched in front of him. 'Fucking hell, he's lost a load of blood, he's fucked. Get back up and get the medics,' the officer shouted over his shoulder. Then repeated shouts of *"Medic"* filled the wing.

By the time he'd been medevaced to the hospital wing, it was too late. The officer had made a valiant attempt to stem the blood flow as Richard was stretchered from the wing, but eventually, one of the prison doctors took his shoulder and pulled him away from Richard's body.

'He's gone. There's nothing more you can do for him now. You did everything you could to help him.'

The prisoner officer wiped his hands down the front of his once white shirt, which was now mostly red, soaked with blood. Looking back at Richard, he saw the laceration on his neck. 'Someone slashed him. He didn't stand a chance.'

A bedding sheet was passed to the doctor; he shook it out, then covered Richards's body where it lay, head to foot. The doctor then looked over to the senior nurse across from him and said, 'Please record the time of death as of now and inform the duty governor.'

A silence hung over the medical bay as the prison officers began to leave. The doctor closed the curtains around the bed and joined the other medical staff at the nurses' station. 'He was an MP, wasn't he?' the doctor asked.

One of the prison officers nodded back to him. 'Yes, he hasn't been here long. The only saving grace is that he wouldn't have known much about it. That was the most shocking rapid blood loss I've ever seen, and I served in Afghanistan. I'm glad I'm not his allocated officer; there'll be stacks of paperwork and questions to be answered.'

The duty governor, an overweight woman dressed in civilian clothing, entered the room. 'How's this been allowed to happen?' she asked breathlessly. 'He was an MP. Why wasn't he on segregation? This is the last thing we need.'

'I'll get onto our police liaison section,' the prison officer with the blooded shirt said before he left the room.

36

Jane got Mandy to give her a lift to the train station. She had got over her paranoia about Mandy being involved in her abduction and was once again enjoying her company. Things were starting to feel normal again, well as normal as could be expected.

Mandy had tried to engage her in conversation about Richard and was keen to tell her that the news of his arrest was in all the papers, social media, and all over the internet.

Jane shrugged and said, 'If you play with fire, you'll get your fingers burned. He got his fingers burned.'

'Do you think he'll struggle in prison?' Mandy persisted, her curiosity getting the better of her.

'Not my problem, Mandy. Who knows?' she said, remaining more focused on checking the mirrors for any signs of police protection surveillance or John and his associates, whom she had no doubt would be following her. But there was no sign of either.

'Are you okay if I drop you here?' Mandy asked. 'I can swing the car into the retail park and do your shopping while I'm here.'

'That's fine, thank you.'

'Do you need picking up later?'

'No, I'll be fine, thanks, Mandy,' Jane replied while stepping out of the car. Then she paused, and leaned into the car. 'Make sure you buy some decent wine. We can have a night in when I get back if you've no plans. Think about what take away you fancy, too. We need to let our hair down after all that's happened. It can't have been easy for you, either.' Jane said, glancing around the pedestrian approach to the railway station. Everything seemed normal, in contrast to her own life. She headed down the ramp and onto the platform, which had seen better days. A relic of splendid Victorian architecture now barely maintained and looking miserable, a shadow of its former self.

There was a scattering of people waiting on the platform. She checked the computerised display screen and was pleased to see the train was on time and hadn't been cancelled for a change. There was just enough time to get a coffee, she decided, and walked over to the kiosk. She enjoyed sipping her drink on the platform while waiting for the train, one of the mundane routines she had dreamt about whilst enduring life in the cell. Enjoying the simple things in the moment.

The train slowly eased into the station, continuing to the far end of the platform. The other passengers began walking towards where they thought it would eventually stop. Jane waited and approached a door when the hissing air brakes stopped the train.

She pressed the entry pad, and the doors opened with a bing-bong sound. The carriage looked pretty new, clean and tidy. Her attention was taken by a family spread over both sides of the carriage, laden with suitcases—no doubt on their way to Manchester Airport for a family holiday. She smiled at the mother and envied how contented and happy she looked, enjoying quality family time.

Jane continued past them along the carriage and selected one of a pair of forward-facing seats. The sliding door connecting to the next carriage acted as a mirror. There was still no sign of John, and she was sure

SILENT BETRAYAL

no police protection team was on her tail. The only issue causing her concern was that she didn't know what 'H' looked like, the man who wanted her dead, for sure.

As she drank her coffee, her mind returned to Mandy asking about Richard. She smiled, amused at what a gossip her cleaner was. Then, her mind switched to seeing him in the church garden for the last time. How pathetic he looked, waving, trying to get her attention, and then his gormless look of confusion as she took off.

A smile spread across her face again. His half-witted plan had failed miserably, like most of his plans did. Returning to Mandy's question, she relished the thought of him doing jail time, knowing how he would struggle. But it was only second best to John having got his hands on him. A pang of guilt jolted her. Did she really want Richard dead, or was she overreacting? Was that what she *really* wanted? Her phone rang, saving her from answering the question.

She rummaged through her bag to locate the phone which was lodged behind the tin foil package she'd brought. She pushed it aside, relieved that she hadn't forgotten it, and grabbed the phone, placing it to her ear.

'Hi, Lee,' she answered, surprised to hear from him so soon.

'Afternoon, Jane. We need to meet. I have an update for you. Where are you?'

She suddenly felt uneasy. She couldn't break away from her plan today. Everything was in place, and she had to see it through. She had no time to meet anyone, especially the police. John would understandably become suspicious if she met up with Lee.

She was about to tell a lie when she realised that she could still be being watched, but then why would he ask where she was? 'I can't. I'm on the train, going to meet my brother,' she said.

'Look, it's serious stuff,' Lee said. 'I could really do with meeting up. It's not a conversation to be had over the phone.' He paused then asked, 'Can you not delay meeting your brother until later today?'

Jane's mind started running through worst-case scenarios. What the hell did he want to tell her that was so serious? 'I'm fine, Lee. After everything I've been through, I'm sure I can cope with a serious update over the phone.'

'Okay, fair enough,' Lee said. 'It's your call… Richard's dead. He was attacked by another inmate on the wing at the prison a short time ago. The prison officers did their best to save him, but he passed away.'

'Dead? How's he dead? What happened?' Jane asked, feeling a sense of numbness washing through her mind in response to the news. 'Has he killed himself?'

'He was attacked by a group of inmates…are you sure you don't want to meet up, Jane? It's not right discussing this over the phone,' Lee asked awkwardly.

'No, no, I'm fine,' she said as the shock began to settle, allowing her to process the news. She fell silent as she recalled John saying Richard's incarceration wasn't a problem, because he had contacts everywhere. The confusion manifested itself in competing emotions. She felt guilty, but why? She'd wanted him dead.

Lee broke the silence. 'Are you okay? Let's meet up, this can't be easy for you.'

'How did they kill him?' Jane asked.

'A laceration to the neck. Massive loss of blood.'

'I need some time to process this. Don't forget, Lee, he paid to get me killed.' The feelings of guilt and sadness were giving way to an ambivalence. 'He started this, he tried to kill me. What a fucking mess.'

'I can arrange for a family liaison officer to call on you, if you like, to give you some support,' Lee offered.

'I'll think it over, thanks. Right now, I just need some time alone. Thanks for letting me know.'

'No worries, Jane. Call me if you need anything, okay?'

'I will, thanks, Lee,' she said before ending the call. She looked out of the window at suburbia flashing by at speed. What goes around comes around, she supposed, especially if you piss someone like John off, she mused, guessing he must have had some involvement. The thought made her more determined not to give John any reason to kill her. Her life had gone wild, like being in an action thriller. All she craved now was normality.

*

'The train is now arriving at Deansgate, Manchester,' a voice announced over the intercom as the screeching brakes brought the train to a gentle standstill.

Jane stood up and slung her bag over her shoulder. She stepped off the train onto the platform encased by red brick walls. It was somewhere she was familiar with and knew her way around. She joined the crowds, heading down the steps and back into the fresh air. Deansgate locks came into view, along with fond memories of happier days frequenting the restaurants and bars occupying the old Victorian railway arches.

She continued along Deansgate towards the centre of Manchester. Usually, this well-trodden route would have taken her to restaurants, pubs, and perhaps the theatre, but today she was focused on unfinished business.

Once she stepped into the bank, she was directed into a waiting area beside the retail banking operation. On previous visits, she hadn't needed to wait long, so she didn't bother flicking through one of the glossy magazines on offer.

Sure enough, a good-looking male in his forties, with gleaming white teeth and wearing a pinstripe suit, approached her. 'Ms Smythe, would you like to come this way, please?'

Jane smiled, stood, and followed the man through a private door and down a flight of stairs into the basement.

The corridor lighting was soft, creating a calm ambience, together with the low hum of the air conditioning system. They reached another door, where Jane was asked to complete the facial recognition identification process. 'That's great,' said the banker on completion, as if she'd successfully completed a round in a TV game show.

There was a metallic clunk, and he pushed the fortified door open. 'Follow me, please.' She followed him along a shorter corridor that led to four other doors. He then stopped at the third door and pressed the numerical code key, which gave them access to a small room lined on two sides with safety deposit boxes and a desk with two chairs in the centre of the room.

'If you're ready, let us proceed,' he said, holding out the key. Jane took her key, and together, they simultaneously pushed them in and turned them to the right. There was a satisfying metallic clicking noise, and the door was released.

Jane took the box handle and slid it out from the secure housing. As she turned and placed it on the table, the banker edged towards the door. 'I shall wait outside, Ms Smythe; please knock when you're ready to leave.'

She smiled courteously and sat at the table, loving the irony of being called by her maiden name, which was still her identity as the account holder.

Alone in the room, she undid the box and peered inside, immediately seeing the large leather folding wallet containing the Krugerrands. She ignored the other items in the box and unfolded the leather compartments to reveal the coins. Satisfied with its contents, she folded the wallet back into its compact state and lifted it to assess its weight. Content that she wouldn't have problems carrying, only just mind, she placed the wallet in her bag and replaced the safety deposit box before knocking on the door.

The banker opened the door and led her to the bank's public area, asking her if she would like to meet with the senior financial advisor while she was in town. He explained it was a service they offered only to their VIP customers.

Jane declined the offer, wondering how much commission he had missed out on because she hadn't accepted.

37

The handle of Jane's bag was digging into her shoulder due to the weight of the Krugerrand coins, and she adjusted its position. Unfortunately, it didn't make much difference. She slowed her pace to counteract the discomfort and carried on to her favourite delicatessen shop.

She was about to enter when her phone's ringtone activated from her jacket pocket. She grabbed the phone and placed it to her ear, scanning the immediate area to locate John. Once again, he was nowhere to be seen. She was convinced that he was monitoring her movements via a tracker in the burner phone.

'Where are you going?' John asked over the phone as if she was doing something wrong.

'I'm just calling at the delicatessen. I'm getting us a proper New York Deli sandwich. Remember I said I'd treat you to a real one, after the supermarket version you bought us. I haven't eaten all day and I need some food.' Jane felt anxious awaiting his answer.

'Okay,' John replied, much to her relief, 'I'll look forward to that.'

'I'm here now. There's no queue, so I shouldn't be long,' she said, her confidence returning. 'I've picked up the package, so everything's in hand.'

'I'm satisfied that the police aren't tailing you, so I'll call you back shortly and direct you to the meeting point,' John said, ending the call.

SILENT BETRAYAL

Jane stepped into the Italian-themed deli, glancing around as she did so to locate her tail. She'd been a customer here for years, and it was always busy, as it was now. She joined the small queue and checked out the tantalising ingredients in the refrigerated display cabinet. The ambient chatter and familiar wafting smells from the food and coffee put her at ease — a refreshing oasis in a dysfunctional situation.

She still couldn't be one hundred per cent sure that John wasn't watching, so sandwiches in hand, she headed for the ladies' room to complete the next step of her plan discreetly. Settled in the cubicle with the door locked, she removed the contents of the tin foil and added them to John's sandwich.

A repressed memory from the vaults of her mind floated into her vision like a recurring nightmare. Memories of her father reminded her of the corner she'd been backed into, forcing her to take drastic action to protect herself and her brother in the only way that guaranteed their safety. And now she was preparing to take the same action against a protagonist posing a different threat. She forced her mind to close the memory down immediately. It was a place and time she'd rather not visit.

To prevent any serious fuck-ups, she removed her sandwich and placed it in the main compartment of her handbag. She didn't want to consider the ramifications of eating the wrong one. Once sorted, she left the shop. Outside, she retrieved her sandwich and took a bite. The extra spicy mustard and dill pickle she had requested exploded into a strong, zesty taste, enhancing the exquisiteness of the cured and seasoned meats.

After swallowing the first mouthful, she took another large bite, savouring the best New York Deli in town.

This was definitely now her sandwich out of the two she had purchased.

As expected, her mobile phone began ringing and vibrating in her pocket. She answered the call and scanned the vicinity for John.

'Make your way towards the National Trust Viaduct at Castlefield, and I'll call you when you get there.' The line went dead. His tone was serious and businesslike, with a hint of menace.

Jane began walking, yanking the bag off her right shoulder in response to the pain and swapping it to her other shoulder. The viaduct wasn't far away. She'd visited it before. His choice of location didn't surprise her. The area, a mix of red brick industrial warehouses and other buildings intersected by railway lines, viaducts and canals, was a rejuvenated popular spot far from its recent derelict and shady past—a perfect place to be discreet yet not far off the beaten track.

Over several short phone calls, she was directed along cobbled towpaths by the dark water of the canals, under the viaduct and along deserted small paths in the shadows of the red brick warehouses.

A shiver went down her spine as she became mindful that she hadn't seen another person for the latter stages of her journey. She looked around the vicinity again. It was like a ghost town down here, and the dark thoughts resurfaced. Was this where he planned to assassinate her? The secluded paths and underpasses were the perfect location for an ambush. Her confidence began to wither as her current state of vulnerability was heightened. Had she been naïve in believing her plan had any realistic chance of succeeding? Was he just going to take the Krugerrands and dispose of her in the canal? The worrying thoughts continued in waves as she followed the directions, passing crumbling brickwork, graffiti and dark, secluded nooks and crannies.

Under the ironwork of the viaduct, she suddenly felt the cold embracing her; the shadows were growing longer, creating a sinister atmosphere. Jane began to feel some strong reservations about the plan. But she accepted that she'd gone too far to back out now. He was probably in striking distance already and wouldn't let her leave.

She descended three substantial stone steps and immediately recognised John lurking in a brick alcove alongside the dark waters of the canal. He wasn't holding a pistol. So that was a good start. Her heart started pounding. He looked different than usual, feral almost, staring at her as a predator or mugger might do before striking out.

'Sit down,' he said, tapping the stone beside him. Something about the tone of his voice told her she was going to be okay.

She felt relieved as she slipped the bag from her shoulder and placed it between her feet as she sat down. Without speaking, she reached down and grabbed the leather wallet. Holding it out towards John, she said, 'It's all there,' praying that now he had accepted the payment, he was less likely to do her any harm.

John began unfolding the large wallet, spreading it across his lap. The pristine, shiny Krugerrand coins gleamed before him like pirate treasure. 'I've never received payment in Krugerrands before. They look exquisite,' he said, studying the coins. I've been researching them on the internet. Are they all minted in the same year?'

After a pause, and not bothering to answer his inconsequential question, Jane asked, 'Did you give the instruction for Richard to be killed this morning?'

'Yes,' John said, not flinching and finally lifting his head to look at her. 'That's what you wanted. Right?'

'He got what he deserved,' she answered, fastening the buttons on her jacket. She reached into her bag and then held the sandwich towards John. Praying that the extra sauces had hidden the earthy smell of the additional contents. 'This is a proper sandwich from the best deli in Manchester. Every New York Deli you buy after this one will never be as good. You'll be addicted after tasting it.'

He took the sandwich and placed it on the stone beside his leg. Jane felt a sudden pang of anxiety from his lacklustre interest in the food. She watched as he folded up the leather wallet before she took her own sandwich and bit into it enthusiastically, hoping maybe that would encourage him to eat his.

'My partner has been arrested in Spain. He got sloppy,' John said.

'The guy who killed Hargreaves?'

He nodded.

'I meant what I said before: I'd be interested in working with you. That's if you need a replacement partner now,' Jane said, relieved that she was safe from 'H' for now.

John opened his rucksack and carefully placed the wallet inside before looking up. 'Why would you want to do that?' he asked, puzzled.

'It seems like a natural step, especially in light of recent events. I didn't ask to enter this world. The actions of others placed me here. I've learned a lot about myself and remembered some aspects buried in the past. I'd be quite capable, you know.' She looked at the abandoned sandwich while trying to establish a plan B should he decide not to eat it.

'This is gorgeous, aren't you trying yours?' she asked, knowing it was her last throw of the dice. Any further mention of the sandwich would appear odd.

John picked it up and peeled back the wrapping before taking a bite, nodding as he munched away.

She felt a sudden surge of euphoria and swelling excitement, surprised at the extreme satisfaction and enjoyment as she watched the scene develop in front of her. The cool, experienced assassin had walked hopelessly into her trap. She watched him chew, just as she'd watched her father all those years ago.

'There's a bit of a sour taste spoiling it, but it's very nice,' John said, taking another big bite.

'That's the dill pickle, and she also added parsley before I could stop her,' Jane said. 'She must be a new employee. You don't put parsley on a New York Deli.' Her confidence began to swell following her explanation, as she watched him take another bite. Then another while she enjoyed her delicious uncontaminated food, experiencing a high like no other, almost an out-of-body experience. By her calculations, he had eaten enough already. He was past the point of no return, and it was all downhill from here for him. She waited patiently for the effects of the Hemlock to kick in with a thrilling feeling of revenge and accomplishment. If he'd intended to kill her, he'd missed his chance.

'I might have an opening for you. Keep hold of the phone,' John answered belatedly. He placed the last piece of sandwich into his mouth, then wiped his lips with the back of his hand as he swallowed the remaining remnants.

'I won't let you down,' she said, creating an illusion of future planning to minimise any suspicion as the poison spread into his bloodstream.

John started coughing. 'That mustard must have been hot; my mouth feels so dry,' he said, finishing with a splutter. 'Have you got a drink on you?'

'I brought us this to celebrate our new partnership and to toast Richard's demise,' Jane said, pulling a half bottle of single malt whiskey from her bag. She unscrewed the cap and handed it to John, watching as he took a long swig, oblivious to the fact that the alcohol would react with the poison and speed up his demise.

'Something's not right, Jane, I... I don't feel right,' he said, struggling to get his words out of his dry mouth.

'Shit, do you think you're having an allergic reaction?' she asked with a look of concern.

'I think something was off. It shouldn't have tasted that sour. How was yours?'

Jane shuddered as she suspected a flicker of suspicion in his eyes. She had to be prepared to dive out of his reach at any moment. 'Mine was delicious; you'll be okay. Have another drink of whiskey.'

John eagerly grasped the bottle from by his side and took another long drink, knocking the amber liquid back like it was water. Then he looked towards Jane. 'You fucking bitch—you put something in the sandwich, didn't you?' He snatched at his rucksack, but Jane beat him to it and kicked it away, out of his reach.

She noticed beads of sweat forming on his head and temples, his hand holding the bottle now trembling. He paused, then knocked more whiskey back before closing his eyes and leaning his head backwards. While his eyes were closed, Jane stood and picked up the rucksack, slowly edging away from him, creating a safe distance. She knew it wouldn't take long now.

'My stomach's cr...cramping,' John said, leaning forward, his chest against his thighs, his body trembling uncontrollably. 'You fucking bitch, H was right, I should n...never've trusted you.'

Jane smiled down at him. 'It's too late now, John. The poison will have spread through your body. Enjoy the whiskey. It'll make it quicker and less painful.

Feeling more in control as the minutes passed, she walked further away behind the cover of the iron stanchion supporting the viaduct, watching calmly as John huddled into a ball, trying to alleviate the pain which was now causing him severe distress.

A few minutes later, she stepped back out so John could see her again.

'I sh...saved your life, and you've fucking posh... poisoned me, you bitch.' John's words were forced and slurred and he looked defeated, almost ready to give up the fight. Like he accepted it was his time.

'Yes, John. I have poisoned you. Call it payback or revenge, whichever. But remember, it's just *business*, nothing personal. Drink the rest of the whiskey. It might be a more comforting death.'

John staggered to his feet and Jane took a few more steps back to safety as his legs buckled from under him, causing him to fall onto the cold, hard cobbles in a heap. His breathing was now shallow and very laboured.

He hadn't got the energy, strength, or coordination to reach the whiskey bottle. It was over. The fight had already drained from him.

Jane scanned the area. The last thing she needed now was a nosey onlooker. Fortunately, the area was still deserted, and she cautiously approached John and crouched down by his side. His breathing was almost undetectable. Her gut feeling told her he didn't have long, noticing how pale and ashen his skin tone had become.

She got back to her feet and cleared up the sandwich packaging. Then she checked the area to ensure nothing had been left behind, put on her surgical gloves to prevent traces of DNA, and retrieved the Krugerrands from his rucksack. She then flung the rucksack into the water.

She moved position several times for the last time, covering all viewing angles to ensure no one was about. The area was still desolate. She crouched down by John, his eyes closed and his jaw hanging open, and she was left in no doubt. He'd underestimated her. He was dead and no longer a threat.

Jane grabbed him by the wrist and dragged him the short distance to the canal's edge, where he slipped into the dark water with one final push. His body remained on the surface for a moment before slowly sinking. Jane stood watching until the air bubbles and ripples in the pitch black water died away. There were no emotions: no hysteria, no regret, no panic. Just a feeling of euphoria and satisfaction. She looked around her and luckily spotted the whiskey bottle, which she placed in her bag. Then, she headed back towards Deansgate, sticking to the same route she'd been guided in, knowing John would have ensured there was no CCTV—just another worker heading back to the office after her lunch break. A question occurred to her while she walked: *Was he planning on killing me?* Who knew, it wasn't important anymore. John, or whatever his real name was, was dead.

38

Jane slowly walked along Deansgate towards the train station alongside other pedestrians. The simple act of walking without having to plan what she was to do next to survive or without looking over her shoulder in fear of what was coming felt like a luxury. A reminder of how precious it was to have regained her autonomy and freedom. It hadn't been easy, and she'd had to work hard in horrible circumstances. But she'd achieved it: her scheming rat of a husband was gone along with the threat of John, which Richard had created. A new sense of power and control over what she did next was simmering beneath the surface in her subconscious. Taking on the evil bastards and playing them at their own game made her proud of her achievements. She felt a surge of enthusiasm towards helping those less resilient than her to overcome the monsters casting shadows over their lives.

Jane reached the station and climbed the stairs to the platform. It was late afternoon, and the place was busy. She mingled into the crowd, now looking forward to a relaxing night at home as the train slowly entered the station. Luckily, she chose the right carriage by chance and grabbed a vacant seat. Then she simply sat back and enjoyed people-watching as the train's motion helped her relax.

The taxi driver eventually dropped her at the door and she entered the house feeling exhausted. Mandy was waiting in the kitchen and rushed forward to hug her. It was then, looking over Mandy's shoulder, that she saw the reflection of a man in the window. He was standing behind her.

Jane froze.

Who was it? What had she missed? Her heartbeat was racing at full pelt, off the scale, and she suddenly felt like it was about to burst.

'Hi, Jane, I was just looking around Richard's office, hope you don't mind?'

She recognised the voice immediately—it was DS Lee McCann. She almost melted with the surge of relief that followed. Luckily, Mandy still supported her in their embrace but for a split second, she feared Lee was an associate of John's. Then she pulled away from Mandy, telling herself to get a grip. Lee was fine. She trusted him.

'I'm worried about you, Jane,' Mandy said. 'You've been through so much. I don't think I would have coped with it.'

'I'll be fine. Let's start on my recovery now: open a bottle of prosecco. Would you like a glass, Lee? We won't tell.'

Lee laughed. 'Why not—just a small one, please.'

They retired to the lounge with their drinks, and Lee was the first to speak. 'I called around on the off chance of catching you in,' he said. 'Mandy said you wouldn't be long and suggested I wait for you.'

'That's fine, Lee. I guess we won't be seeing much of you anymore. So, thank you for everything you and your team did for me. I'm one lucky woman.'

'I think we both know that you were instrumental in getting yourself out of there, too,' he said. 'It can't have been easy.' A silence followed, so Lee continued, 'Richard's body now lies at the mortuary in Oldham.

An investigation into his death is being undertaken. I'll keep you updated on the progress. If you wish to view the body—'

Jane interrupted, 'I won't be doing that. I'll stay out of the way and leave it to his relatives. Can we discuss Richard another time, please?'

'Of course, Jane, no worries. I understand.' Lee took a sip of his drink then added, 'The man who killed Tony Hargreaves is remanded in custody in Spain. The evidence against him is overwhelming, so he won't see the light of day for a long time. That brings us to your kidnapper. We're still following some strong lines of enquiry to find him and locate the premises where you were held. I'll keep you updated on that, too.'

Jane nodded, doing her best to look concerned.

'I've completed a "Person at Risk Assessment" to ensure we do all we can to keep you safe while his whereabouts remain unknown. We'll target harden your house and take other measures to look after you.'

'That's great, thank you,' she replied, catching a glance at Mandy's worried expression. 'My gut feeling tells me he won't be back. Hopefully I'm right.'

'I agree. We can never say never, but it would be unlikely that he would return for you. But we won't get complacent. And for now, that should do us. Do you have any questions?'

'Not just yet, but maybe when I see you next time I might,' Jane said, sipping her wine. She liked Lee, and couldn't help thinking he might be a valuable contact in the future.

'That's me done, then. You two enjoy your evening. I'll let myself out.' Lee placed his empty glass on the coffee table and went to his car.

Jane stood at the window and watched as the red tail lights headed down the drive.

'Are you scared that the kidnapper will come back, Jane?'

'He won't be coming back, Mandy. I'm safe now.'

Other crime fiction, page-turning books by CJ Wood.

Available online at Amazon in paperback and digital format.

The County Lines Trilogy...

County Lines (Book One)

There comes a time to batten down the hatches and choose those you trust very carefully. Jason Hamilton's criminal drug dealing operation has made him into a successful, powerful, wealthy man. As the head of a Manchester Organised Crime Group, he is ruthless, violent and feared by his enemies and associates alike. An unexpected sequence of events leads to betrayal, suspicion and paranoia within his firm. Cracks began to appear. Internal feuds fuelled by jealousy, revenge and paranoia of police informants. To make matters worse, the Drugs Squad are also taking an interest in his activities. He has always kept his friends close, but his enemies closer ... now he's not sure which is which... events start to spiral out of control. Can Hamilton turn this around or is it the beginning of his demise?

Crossed Lines (Book Two)

Following his failed attempt to murder a rogue associate, Jason Hamilton wound up incarcerated in prison. But doing time is just an occupational hazard for Hamilton. He has the reputation and tenacity to cope well inside. Also, he isn't planning on staying long ...

Driven by revenge against the under-cover cop who nicked him Hamilton has to decide whether he can trust his organised crime group associates and bent solicitor Frank Burton or whether he needs to take matters into his own hands.

Meanwhile, DI Andrea Statham is determined to crack two murder cases, and all the clues lead back to Hamilton. Now she's watching and waiting for his next move?

But will Hamilton's next move be the last line he crosses ... or will he succeed?

Critical Lines (Book 3)

No one likes a bent cop… especially police colleagues.

Continuing the page-turning gritty crime fiction from CJ Wood's popular books, DS Pete Higgs continues to play the Police and Organised Crime Group off against each other.

But how long can he succeed? Is he entrenched in noble cause corruption, or is he now an organised crime gang member? Either way, he's crossed the line; he's a villain.

DI Andrea Statham is convinced that her one-time trusted colleague and experienced detective, DS Pete Higgs, is embedded within Wayne Davies's organised crime group. But she needs evidence to prove it. And now she is on his case to get him banged up.

The intelligence suggests that he is now involved in dealing drugs and firearms. But he is an experienced operative and covering his tracks. DI Statham knows it won't be easy, but that won't deter her. Only one of them will succeed

One way or another, things are coming to a head…

Printed in Great Britain
by Amazon